For Luke and Jake, my inspirations.
And for Jim, my love, my favorite person in the world,
and my first and biggest fan. LSM

4

BRIDGEKEEPER

By L. S. Moore

THE BIG FIG

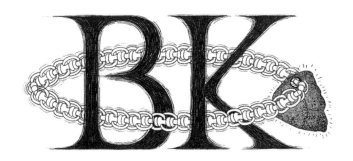

CHAPTER ONE

The more you sweat in practice the less you bleed in battle. True bit of martial arts wisdom there, but tonight I wondered if losing sweat would kill me faster than losing blood. The crowd milling around the tournament made the air as refreshing as breathing water from a hot tub.

Seth held out a gym towel. I traded him my black belt and buried my face, savoring the bleach-scented break from the funk in the air. My brother's blue button-down shirt was dry and pit-stain free. His short, dark hair was *not* soaking wet and plastered to his skull like mine. Nothing made Seth sweat. Really annoying.

"Man, I'm gonna suffocate," I complained. "Don't they have the windows open tonight?" Our dojang took up the second floor of an old hat factory on the town square. The big room looked like a jumbled chess board tonight with our club members in black uniforms, our opponents in white. The ceiling fans spinning overhead might have been creating a breeze, but they were twenty feet up.

Seth craned his neck to look over the crowd and then grabbed my shoulder. "Come on. We'll get you cooled off." The floorboards creaked as he broke a path, and I did my best to keep my bare toes away from people's street shoes.

"Yo, Will!" Nico's charcoal-black hair stuck out like he'd done a few head spins during his fights. Hopping on one leg, he showed me the tattered edge of a familiar pair of sparring pants. "I wore my lucky dobok, see? Didn't help my last bout, but all my leftover luck's for you." He chucked me on the shoulder. "Not that you'll need it, primo."

I raked my soggy hair off my forehead. "Thanks. I'll take all the free luck I can get."

"Here," Seth said. "Stick your head outside for few minutes."

He pushed me toward a towering row of windows. Sometime over the last few hours, Halloween night had rolled up against the building tsunami-style. Ancient glass reflected the room's fluorescent lights in oily black ripples.

Flapping the open edges of his tunic, Nico let out a moan as he hopped onto the sill and leaned out. "Oh yeah, popsicle me." He moved aside to make room for me.

"It's dark out there," I managed, my mouth gone dry.

Nico ducked his head in and cocked an eyebrow at Seth. "It's the cat thing," he whispered out of the side of his mouth. "Been bugging him all day."

Seth caught my eye, concern obvious in his look.

8

"It'll pass like always. Don't *sweat* it."

"Ha-ha," I said with a grimace. The *cat thing* had been part of my life long enough that I should have gotten used to it by now. But every time my chest hollowed out and weirdly alien emotions oozed into the empty space, it surprised me. The first time somebody shivered and said, *Oooo, a cat just walked over my grave,* I knew that was the closest I'd ever come to describing what it felt like to have somebody else's feelings blow through your insides. Seth was right, the weirdness always passed.

Except today when it hadn't. Out there somewhere, my smart-ass cat had paced back and forth over my grave *all day.* Concentrating on my AP calc test had been loads of fun. I got no relief until I stepped across the threshold at the dojang tonight. So, as great as a cold slap of autumn air would feel, I was nervous. What if sticking my head outside invited the cat back? That kind of distraction during my final bout could leave me bloody.

Seth reached to undo the Velcro fasteners on my sparring vest, but I pushed his hands away. "I got it, *Mommy.*" He smirked and propped a shoulder against the brick wall.

The wide, stone windowsill glistened invitingly with icy drizzle. I squared my shoulders, peeled my vest off and handed it to Nico. Goosebumps rose across my belly as I pressed my face cautiously past the brick wall, out the open window . . .

. . . and into the dark.

A groan rolled through my teeth as sad, achy regret seeped into the hollow of my chest. All day, I'd been

9

trying to connect the feeling to some shitty thing I'd done or said. I'm no saint, but nothing *I'd* done justified this heartache. *Damned cat!*

Jerking my head inside, I let out a relieved breath as the feeling faded. "Not happening, guys." Seth and Nico followed me back into the dojang exchanging worried glances. It was time to steer the conversation in a new direction. "So, who's in the final round with me?"

Looking resigned, Nico tossed me my vest. "Some older guy from the other dojang."

"Nobody we know?" I shrugged on the gear and tied my belt. Nico shook his head.

"I've been watching him," Seth said. "He's only a brown belt. Can't figure out why he's winning, except he's got thirty pounds on almost everybody else."

"Weight shouldn't matter," Nico and I said together, and then grinned.

We'd dubbed our Hapkido instructor *Jet Li's mini-me.* Ms. Beverly weighed a hundred pounds soaking wet and had no trouble kicking our asses, so she never let any of us use size as an excuse for losing. She'd probably invited the other club to our friendly melee tonight specifically because they had a couple of older, bigger members.

"What's the guy's name?" I asked.

"Never caught it, but he's over there." Seth nodded to a knot of people against the far wall.

I picked out my opponent by the brown belt around his thick waist. As I watched, he spat a Day-Glo orange mouth guard, slick with slobber, straight into the waiting hand of a girl who looked at him like he was a rock star. From her other hand, she produced a chewed wad of

10

gum which she popped into his open mouth.

"Dios," Nico whispered. "She didn't just . . . I'm gonna puke."

"Crap, I hate those things," I said. Mouth guards screwed up my breathing, stank, and made me drool.

"You should wear one," Seth said without turning away from the gum-chewer. "Protect your teeth."

"Thanks, brother-hen," I muttered. "Who'd he beat in his last round?" The guy didn't look light on his feet.

"It was Dave," Nico said. "I heard he pinned him. Dave tapped out."

My eyes widened. "*Dave* tapped out?"

Nico nodded solemnly. "He went home already. Might be hurt."

You only tapped the mat to surrender a bout if you were hopelessly pinned or hurt, because when you did, the fight was over, you lost, no matter who'd racked up the most points. Dave and I sparred a lot. I'd never seen him give up a match.

I took the gym towel from Seth again and sopped up a little more sweat while I studied my competition. The girl offered him a water bottle, but he swept an arm out and pushed her aside to lean over and say something to the guy next to him. They laughed, but the girl blushed deep enough that I could see it across the room. My gloves creaked on clenched fists.

"Kick his ass," Nico muttered.

Seth nodded. "Agreed but keep your head in the game. Figure out how he's winning."

Maybe the cat had been haunting my grave all day to keep me on my toes for tonight. All I needed to do to get rid of the heartache was win this bout, teach that moron some manners. It was a good theory and I intended to run with it.

Most of the crowd looked friendly when the ref called us up. My opponent wasn't a real popular guy even in his own dojang. Hardly anybody in white uniforms had stuck around to watch him fight. The chomper gave me a Day-Glo smirk as he stepped onto the mat and sized me up.

I sized him up right back. He'd favor punches over footwork. He had one of those bodies with muscles up top, skinny, neglected legs below. He'd want me in close. I bounced a little on my toes.

"Atten-tion!" the ref commanded. "Bow."

I made my bow, respectful, cool and gave the guy my name, "Will McCurty. Good luck."

Jaw bunching and loosening on the guard, Chomper barely tipped his head. "Gluuphys Mwaff," he said.

I tried to work out what the hell he'd said, but decided I didn't need to know his name to kick his butt.

The ref raised his hand. "Ready." He swept it down. "Begin!"

Chomper telegraphed his first move like a bull pawing the ground. I went in fast. Front kick to the chest. He stumbled back, eyes wide. Two points for me. He charged, but I lunged aside and grabbed one thick wrist as it passed. Momentum sent him stumbling to the edge of the mat like he was wearing clown shoes. I hit him again, a roundhouse, right side, ribs. Switched feet. Left side, ribs. Four more points for me.

In the next minute and a half, I went through a martial arts catalogue of kicks, racking up points for each solid contact. Finally, he got in close enough to land a punch. I blocked, but his glancing blow knocked me sideways. The guy wasn't pulling his punches! Everybody pulled their punches! It's instinctive in a tournament, for sane people at least.

Splotchy cheeked, eyes blazing, Chomper crowded me at the edge of the mat. I ducked, spun, then punched. He knocked my fist aside with a clumsy block that sent fire flashing up to my elbow. That arm was out of commission, so I punched left-handed. His block hit my wrist bone. Searing pain roared all the way up that arm too! He slammed a fist into my chest and despite the vest, I coughed, blinking watery eyes. Chomper's lips stretched, showing me that Day-Glo grin.

Son of a bitch. He was hitting pressure points! Strike one just right, and intense pain could cripple a bigger, stronger attacker. They're for real-world, getting-robbed-in-an-alley stuff, situations where you need time to run like hell. Shaking out my arms, I kept circling, struggling to get my breathing evened out.

"Shrug it off, Will. You got this!" Nico's voice. Beside him, Seth looked like he wanted to charge onto the mat. He may not have figured out how, but he knew I was hurt.

Chomper wasn't as sloppy as I'd thought. Brilliant. Mean. And sneaky. His wins tonight weren't skill or strategy. He wore his opponents down with pain.

I charged, dodging a wild swing, and kicked the back of his knee. It buckled, but he twisted and grabbed my vest. Ref finally called a penalty, but we ended up in a bear hug with me taking most of his weight. I found my fingers locked onto a pressure point at the back of his

13

elbow. All I had to do was dig in and he wouldn't be using that arm for a while. I'd be perfectly justified. He started it. Just a bit of pressure.

But I was the black belt. Size shouldn't matter. I might win, but could I hold my head up afterward? This debate flashed through my mind in a couple of seconds. In one of those seconds, Chomper threw a sharp, blade-hand strike at the same spot in the middle of my chest. I buckled feeling like my breastbone had split in half. He dropped on top of me.

"Tap out," he slurred around the mouth guard.

"Screw you." I got my hands under my shoulders, gritted my teeth, and lifted us both. He let out a yelp. Another inch and I'd get a knee under me, tip him off.

Chomper pulled my arm out from under me and jerked it up. I bit back a groan. It was a simple arm lock, but with him on top of me, I couldn't get out of it. There was just no way.

"Tap out," he said again and wrenched my arm a little more.

I wanted to tell him where to stick his surrender, but it was all I could do not to scream.

"It's over!" The ref yelled. "Opponent is pinned. Inescapable hold."

Chomper bounced to his feet, blowing spit past his Day-Glo grin. I swallowed another groan and twisted my arm back the way nature intended it.

The ref lifted Chomper's fist high. "Winner!"

The final match was over. I blew it.

CHAPTER TWO

Ms. Beverly handed out trophies in a ceremony that didn't last long, thank God. I spent the whole time, fists clenched, barely resisting the urge to walk over to the guy and start my first *real* fight.

In no mood to pretend to be a good sport, I bolted for the locker room before the crowd had a chance to break up. Flinging my sparring gear at my open locker, I missed, slammed the door, then punched it. "Owwwww! Idiot!"

"Can't argue with you there." Seth stood in the doorway, coat folded over his clasped hands, looking coolly amused. "Ref was blind, Will. It wasn't your locker's fault."

I flexed my sore fingers letting the middle one rise. Seth gave a soft laugh and leaned against the doorframe to watch me pace around the wooden bench.

"You know what he was doing?" I fumed.

"Pressure points. Nico figured it out."

"I lost my cool. Should have kicked his sorry—"

"*You* won that fight. Everybody out there knows it."

I snorted. Seth was twelve when our dad took a bullet to the chest, I was eight. Since then, he'd been my one-man cheering section. Mom wasn't the kind of cop's wife who bounced back from death in the line of duty. Grams, the only other family we'd ever been close to, hit the road after Dad's funeral to work through losing her only son, I guess. She never came back.

It made me an ungrateful bastard, but I was sixteen years old now. It was long past time for Seth to get a life. His own. Tonight, on top of the persistent cat, losing my bout, and the damned locker, his hovering presence pissed me off. I slumped down on the bench and peeled off my sparring gloves. "Where's Nico?"

"Running around looking for a bottle of hot sauce. Said something about spicing up somebody's mouth guard. Get dressed." Seth tossed me my rolled-up street clothes. Rowdy laughter echoed down the hall, and he poked his head out the door. "Uh-oh. The Big winner's headed this way."

Shit. "Just hand me my shoes and the rest of my stuff." I tossed the roll of clothes back to him.

"It's cold out, you know."

In answer to my glare, Seth gave me an, it's-your-funeral shrug and passed me my phone and leather bracelet. We got out just as the champ and his entourage rounded the corner down the hall. The guy was still working that wad of tutti-frutti. My feet slowed.

Seth knocked my elbow. "Shoulda, coulda, woulda," he whispered. "Next time. Come on."

"That's a promise," I muttered as we scooted out. We took the stairs down to street level two at a time, and I flung the door open spilling steamy air onto the sidewalk. Icy cold molded around me like shrink wrap as drizzle mixed with the sweat on my skin. It was heaven for about half a second, but then the cold sank deeper.

My cat was back. Claws out. A revved-up sense of urgency came with the deep regret I'd been feeling all day, making the whole alien stew even worse. *Great.*

Seth blew out a breath of fog. "Is this a perfect Halloween night or what? Spooky!"

"Fun spooky or *real* spooky?" A shiver that had nothing to do with the cold made my fingers clumsy as I worked the braided knot to fasten my bracelet.

"You okay? Are you still feeling the—"

"Nope." I forced myself upright. "You were right. Cat's gone. *Stop* hovering." Seth backed off with his hands raised.

"Hey, Will!" Nico waved my trophy, a silver ninja doing a six-inch sidekick, as he maneuvered through the crowd that was streaming out the door at the base of the steps. "Found this in the locker room. Second place! Where'd they find that ref, right?" He didn't care about *his* losses tonight. His sour grapes were all for me. "Still, shiny trophy! You rocked tonight. Really."

"Right. You keep the trophy."

"Oh no you don't." Seth whisked it out of Nico's hand and wedged it into his pocket. "Did you find any hot sauce?"

"No, damn it. Couldn't find any Super Glue either." Nico squinted up into the drizzle as he fought the zipper of his hoodie. "Nice weather, huh?"

Watching that zipper close to his chin, I regretted leaving my dry clothes back in the locker. I eyeballed the line of cars parked along the sidewalk, hoping to see Mom's. *Crap.* I checked my phone. Seth confirmed what I feared with a disgusted shake of his head. Obviously, Mom's hot and cold parenting style was running cold tonight. "Great," I said. "Just great."

"What's up?" Nico followed my gaze and frowned. "Oh. Your mom didn't show up?" Nico didn't like our mom. We usually pretended I'd hatched.

"No big deal," I lied. After the hundredth time a person lets you down, you ought to be ready for it. But my future depended on Mom getting her act together. Seth graduated from high school two years ago and still hadn't moved out. As long as he showed up and stepped up, he made it easy for Mom *not* to. She screwed up, he worried. As long as he was worried about me, he'd never leave. Freakin' Catch 22.

A beautiful, old Ford pickup pulled up to the curb. "That's my ride," Nico said, waving to his dad. "We can give you guys a lift."

Dr. Muro trained rescue dogs in his spare time and two of his bloodhounds, Lola and Che, lolled in the front seat next to him. He leaned around the dogs. "Holá, guys."

"Hey, Dr. Muro." Seth nodded from the sidewalk.

I got a whiff of doggy breath and a quick lick on the cheek from Lola before Nico scooted her over to squeeze onto the edge of the seat.

"Sorry. Looks like a no-go on the taxi service," Nico said.

"I could come back for you boys," Dr. Muro offered. "You could wait at the café."

"You don't have to do that," Seth said. "It's not that far, we can walk."

Since I'd just denied the creeping cat, I had no grounds to argue for inconveniencing Dr. Muro, so I reluctantly closed the truck door. "Yeah, we'll be fine. Thanks anyway."

Nico cranked the window down. "Hey man, the Fall Fling's Saturday night. Start thinkin' about a costume."

"We'll see," I said in a voice lacking a single drop of enthusiasm.

Nico grinned. "That's the spirit! See ya at school."

Way too many dark doorways and suspicious shadows snagged my attention as Seth and I started down the sidewalk. I fidgeted with my phone, wanting my hands free. *For what? You going to take down the Boogey Man if he jumps out? Get a grip, McCurty.* Still, I held the phone out to Seth. "Take this, will you? No pockets."

"What's up with you tonight?" he said as he slipped it inside his jacket. "Don't say, nothing."

"I wish we'd come in the Mustang, that's all," I said, trying and failing to stop looking over my shoulder.

"We walked because you're all about saving the planet. I'm showing solidarity with your refusal to get a driver's license. Stop avoiding my question."

"Fine!" My jagged nerves shredded my filters. "You've got to leave the nest, man! I graduate in two years. If you're still at home, it'll ruin college for me. I can't leave you and Mom alone. You'll kill each other." The roof of our house rattled like a pressure cooker with the two of them under it. "Why aren't you at some haunted house on campus tonight instead of playing Dad?"

I wanted to suck the words back the second they left my ungrateful mouth. Seth stuffed his hands into his pockets looking hurt and stunned. Kicking myself, I wrapped my arms around my chest and turtled into my tunic.

Up ahead, the door to the Heartland Café opened spilling voices and the sound of clinking dishes onto the sidewalk. A couple of girls dressed as zombie Kardashians toddled down the steps in six-inch heels and we did the excuse-me-shuffle at the bottom. Fake eyelashes as big as feather dusters fluttered at my brother. There was a lot of giggling. Nico swears that Seth is the love child of Captain America and Marie Curie, a chick magnet with the personality of a science nerd.

"You suck," I told my oblivious brother as the girls toddled off. Seth walked ahead, ignoring my lame attempt to banter away the tense silence.

I trailed him around the corner, and we left the town square behind. One lonely car sped past, its tires making a ripping sound on the wet pavement. "Look, I'm sorry," I said, "but don't you ever wonder what you're missing, stuck here in Eagle Shoal?"

"I'm not stuck. I'm where I need to be," Seth said quietly.

"Why? Why do you need to be *here?*" Before he could answer my question, a wave of tension crested in my chest. My feet slowed. "Seth, something's not—"

20

Pop. Pop. Pop! Streetlights all down the road plinked out. No tinkling glass, no blown transformer sparks, just instant blackness.

"Craaaap." Waving my hand, I found Seth's shoulder and pulled him around to face me. My breath caught. His drizzle-slicked face looked like he'd taken a bath in glow-in-the-dark paint. I wiped water out of my eyes. "Sssseth. You're glowing."

He gave me a snort. "Uh-huh, sure."

"I'm not kidding." His weird light grew stronger. "You're actually lit up like—"

"Shh! Did you hear that?" Seth jerked his shoulder out of my grip. He cocked his ear. "Somebody's calling my name."

"What? I don't hear anybody." I checked up and down the road. There was another car, but it was so far away the headlights blurred into a single blob. Seth stepped into the street. I made a grab for him, missed, and hung there, toes over the curb trying to breathe. His glowing skin made a white smudge on the inky gloom as he knelt and reached out a hand.

Dread scrabbled up the back of my throat like a spider in a bathtub.

A woman materialized in front of Seth. Silver-haired, only half conscious, she lay sprawled in the road. How could I have missed her? My head cleared with a jolt of adrenaline. "Toss me my phone! I'll call 911." Wearing a weirdly serene expression, Seth ignored me and slid one arm under the old lady's knees to lift her. "Don't! Don't move her! You're not supposed to—"

Too late. With the woman in his arms, Seth tried

to stand, but she gave a pitiful little cry, stiffened, and threw her arms around his neck. He fought for balance, tottered, then took a nose-dive onto the street.

A squirmy feeling shot between my shoulder blades. That faraway car's headlights weren't a distant blob anymore. They were charging supernovas.

"Move her! Move her!" I yelled, jumping off the curb. Heart in my throat, I planted myself in front of my brother, waving my arms like an inflatable, flailing tube man. The headlights charged on, as if I was invisible. My black sparring gear—it made perfect night camo! I stripped my tunic off, and light flared on my pasty pecs.

"Stoooooooooooop!" I yelled, thrusting my arms out Superman-style.

Brakes screamed. The car canted sideways. Pancakes, smashed pumpkins, and roadkill swam across my vision.

Then nothing. I slitted one eye open.

An SUV sat two inches from my outstretched hands, engine rumbling like a fat, white cat. "Holy crap!" The warm, slick hood was close enough to catch me when my knees gave out. "That was . . . holy crap," I wheezed.

When the dome light flicked on, a bell *ping, ping, pinged.* Cell phone clenched in her hand, a girl in a clown wig and street clothes scooted off the front seat. "OMG, Janine! I almost ran over a guy in black pajama bottoms! No, I'm not kidding. Look!" She aimed her phone at me. "Hey, are you okay?"

I stumbled back, shaking from my adrenaline overdose, and looked myself up and down. "Yeah. I guess. Seth?" The road behind me was empty. My trophy lay cracked in two, the pieces glinting on the pavement. "Seth!"

"Will, over here."

"Damn," I gasped, doubling over. Back on the sidewalk, the SUV's headlights lit one side of Seth's body and a long black shadow stretched from the other. Road grit clung to one sleeve, but he was upright, breathing. "Are you hurt?"

Dazedly, he lifted one fist into the beam. Bright red glistened on his knuckles. "Just scratches." He let his hand drop.

He'd lost the glow, but his zombie-like calm was just as disturbing. "Did you hit your head?"

"Looks like he's okay," the girl said to her phone. She hitched a hip onto the front seat looking annoyed that we'd interrupted her conversation. "Stay out of the street, you guys. You could've gotten yourselves killed." She slammed her door and the engine revved.

"No, *you* stay out of the street!" I yelled as our only source of light sped off. Mumbling a curse, I lifted my arms and stretched out a toe, trying to feel my way to the curb and Seth.

Some cosmic joker flipped a switch. The streetlights popped back to life, and I threw my forearm up to block the sudden glare. "Ahh! Sure, *now* you come on! Do you believe this?"

A scent wafted to me that cut off my rant. The strange, out-of-placeness of it made my nostrils flare. *Cinnamon rolls?* It was so strong and sweet that I could almost feel the heat of an open oven door brush my skin. Goose bumps rose on goose bumps across my bare chest as I turned around.

A woman, *the* woman Seth had rescued, stood beside him. For a second, I wondered if I'd been the one who hit my head. I'd totally forgotten her. She must have been hidden in the shadow Seth cast in the headlights. With her hand tucked into his elbow and her mouth turned up in a little smile, she looked totally unfazed.

Unfazed and familiar. I recognized her like I recognized the heavenly smell of those cinnamon rolls. They both belonged in a little kid's memories from a long time ago.

"Grams?"

CHAPTER THREE

"Hello, Will."

I remembered Grams' face like I remembered Dad's. Part real details, part stories made up to go with the pictures that I used to sneak out of Seth's dresser. Her short, silvery hair and green eyes, I knew. But that fragile body, thin enough to blow away? That was new. I used to fantasize about the day she'd finally come back to us, but my imagination wasn't nearly good enough.

"What are you doing here? How . . .?" Years-worth of questions tangled my tongue. "Grams, where have you been?" Her eyebrows drew together pulling wrinkles that I didn't remember along with them.

"I wish I could have come home sooner. I'm so sorry." She traced a line along Seth's jaw with the backs of her fingers and that little gesture, so familiar, made my breath hitch. "You look so much like your father," she murmured. And then turning back to me, "That was quick thinking, taking off your tunic. I'm proud of you."

"That was pure desperation. Grams, *what* are you doing here?"

Instead of answering, she patted Seth's shoulder. "I'll explain everything, but Seth needs to sit down. Let's find a warm spot where we can talk. Collect your things." With both hands tucked around Seth's elbow, she steered him back toward the town square.

It took a massive shiver to get my feet moving. It didn't help that the damned cat, despite being a lot gentler about it, was still kneading the top of my grave. I wrestled my cold, wet tunic over my head and then scooped up the pieces of my trophy as I ran to catch up. "Seth, are you sure you're okay?" I asked, teeth chattering.

"Your brother is strong. He'll be fine," Grams said, as we turned the corner.

Seth obviously *wasn't* fine. He hadn't said *boo* to our long-lost grandmother. When my trophy hit the trash can on the sidewalk, he barely reacted. If he hadn't hit his head, was this zombie routine some kind of shock?

Grams led him up the steps to the Heartland Cafe, and I crowded behind them. A bell tinkled as we walked inside. Air, warm and thick with the scents of frying meat and toasted bread, eased my shivering. Gently drawing Seth along the aisle, Grams settled him into the last booth by the windows. I huddled into the lumpy, red vinyl seat on the other side.

"Happy Halloween," the server said.

Pulling worried eyes away from Seth, I looked up.

Clouds parted. The sun came out. The angels sang.

My mouth made a lopsided grin. "Hey, Maureen. I didn't know you worked here."

Maureen Gardener, she'd literally been the girl-next-door before the grandmonsters moved us out of *that little cracker box* after Dad died. I proposed to her when we were both five and hadn't seen her much since then. But Eagle Shoal only had one high school, and this year, I was back in her orbit.

"Will, hi," she said with a polite I'll-be-your-server smile. "Yeah, it's my first weekend. And I go by Reen now. Maureen's my grandma's name too. It was confusing."

"Sure, I get that." Sparkling jack-o-lantern pins caught the dark curls trying to escape her ponytail. She had skin like chai tea, eyes the color of perfectly toasted toast and a curvy body that looked soft and strong at the same time. Naturally, I devolved into a jabbering idiot. "Reen's nice. It fits you. I like it." *Shut up. Shut up.*

"Thanks." When she turned to Seth, her pencil and pad ready, she gasped. "Oh!"

"What?" I asked. He didn't look *that* bad after his roll in the street. Like always, he looked too damned good.

"Sorry," Reen said, hugging herself. "Cat just walked over my grave. Do you ever get that feeling?"

"All freakin' day," I said, starring at the girl. She felt it too?

Reen laughed like I was kidding and gave a decisive nod. "Chocolate will fix that darned cat. Hot cocoa's the Halloween special.

"I'll try anything." Remembering our surprise guest, I looked over at Grams to see if she'd take the cure too, but she shook her head. Seth didn't even look up. "Make it two. Heavy on the hot."

"Okay. Be right back."

I watched her walk away and would have kept watching, but Seth's pale face and Grams' level gaze pulled me back. I took a couple napkins out of the chrome holder and passed them over to Seth. "Here, clean up the blood a little." He took the napkins, but I could tell he didn't know what to do with them. "Your knuckles, man."

"You don't have to worry about your brother tonight," Grams said, patting his arm.

Something about the way she said, *tonight*, made me worry harder. "So, this is your idea of a family reunion? Kind of dramatic don't you think?"

Gram's slender fingers curled into a fist in the middle of the table. "Did the incident teach you anything?"

I frowned. "That I should be thankful for anti-lock brakes?"

She looked at me like she had when I was little and she caught me with my finger up my nose. "You followed your instinct to protect your brother, as I knew you would."

Either she'd been less confusing when I was five or I'd lost some kid-like ability to follow her train of thought. "You knew I would? What are you talking about?"

Reen came back with two steaming mugs of cocoa and set them in front of Seth and me. "Can I get you anything else?"

"No, nothing. Thanks." I took a scalding swallow as Grams watched me like she could wait all night for me to get a clue. I shifted on the seat. "Are you trying to tell me that you were lying in the street waiting for us to walk by? You set us up?" I tried a grin to show I was in on the joke. Her familiar green eyes didn't waver. "Grams, that's just . . . Nobody could pull off a stunt like that." She couldn't have known we'd be there. Every streetlight on the block went out. How'd she manage that? And *why*? I scrambled for some reasonable explanation. Practical joke? Hidden cameras? Nuts. But explaining all this drama away as mere coincidence? That was nuts too.

"You've become quite skilled at martial arts," Grams said, nodding to herself like she was checking off my score on a test I didn't know I was taking. "I'm here tonight to make you an offer."

"An offer?" I asked, my throat suddenly dry. Grams leaned across the table and the vinyl seat gave a long, low scrunch as I leaned hard the other way.

"William Ian McCurty," my grandmother said. "I've come to offer you your destiny."

CHAPTER FOUR

estiny? Knee-deep-in-average guys like me didn't have destinies. "That's a pretty heavy word, isn't it, Grams? Marvel comics stuff?" I could feel the goofy, confused look on my face, but she ignored it.

"Did you ever wonder how your father solved so many difficult cases while he was on the police force?" Grams asked.

A familiar ache came with the memories of Dad. When I was a kid, being a cop was right up there with being a Power Ranger. I'd wondered for years what went so wrong that night that a superhero couldn't handle it? And why couldn't Mom get over it?

"Your father practiced more than good police work. He'd begun to teach you. Do you remember?" Grams glanced hopefully at Seth who freaked me out by giving her the tiniest nod.

"All Dad taught *me*," I said, "was *Stairway to Heaven*

on his guitar. That's not what you're talking about."

Grams straightened, lifting her chin. "Will, your father was a medium. A human Bridge between the living and the dead."

Another beat went by while my brain replayed the nonsense words my ears had just fed it. *Bridge-between-the-living-and-the-dead?* Okay, now I knew there were hidden cameras. "Dad was into séances?"

"Séances are for amateurs and charlatans. Please listen." She went on as calmly as if she was explaining that Seth and I came from a long line of accountants. "Spirits traumatized by the circumstances of their deaths can become trapped In Between. They're fixated on the living, watching loved ones, following enemies, unable to turn away and journey on to the Light. Our family's gift, mine, and your father's, is to provide a temporary path back to this plain. Just as someone steps onto a bridge to cross a stream, so the dead step *into* the medium to cross the veil. We give them a voice, quite literally. This ability passes to the first-born in each generation. I had it, then your father, now . . ."

We both looked at Seth. Grams' little smile had an edge now and her fingers tightened on his arm.

"Seth, are you hearing this?" I asked him.

"The heir can't bear the weight of a second soul and listen too," Grams said. "He needs someone willing to join him in his mission and ensure his safety. He must bond with a partner, his Keeper."

Keeper. The word floated across the table, hit me in the chest and sank in.

Grams raised a pale finger to tap her temple. "The

Keeper remembers. He stores every word uttered by the dead. He's a protector and a source of strength, sometimes great strength for the Bridge. Together, Bridge and Keeper resolve the earthly troubles that prevent souls from passing into the Light." She smiled in a proud grandmotherly way. "I believe, your brother chose you the day you were born. And you proved tonight that you're ready. The bond between you is strong and clear."

I looked at Seth's pale face and frowned. Maybe, if I stretched credibility past the moon's orbit for Grams' sake, I could accept that he'd inherited some psychic gift from Dad. But why drag me into it? His Keeper-protector? A source of great strength? If he chose me the day I was born, why hadn't the subject come up in the past sixteen years? Her story was full of holes.

But something squirrelly and insistent in my gut argued with my rational brain. *It's all true,* it whispered. *One hundred percent. And you know it.*

"I don't have a super memory," I said, studying my hands, white-knuckled on the wad of napkins smudged with Seth's blood.

"But there are other things. Sensitivities?" She arched an eyebrow in question.

I looked up quickly. "The cat walking over my grave thing?" I rubbed my chest where the damned thing was still pacing back and forth. "That's just random weirdness."

"You've always had empathy in the presence of spirits. Other abilities will come to you if you accept this responsibility." She paused then added gently, "The burden is yours to take up or deny, Will."

Searching her lined face and earnest eyes, I looked for a soft spot that would prove my squirrelly gut wrong. No luck. "What happens if I say, no?"

Grams' brows knitted together. "Seth made a choice tonight too. He can't go back. Without you, he'd need to choose another Keeper."

Across the booth, Seth sat still, eyes down, not showing a hint of what *he* wanted.

I swallowed hard. Telling Grams, *no,* would mean Seth could finally go off to get his own life. A weird life, but at least I'd be free to figure out mine, and Mom might pull herself together. The possibility should have cheered me up. Instead, my body felt heavy.

My brother had made dysfunction functional in our messed-up household since he was twelve. Even if this was just some crazy hallucination, saying, *no,* felt like the worst kind of betrayal. Who'd care enough to protect Seth better than I would?

There was only one answer. I had to clear my throat twice to get it out. "Yeah, I'll be his Keeper." The alien sadness and regret churning in my chest settled as if the cat had curled up on my grave and begun to purr. Grams gave me a proud, relieved smile and slid to the edge of the booth.

"Wait. That's it?" I asked, rising from my seat. "You can't leave. What happens now? What do I have to do?"

"Your abilities will strengthen along with Seth's over the coming days and weeks. Marcus will come. He'll teach you what he can."

"Marcus Dean? Uncle Marcus?"

She nodded. "He was your father's Keeper."

My eyebrows climbed. What I remembered about Marcus Dean was that he was our adopted uncle and Dad's partner on the force. He'd been shot the same night Dad was killed. "Where's he been all this time? With you?"

Ignoring the question, she reached the edge of the booth, her fingertips still resting on Seth's arm. "Bonded siblings are rare in modern times. We've forgotten so much of the lore. I can't predict what abilities you'll manifest. Cultivate every resource. You'll need them for what's coming." She looked tenderly at Seth. "You've been a strong Bridge for me, child." Turning back to me, she sighed. "My visit has drained us both. I'll stay nearby, but we won't meet again, Will, not like this."

"What does that mean?" Her free hand drifted slowly over the table toward me. An icy chill flowed from it.

I blinked. It was like one of those optical illusions you've looked at for hours thinking it was a rabbit, and then all of a sudden you see a duck. Everything that had happened since the tournament clicked into a new focus. Cold dread froze my lungs, and I shrank back. As her hand, gentle and terrifying, drew close to my cheek, her fingertips lifted from Seth's forearm.

His breath rushed out. He slumped forward.

I felt a bubble break like my ears had popped.

And our grandmother disappeared.

CHAPTER FIVE

I stared at empty air, studied every molecule till my eyes burned. *NO. We did NOT have hot chocolate with a ghost!* But Grams was gone, and so was my grave-loving cat. Trembling, Seth hunched his shoulders, and I slid over next to him. "Are you okay?"

"C . . . cold," he mumbled.

I fought the urge to throw my arms around him right there in front of God and everybody. "I think Reen slipped pharmaceuticals into our cocoa, man." His face was pasty and slicked with sweat. I pressed the warm mug into his hands. "Drink it anyway." Catching Reen's eye, I said, "Scuse me, would you come here for a second?"

"How can I help you?" she asked, glancing worriedly at Seth.

"Listen, the woman we came in with, did you see where she went?"

Reen frowned. "Just the two of you came in. If a lady joined you, I didn't see her." She gave me a confused, apologetic smile.

Oh hell. "Could we have the check?"

It took forever to walk home, me talking the whole way, hoping Seth would snap out of it. The longest sentence he managed was, *Please, shut up.*

Mom's car wasn't in the garage, which would have worried me any other night. Tonight, I only felt relief. I couldn't explain what just happened even with Grams' every word, every gesture running through my mind in 3D, hi-def with smell-o-vision. Super memory. Just like a good little Keeper.

I fought down panic. If I was already changing, what was happening to Seth?

My body was numb with cold by the time we made it up to his room. I barely managed to wrestle him out of his clothes and get him under a pile of blankets before my knees buckled. He was asleep, or passed out, before I knelt beside his bed to catch my breath.

A replay of Grams' hand—dead Grams' dead hand— reached across the café table. Some deep-down instinct told me that if she'd touched me, even for an instant . . . I clenched my fist around Seth's blanket. She'd had her hand tucked in the crook of his arm for what? Half an hour? More?

"Grams wouldn't hurt you," I whispered, determined to convince both of us. I pressed my palm against Seth's back until I felt the thud of his heartbeat and my breathing slowed.

Stumbling to my room, I muttered, "Psychotic episode. Had to be." Fixable with medication and a lot of therapy. It was that, or ghosts were real. I'd just promised one that I'd *join Seth as his Keeper* doing who knew what for who knew how long. *There better be a hell of a silver lining to this mess.* I felt around for pajama bottoms and crawled under the covers exhausted . . . but sure, I wouldn't sleep . . .

I sat cross-legged on a blanket in a cemetery, with Seth and a giant, black teddy bear that I somehow knew was Uncle Marcus. Weird place for a picnic, my dream self was thinking when my stomach took a sickening swoop. A craggy tombstone ten stories tall, tilted toward us. In a blink, I was a mile away screaming for Seth to run. *Run!*

Gasping, I fought my way out of tangled covers and stumbled to Seth's room. With my hand turning the doorknob, I woke up enough to realize that the chance of him being in there crushed under a tombstone while a giant teddy bear looked on was pretty slim. I dragged myself back down the hall.

Mom's car pulled into the garage at about two. The next thing I heard was my alarm, Jimi Hendrix's Star-Spangled Banner, wailing from my phone. When I rolled out of bed, my shoulder and chest complained about the abuse they'd suffered in the final round of the tournament, but I trudged to the window and pulled up the blind.

"Huh. Real world's still out there." I pressed my forehead against the cold glass and stared down at the rusty maple leaves lining the birdbath in the backyard. "Halloween's over. It's a brand-new day."

Kneading my shoulder, I headed for the bathroom. With the shower splattering into the tub, I leaned against the sink fingering the tender bruise on my breastbone.

Steam fogged the mirror, and I swiped it away to look myself in the eyes. "McCurty, you had a real life before you had a destiny, *damn it.*" My life had needed some sorting out, sure, but I had a plan.

The scents of rosemary and mint wafted from the soap as I lathered up in the shower. My brain perked up a little more. *I'll be his Keeper,* I'd promised. Okay, but was there a grace period in this BridgeKeeper contract, some transition time before whatever started, started? I let my unnaturally vivid memories replay. *The heir can't bear the weight of a second soul and listen too.* Seth was really out of it last night. Did that mean he hadn't been listening? *The Keeper remembers.* So, Seth didn't?

My shoulders straightened. Suds rolled down my back. If I neglected to mention it, could we *both* forget that Grams had dropped the BridgeKeeper bomb into our laps?

Out in my room, I almost did a face-plant pulling jeans on over mostly wet skin. I tucked a blue t-shirt under my arm and sat down to put on my shoes. "My hoodie and backpack are in the kitchen," I whispered as I tied the laces. If my theory was correct, Seth, oblivious to everything that had happened on the way home, would be in his room as usual, so deep in a physics text he wouldn't notice a horse gallop down the hall. I'd sneak out, spend the day at school, hit the dojang afterward, get home late, and then lock myself in my room. Avoiding Seth today would give me a chance to come up with a more long-term plan. I squashed a pesky pang of guilt. "Buying myself a little time won't hurt anybody."

The smell of coffee filled the hallway when I stepped

out of my room. Mom wouldn't be up for hours, so that meant Seth was already downstairs. *Shit.* I crept down the steps and peered around the kitchen door.

Seth stood with his back to me staring out the bay windows. His hair was wet from a recent shower, but he had on sweats and his knobby, green robe. My stomach twisted uneasily. Was he sick? Did Grams' touch hurt him after all? "Damn it." I stopped lurking and headed for the caffeine. "Why aren't you dressed. You're not ditching class, are you?"

Seth turned. "Good morning to you too. Yeah, I am, but it's only American Lit. I'm caught up." He watched me pour fresh brew into my mug. "You look kind of rough. Bad dreams?"

"That's a theory." I took a sip of searing bliss, then used the t-shirt to sop up the last few drops of my shower. As I pulled it over my head, I fixed up my poker face. "You feeling okay?" He didn't look any different, not glowing like last night.

He massaged his stubbly chin. "I'm feeling mildly terrified actually." The glint in his eyes said he meant terrifying like a great roller coaster ride. He studied the scabbed-over scrapes on his knuckles, and I fought the urge to squirm.

"I can't remember much about last night. Your tournament is crystal clear, but then things get foggy." He smiled for a second. "Foggy, get it? The rotten weather. I remember that." He let his hand drop and then stared into the empty space between us. His voice was hushed. "I woke up this morning feeling like I'd shed my skin. Literally, like I stepped out of a rubber Seth suit for the first time in a long time." Another smile grew on his face. "I feel good, really good. I just wish I could remember."

I bit my lip as Keeper memories jumped to the tip of my tongue and kicked the back of my teeth. *Tell him. Tell him.* I took a scalding gulp of coffee. "Probably a good idea for you to stay home," I managed. The thought of him leaving the house without his skin totally freaked me out. "Stay inside. Don't go anywhere."

Seth gave me an odd look. "Will, what's up? What happened?"

Don't ask! "Gonna be late!" I dumped my coffee in the sink, grabbed my backpack and hoodie off the hook by the back door, and started out. "See you tonight."

Standing outside on the porch, I tried to stop trembling. It took everything I had to take my hand off that doorknob and go to my bike. "What the hell is wrong with me?" *The precision of your memory and other abilities will come to you.* Yeah, it felt like I had some major cranial renovations going on. More stiff muscles complained as I threw my leg over my bike and forced myself into a sprint. Distance, I needed distance!

At the end of our driveway, the air thickened with the scent of cinnamon rolls. "Grams!" I almost hopped the curb owling around looking for her. The fact that I couldn't see her didn't make me feel better. *I'll stay nearby.* She was here, alright. Disapproval polluted the sweet doughy scent, turning it sharp and sour.

"Yeah. I know I promised," I huffed out the words as I pedaled hard. "I will, I am. Just not yet." The tinge in the air twisted from disapproval to disappointment. Only a ghost could make cinnamon rolls smell judgy.

"Grams, give me a break. *Please,*" I groaned. A hot tear cut a path across my cold cheek. Her scent faded almost to nothing.

Almost.

CHAPTER SIX

Cresting the hill, I straightened, letting the wind dry my face. Putting distance between me and Seth helped tone down the vivid memories, and space opened in my mind as I rolled into the high school parking lot. Unfortunately, the thoughts that filled it weren't encouraging.

I'm stuck, really stuck. Grams would haunt me for the rest of my life if I didn't fess up to Seth. One destiny offered and accepted over cocoa, and he and I were bonded, joined at the hip. He'd never leave home. He and Mom would stay locked in their silent war of wills forever. Yesterday *all* the majors at *all* the colleges had seemed like legit possibilities for me. Could I even go away to school now?

Afterlife University, Ghost Studies major?

At the back entrance, I shoved my bike into the stand and took deep breaths to stave off a wave of panic. *Calm down.* Dad went to college, got married, had a life. Uncle

Marcus may have been a Keeper, but he had a career as a cop too. And reassuringly, he could put two sentences together. *His* brain hadn't seemed overrun with full-immersion memories.

"Hey, dude." Slack-faced, half asleep, Nico poked a finger at the crust in the corner of one eye.

A flood of relief left me breathless. "Man, you're a sight for sore eyes. Combed your hair with your pillow again I see. Adorable." My best friend had *not* changed overnight. He'd probably stayed up studying after the tournament. I threw an arm over his shoulders and got him shuffling toward the building. "You would not believe the night I had."

"Hmph," was Nico's unimpressed comment. He slanted me a look. "What's up with you? You look different. Or something."

That was my cue to lay out the whole ghost story, give it an airing, and see how well it held together. But then we squeezed through the double doors into school. Voices punctuated by slamming lockers boiled up in an avalanche of echoes. The chaos wrapped around me like a warm, comfortable blanket. Real life. I couldn't bring myself to ruin it.

"Nothing's up with me," I said and dropped my helmet into my locker.

"Hmph," Nico said again, pawing at his hair. "Well, you look weird."

"You're not awake yet."

He nodded his agreement. "Workin' on it. Gotta ace a chem test today. See you at lunch." He turned and dove into the crowd that flowed down the hall.

"Real life, here I come," I muttered. *You followed your instinct to protect your brother, as I knew you would.* "Nope! No more of you, Grams." I pulled my phone out, pointed my eyes at the screen, determined to be distracted as I started to class. A Star Wars gif came up, somebody's D&D avatar, two guys sparring, one in black, one in white . . . Wait, that was me getting my ass kicked last night. Who posted that? *You've become quite skilled at martial arts.*

I squeezed my eyes shut. "Errr, brain, leave me alone. Ooof!"

Dan-the-man, football, baseball, track and field star, made an excellent wall. "Sorry, man," I said, easing around him.

"Wait." He put an arm out.

The stream of kids broke and flowed around us like we were two boulders in a riverbed. Well, a boulder and a pebble. Dan looked down at me with a dark, worried gaze. Instant empathy tightened my throat. "What's wrong?" I croaked. He put his lower lip between his teeth. *No, please. You're not gonna cry.*

His troubled eyes roved over my face. "What's your name?" he rumbled.

"Will McCurty."

Looking confused, he nodded slowly. "You're that karate kid. I don't know you."

"No, not really." I patted his shoulder. *Don't pat his shoulder! What are you doing?* "You okay, man?" I winced dreading that he'd tell me exactly why his world seemed to be imploding.

"Dan-the-maaaaan!"

Dan rocked sideways as a couple more boulders

44

from the football team barreled into him. His despair vanished, replaced by a giant, plastic grin. He shoved me past him with a sweep of his arm and put one of his teammates into a headlock.

Okay, what just happened? I stumbled backward down the hall. Had I imagined all that pain? The lump in my throat said, no. Dan seemed as confused about why he'd stopped me as I was. I hoped that he found the right person to talk to. Seemed like he really needed help.

I walked into Poli-sci looking forward to Ms. Piebottle lulling my overactive imagination into a comfortable stupor. A good doodle was what I needed. Opening my notebook, I started to draw.

Damn. What the hell? A giant, black teddy bear had appeared at the end of my pencil. Flipping to the eraser, I started scrubbing away the image, but an itchy feeling made me look up.

At her desk, Ms. Piebottle's eyes met mine over her cat-eye glasses. She stared, even more bewildered looking than usual, and tilted her head to the side. Her chin began to tremble. She half rose from her seat.

Nooo, no, no, no. Don't come over here. Don't—

"Morninnng!" a couple of girls sang as they walked past her desk.

Blinking, Ms. Piebottle seemed to remember where she was. She straightened her sweater vest and then pulled down the screen to start class. I didn't dare look up from my notebook again for the next forty minutes. What was going on with people today?

Ducking into the john, I checked my reflection over the shoulder of a short guy hogging the sink. Yeah, that was me staring back. There wasn't a neon sign over my head flashing *confide in me,* but I couldn't figure out what else was getting me all this attention.

Raking my fingers through my hair, I accidently clipped the top of the short kid's head with my elbow. "Scuse me. Sorry."

Turning, he speared me with *the stare.* Damn, I was beginning to recognize it. His was an angry, hurt stare, a Unibomber stare. His neck was too skinny for the collar of his beat-up army jacket. He had a DIY haircut and dark circles under his eyes. The funk drifting off him told me it'd been a few days since he'd showered.

Unibomber Junior didn't say a word, but he reached out and clutched my sleeve.

"What do you want from me?" My voice echoed off the bathroom tiles and he flinched, jostling loose a tear. *God, I'm such a jerk.* I took a deep breath. "Sorry, that was a douche move. Go ahead, tell me . . . whatever." I tensed. The kid licked his lips.

A couple guys came in, loud and laughing. Unibomber Junior dropped my sleeve, gave me one last desperate look, and rushed out the door.

"Wait!"

"Lover's quarrel?" One of the jackasses asked. His friend chuckled.

Fists clenched, I turned very slowly. "Cut us some slack."

The jackass opened his mouth, looked at me, closed it again. Both guys concentrated hard on hitting the urinals.

I'll never take a piss at school again. At my locker I

46

leaned against the cold, metal door and spun the lock to give myself time to think. One random emo encounter I could write off, but three in one day? Ms. Piebottle hadn't burst into tears, but she sure looked like she wanted to. What did she and Dan have in common with Unibomber Junior? Not me, that was for sure. Not before today. What *the hell?*

Nico would be wide awake by now and more clear-headed than me. The anticipation of how badly he'd freak out when I told him about last night, gave me the strength to push away from my locker and get my feet moving.

The lunch lady who'd never in the history of the school smiled at anyone, winked when I made the mistake of looking up. She gave me extra fries. Did that count? Was she number four? A little panicky, I clutched my tray and headed for the table by the Eagle Shoal mascot mural painted on the wall. Nico always got there ahead of me, and I couldn't wait to see his familiar face.

Hell no. Give me a break!

Under the giant eagle diving in for the kill, Nico wasn't alone. A girl in a crimson and black pep squad jacket sat leaning away from a fidgety kid wearing an honest-to-God pocket protector. And just to put frosting on the cake, Dan-the-man, *and* Unibomber Junior were there too. I looked around for Ms. Piebottle, sure she'd ditch the teacher's lounge and join us for lunch. A weirder combination of people at one table wasn't possible.

Could this day get any worse?

CHAPTER SEVEN

I'll ditch the tray and find a secluded corner in the library to starve in.

Nico stood up, waving like he knew exactly what I was thinking. "There he is! Saved you a spot."

I trudged closer, praying that this bizarre gathering was part of Nico's campaign to get elected president of the Snow Ball committee and had nothing to do with me. He slapped me on the shoulder, a little too hard, as I sat down under the eagle's left talon.

"See, he's not scary. Don't let the dark, broody vibe fool you."

My cheeks went hot. "So, what's goin' on?"

"Just talkin' about you, dude," Nico said, through a toothy, fake smile.

"I'm Sanna. We have Poli-sci together," Pep Squad Girl whispered, leaning my way. "I've seen you here before."

"Yep," Nico said, loud enough to remind her that she wasn't having a private conversation. "Monday,

48

Wednesday, Friday. Same table. It's just amazing."

Dan perched on the corner of the bench with his legs facing away from the table. He twisted awkwardly around, glaring. "What's your deal, man? What's she doing here?"

"I was here first, Dan." An angry flush swept Pep Squad Girl's face.

Pocket Protector Kid was all painful smiles. "I just wanted to talk. I think." He ran his fingers up and down the edges of his tray. "But I could come back another time. Or catch you later, or—"

"Stay right where you are," Nico said. "It's a free table." He slanted a look at Unibomber Junior who crammed tater tots into his mouth like he didn't expect to eat again for a week. "Absolutely anybody can sit here. Who wants to talk first?"

Four sets of eyes went straight to their trays. Mine did too. I tipped a paper cup of ketchup onto my burger hoping to remind everybody that this was just lunch. *Eat already.*

"May I sit with you, guys?"

My fingers spasmed on the cup. "Reen! What are you doing here?" *Find a napkin. Find a napkin.* "Uh, I mean of course you're here." *Oh, my God, please shut up.* It wasn't like this when we were kids. Why couldn't I be as suave as I was when I was five?

"Yeah. Long time no see," she said with an adorably lopsided smile. "Hi, Sanna, Anthony." Unrattled by the support group vibe around the table, Reen set her tray down and climbed over the bench.

A tomatoey scent wafted up from my shirt. With a

tiny smirk, Unibomber Junior, Anthony apparently, handed over a wad of slightly used napkins. I wiped off the ketchup, hoping my face didn't match it.

Reen had taken out the sparkly jack-o-lantern pins she'd worn last night and corralled her curls with a flowery headband. Her fuzzy, purple sweater made me want to reach over to see if it felt as soft as it looked. In some alternate universe where I still had my five-year-old charm, I'd do it. *Welcome to the table of misfit toys,* I'd say. What a great line.

Narrowing deep brown eyes at me, she picked up a stubby carrot from her plate and took a nibble. "Will," she said, drawing out my name.

"Yeah?" Her eyes were luminous.

"Have you noticed that your aura's going crazy today?"

"Oh?" I murmured. There was a dreamy, rom-com musical soundtrack running through my head.

"I don't see anything." Nico squinted at me.

"Believe me, he's gone all deep purples and lava reds."

Reen used the carrot to trace the outline of my body. With the movement of her hand, a deep red crystal and a pentagram tinkled among other charms on her bracelet. I finally registered what she'd said. The movie music faltered.

"You all sense it, don't you?" Reen asked, looking around the table.

Pocket Protector Kid shifted nervously, but Anthony and Sanna nodded. Even Dan looked intrigued.

"You did look shiny this morning," Nico said and then turned to Reen. "Do me next! What color's my aura?"

Was this another Keeper modification? I had a shiny

new aura that attracted troubled strangers, now? That was all I needed. But it had attracted Reen too. Maybe she'd be my silver lining.

Nibbling the carrot, she turned back to me. "How's your brother feeling? He looked kind of wobbly last night when you left the café."

My breath caught as a vivid replay of Reen carrying two mugs of cocoa gave me double vision that overlayed the current gorgeous girl across from me. I hunched over my burger and took a bite.

Nico snorted. "Seth, wobbly? Seth's never wobbly. What's up, dude?"

"He uh, got really cold last night walking home from the tournament. You know the weather was, uh . . ." I chewed a french fry, swallowing past a roiling flood of images. Seth's glow against the dark, my trophy in two pieces, Grams' lined face. With Reen's quiet, persistent gaze, she seemed to be picking the memories right out of my brain.

Abandoning any more attempts to eat lunch, I gripped my tray with shaky hands and stood. "I better check on him. I'll text you later."

"All of us?" Nico asked, one eyebrow arched.

"No, not . . ." *Smart ass.* "Later."

"Will, wait." Reen scrambled off the bench and caught up with me. "Hey, I'm sorry if I freaked you out."

"You didn't," I lied. "I just never knew you were into that witchy stuff." I dumped my plate into the trash and winced hearing the echo of my broken trophy clattering into the can outside the café.

"It's Wicca stuff mostly, with a little voodoo from my

51

mother's side. Doesn't matter. Are you okay?"

"Yeah. Just a headache. Listen, I gotta go."

"Okay, but . . ." She touched my arm. "Can I have your phone for a sec?"

A starburst of warmth spread from her touch. "Sure."

"Here's my number in case you ever want to talk about anything."

"Thanks." Did she want to talk because I was hot or because I looked so pathetic? When she handed back my phone, I could only meet her eyes for a second. It was too weird seeing my phone in her hand overlaid with the pad and pencil she'd taken our order with last night. "See you later."

Out in the hall, I dropped my pack and slumped against the wall. With a few slow, deep breaths and a lot of effort, the Heartland café, screaming headlights, and Seth's bloody knuckles sank into the background of my thoughts again.

"Lunch isn't over for ten more minutes, son."

My eyes flew open. Across the hall, a security guard stood in front of the message board. "Yeah, I know, sorry." I pushed away from the wall. "Just heading to, uh, the library."

A girl with straight, blond hair smiled out from the flyer he was putting up. *MISSING*, ran above her head in tall letters. The guard noticed me looking, ripped the flyer off the board, and crunched it in one fist. So, he was taking it down, not putting it up. I hadn't heard anything about a missing girl.

"What's your name, son?" he asked, stepping toward me, putting a lot of energy into pulverizing that flyer.

"Have we tangled before?"

"Tangled? No sir." I picked up my pack.

"Your name?"

"Will McCurty." I could almost see him etching me onto his shit list. *Great. Just great.* He swung his hand in a move-along gesture. I moved.

Time crept by like a sloth in no hurry. Barely able to keep my butt in the chair for the last few minutes of class, I rubbed a spot between my eyes where a weird buzzing headache had started. A brutal workout at the dojang was what I needed. I texted Nico. *Dojang 3:30. Can I come over for dinner? We need to talk.* At 3:02, I grabbed stuff out of my locker and lunged for the back door like I was abandoning the Titanic.

The yeasty smell of cinnamon rolls hit me the moment I stepped outside. Instead of Grams, I spotted my dad's, lovingly restored, dark blue '68 Mustang idling at the curb. Seth's car. *Ohhhh shit.*

He leaned out and waved. "Will! Put your bike on the rack. We need to talk."

CHAPTER EIGHT

Fumbling with the seatbelt, I could barely see anything beyond the surge of replays running against my eyelids. In close quarters with Seth, the senso-rama doubled, crashed into my headache, and doubled that too. I hardly dared unclench my jaws for fear I'd spew the whole story of Grams' visit. "What are you doing here?" I managed.

Seth squeezed the steering wheel like he was reining something in too. His eyes were bright, his mouth set in a little smile that he kept trying and failing to turn down. "I figured out what happened last night." He nosed the Mustang into traffic "I understand why you don't want to tell me. I mean, it's crazy, right?"

He was fishing. He still didn't remember a damned thing. We turned left out of the parking lot instead of heading home. "Where are we going?"

"I want to take you somewhere we haven't been in a long time." He was almost bouncing in his seat. My

54

brother did not bounce. "You remember how Dad taught you to read?"

"No," I lied. Other dads took their kids to ballfields or parks on Saturdays. Dad and Seth went to cemeteries. If Mom didn't have my weekend booked up with kiddie classes for future geniuses, I tagged along. I learned the alphabet sounding out names on tombstones.

Seth grinned. "Well, I'm hoping Muddy Bend will jog your memory."

Muddy Bend Cemetery, ancient shade trees, jonquils popping up in the spring, peonies in the summer, all thriving on people fertilizer. Seth might not remember the details of last night, but it sure seemed like he knew that Dad and Uncle Marcus were BridgeKeepers. *And he never told me!*

"What?" Seth asked. "Why are you looking at me like that?"

"Watch the road."

Seth's smile grew as the Mustang's tires crunched gravel. A split-log sign read *Muddy Bend Cemetery Established 1884.* We drove along the narrow car path and parked under an old, crooked mulberry tree. Somewhere at home, there was a picture of my grinning face smeared purple with mulberry juice.

The cinnamon scent was so thick it felt like Grams was in my lap and the moment Seth cut the engine, I jumped out of the car. A chill breeze brushed my sweaty face and rippled the tall grass beyond a barbed wire fence. *Grams' fingers, gentle and terrifying, reached for me across the table.* I shoved my fists into my hoodie pockets, seaming my lips against the pressure of words that wanted out.

"Will, I know what happened to me, but I'm not sure what happened *to you*. I'm going to ask you to do something."

"Don't," I gritted out.

"I have to know."

Don't ask.

"Will, tell me what happened last night."

Those seven words smashed the dam I'd spent all day shoring up.

I. Couldn't. Stop myself!

Pop, pop, pop, streetlights cut out. Seth followed a sound into the road. Grams materialized. Brakes screeched. Cinnamon rolls. Word-for-word, I told him everything Grams and I had said across the table in the café. Even things I hadn't said out loud, all of it rolled out of my mouth. By the time I got to, *Poof, she disappeared,* I was crouched against the Mustang's tire, Seth in front of me, his fingers digging into my shoulders.

"Will! Breathe. It's over. Hey, are you okay?"

Breathing seemed like a good suggestion. I gave it a try. First thing I noticed when my heart stopped hammering was the blessed silence in my head. I had that relieved, shaky feeling you get after a really good puke. No weird buzzing headache. No replay. Cautiously, I teased up a memory and found that I could think back to Grams' visit without a full-on flashback attack. Seth was right. It was over.

And . . . I . . . was . . . pissed! "Get off me. How did you do that?"

"I didn't know it would work like that. I'm so sorry."

"How'd you *do it?*" I snarled into his worried face.

56

Seth grimaced. "Dad and Marcus showed me once. It's called a Sharing. It's the way a Keeper brings his Bridge up to speed. You feel better, right?"

Seth followed as I got up and stumbled around the car. "How long have you known you were a Bridge? Years? And you never told me!"

He raised his hands. "I didn't know for sure. I hoped it would happen, but I couldn't tell you anything. I swear, I couldn't."

"Bullshit! Why not?"

"Mom. She thinks I'm cursed."

"Are you? Are we?"

"No, no way. Cursed is her word, not mine. After Dad died Mom was a mess. You remember that her parents had her committed to that sanitarium?"

I frowned. "No, I thought . . . I don't know what I thought. I just remember we lived at Nico's for a while. What's that have to do with this?"

"I think it was some kind of brainwashing therapy. When Mom got back from that place, she tried to cut me off from BridgeKeeping completely, forbade me from talking about it. If she could have wiped every memory of Dad being a Bridge out of my mind, she would have. You were so little, Dad never really explained it to you. I didn't think it was possible for you to become—"

"Your human memory bank? Your minion?"

"It's not like that."

"No? That Sharing thing was against my will!"

"Why?" Seth asked, spreading his arms in exasperation. "Why didn't you just tell me?"

Because I want a normal family! I want my own life!

Raking my fingers into my hair, I paced away from the car and the mulberry tree, realized I was heading deeper into the cemetery, and paced back. "My brain's been on fire since last night! You wouldn't believe the shit I went through today." I jabbed a finger at him. "You've had your whole life to get ready for this. I had one conversation and now I'm supposed to be okay with it?"

"I'm sorry!"

"Well, that makes it all better, doesn't it?" I kicked a rock that shot across the barbed-wire fence.

"I was ten when Uncle Marcus explained that I'd choose a Keeper someday. I told him I already had one. You. But Dad said it wasn't possible, you couldn't be my Keeper."

"Well, thanks a lot for ignoring him." Seth bit his lip and swallowed hard. *Shit.* For the second time today, I forced the asshole tone out of my voice. "Why would Dad say that?"

"I don't know. Maybe he knew how Mom would react. Or maybe it was the sibling thing. Grams said sibling partners are rare in modern times, but not impossible, right?" I nodded slowly. "Okay, so, obviously Dad was wrong."

"Well, that's just great. What little information we have is wrong."

"I wish I'd asked more questions, but our lessons got cut kind of short!"

By a bullet to the chest.

Seth's eyes went watery. But I was the first to look away.

"Dad made sure I understood one thing," he said after a long silence. "What he and Marcus did, what *we* do

58

now, saves people, living and dead. It's important. Vital."

I slumped against the Mustang. "Listen to yourself. I'm a sixteen-year-old without a driver's license. You still live with your mother."

Seth swiped a knuckle under his eye nodding. "I know. This is crazy." He leaned beside me, and we stared out at the wobbly lines of lichen-crusted tombstones.

"Mom's breakdown, or whatever it was, happened years ago," I said. "Maybe she's mellowed."

Seth glowered. "She still has her parents whispering in her ear."

"The grandmonsters," I muttered, my lip curling.

"Mom hoped she could force me to make a more respectable choice when I came of age."

"You had a choice?"

He nodded. "I could have ignored Grams' voice out in the street. Could have walked away and gone on with my life."

"Seth, man! Why didn't you?"

He looked at me like I'd asked him why he hadn't torn up a winning lottery ticket. "I've been waiting for this my whole life. And you said yes too, little brother." He leaned toward me until his shoulder bumped mine, one side of his mouth turned up. "Thanks for that."

I snorted softly. "Temporary insanity." It wasn't fair, this skinless version of my brother. Exposed to his determination to follow in Dad's footsteps, my doubts softened around the edges. And damn it, I did feel better after the Sharing.

At the bottom of a rolling hill beyond the barbed wire fence, a pond glistened under the low, orange sun.

Scents of burning leaves and cattle rode the breeze. No more cinnamon rolls. Grams seemed to have left us now that I'd told Seth everything. My pang of disappointment surprised me.

"So, what's next?" I asked. "How do we do this BridgeKeeper thing?"

"I'm not totally sure. But, that's why Uncle Marcus is coming, right?"

"Right. I guess."

Seth straightened, rubbing his palms together, and walked down the slope toward the graves. "In the meantime, how about a little practice?"

"Whoa, whoa, whoa! You can't be serious?"

"That's why I brought you here, and why Dad used to bring *me* here. Everybody buried at Muddy Bend passed on a long time ago. There are only echoes left, no actual lost souls. I'll remember everything that happens. That cat of yours is quiet, isn't it?"

"I don't feel anything," I said, rubbing my chest. "But who knows if we can trust that?"

"Trust *me*. This'll be fun."

"Fun?" I looked up. "Seth. Stop!"

"Whaaaat?" he groaned, half turning back to me.

"You're glowing again. No, don't blow me off. It happened last night too, right before Grams showed up." He pushed his jacket sleeves up above his wrists, and I said, "Really? You don't see that?"

"Nothing. I don't remember Dad glowing either." He shrugged. "That's our first question for Uncle Marcus. Come on."

"It doesn't bother you how clueless we are?"

60

"You're clueless. Just follow me, Keeper. All you have to do is watch."

"Sure, in a graveyard, at twilight."

Seth laughed and I smiled. I couldn't help it. His excitement was contagious.

When I tagged along on Dad's cemetery fieldtrips, we'd play hide-and-seek among the tombstones, practice reading, and then Seth and I would follow him down the rows. I had no idea what was really going on and thought he was just making up awesome stories. Tonight, in the semi-darkness, Seth's hand stretched toward the markers just like Dad's. He passed a headstone carved like a tree stump, a rusty wrought-iron cross, and then finally cocked his head toward a plain, marble stone poking through the shaggy grass.

"Ready or not," he said, and winked.

The hairs on my arms stood up as he knelt. "What do you hear?" I asked.

Seth's glowing hand slid down the rough edge of the stone, and then he pressed his palm flat on the grave. "Shhh. This isn't as easy as Dad made it look."

If my pounding heart distracted him, he'd just have to deal with it. I held my breath, focusing on the hollow place in my chest. It stayed empty. No alien emotions. Seth moved his head like he was tuning into a weak radio signal. His glow grew stronger, and my eyes widened.

Nico and I used to stick flashlights in our cheeks so that blood red light shined through us. Seth's glow was *not* like that. Milky white everywhere his bare skin was exposed, it sharpened his cheekbones, turned his eyebrows into black slashes, and made tiny blue capillaries stand out along his jaw.

"I'm getting something," he whispered. "Images, feelings. It's all jumbled up. Ugh, how did Dad make sense of this?"

"Hey." I crouched beside him. "Take a breath." I drew in a deep one, and Seth, eyes closed, nodded and breathed with me. With the sun tilted so low in the sky, it was hard to make out the chiseled inscription on the stone. Seth's glow stayed under his skin. His hand didn't illuminate a single blade of grass. I leaned closer. "It says, Nancy Kinney, wife of . . . somebody. She died in nineteen-nineteen."

"I think I'm getting her last few days. There was fever in the house." Seth bowed his head. "Sickness came with the summer heat. She was . . . God, she was so tired, but nursing the kids kept her going until . . ." He winced and slowly looked down the row where three markers, miniatures of Nancy's, huddled close.

I whispered, "Those were her kids?"

Seth jerked his hand off the ground and sat back on his heels, letting out a shaky breath. "Yeah." He didn't seem inclined to touch the grave again.

There were no strangely inappropriate scents on the air. No apparitions rising from the graves. A relieved smile curved my lips. Maybe, just maybe, this new hobby of ours would turn out to be something awesome after all.

"That was incredible, right?!" Seth shouted, jumping up beside me as I stood. A sleepy cow let out a ticked-off moo as Seth's voice echoed down the hill.

"Shhhh! Have a little respect. That's enough fun for one night." I wrapped my arm around his shoulder and dragged him toward the car.

"I get why Dad called them echoes," he said excitedly. "There was nobody there. It was like watching an old, degraded film, with smells and feelings. Does that make any sense?"

"No. But I'll take your word for it."

He turned to face me his eyes wide with awe. "The coolest thing? The echoes aren't just floating around for me to pick out of the air, I had to *pull* them out of her grave."

I looked back at the shadowy line of Kinney gravestones. "From her corpse?"

Seth's smile dimmed. "I guess so. Dad said old cemeteries are quieter. The remains here are mostly dust by now."

"So, in a new cemetery where people are pickled in formaldehyde and buried in airtight vaults, it'd be a lot noisier?"

"That's a theory." He slapped me on the shoulder. "We'll have to test it out."

"Not tonight." I lunged for the Mustang to open Seth's door. His glow had faded. He looked like his old self again, except for the happiness humming in every line of his face, lightening the way he moved, putting a lilt in his voice.

"I freaked you out, didn't I?" He looked pleased instead of sorry. "Don't worry so much. Uncle Marcus will teach us everything we need to know."

"He'll teach us everything he *can*. Those were Grams' exact words." I tapped my temple as I went around to the passenger side and got in.

Seth started the car, grinning. "What more could we need?"

CHAPTER NINE

After the night and day I'd had, the Mustang's rumbling bucket seat would have lulled me to sleep except for a nagging impatience to get Seth home . . . where he'd be safe. I'd felt the same whispered warning this morning. What was that about? My shoulders slumped with relief when we pulled into the garage.

"Mom's home," Seth said.

"Don't tell her what happened," I said, following his gaze to Mom's shiny BMW. "Not tonight."

"Why not? I doubt she's mellowed on the subject of BridgeKeeping," Seth trailed me as I lifted my bike off the trunk rack, "but it won't be a total shock. I can handle her."

"Since when? You two can't agree that the sun's come up. Let's wait until Uncle Marcus gets here." *Damn, the man better be teleporting from wherever the hell he is.* "Look, I get that you want to rub her nose in it a little, but even if she's not shocked about your choice, she will be about mine." I leaned against the bike. "Please. I've had way too many emotional conversations today."

Seth's jaws bunched and a word slipped from between his teeth. If I hadn't known that pigs would fly through an ice storm in hell before my brother uttered a curse, I would have sworn that word was spelled with four letters. "Fine, I'll wait for Uncle Marcus."

"Thanks," I said, relieved. "It's Friday, Mom's probably on her way out anyway. Avoid her until the coast is clear."

I opened the kitchen door and knew instantly that something wasn't right. A hot cheesy scent made my stomach rumble. It was as out of place as the cinnamon rolls in the street last night. Nobody in our house cooked. *Another ghost?*

"Will, you're late!"

"Mom?" I took a cautious step inside. Mom stood by the open oven wearing a white silk blouse with designer jeans and a little apron tied around her waist. The grandmonsters bought us a subscription for weekly deliveries of Showy Chef frozen meals. Our normal dinners were every man for himself.

"What's all this?" Seth asked like we'd walked in on her cooking meth instead of dinner.

Every light in the kitchen was on, the counter tops gleamed, the chandelier sparkled. The table was set with three white China plates on blue placemats that I'd never seen before. It looked perfect enough for one of Mom's interior design shoots.

"We having company?" I give her a sideways hug.

66

Mingled with the scent of her perfume, I caught a whiff of vodka. Whatever was going on, her timing couldn't have been worse.

"No company." Mom wiped clean hands on her spotless apron. "It's spinach lasagna, your favorite. I felt bad about missing your karate match last night."

"It's Hapkido," Seth said. "He won the tournament."

"Second place," I said, giving him a don't-start-anything look. "No big deal."

My phone bleeped its text alert. *At the dojang. Headed home. Where r u?* A string of emojis followed Nico's message—puzzled face, pissed face, worried face, dog pile. I typed, *Sorrysorrysorry!!!! Mom made dinner.* That would shock him out of being mad. *Tell you about it tomorrow.* Nico's response came fast. *You better, at the Fling. Pic u up at 7. Costume!!* I groaned. I'd forgotten all about the Fall Fling. Another message came before I could text him an excuse to get out of it. *No excuses! Reen will be there.* A wink emoji. *See ya.*

"You won't be on the phone through dinner, will you?" Mom asked. "I have a little news."

Shaking off the lame smile that had appeared on my face at the mention of Reen's name, I said, "Nope. Done. So, what's your news?"

"Let's start dinner first."

Mom carried over a foil pan of spinach lasagna big enough to feed a football team, and Seth and I hovered beside the table. Neither of us knew where to sit. Untying her apron, Mom picked up a glass of tomato juice on the rocks and when she sat, we took seats on either side of her. I hurried to wrangle a hunk of lasagna onto Seth's plate. *Eat, don't talk.* Cheese stretched and sagged onto his blue placemat.

Mom opened her napkin. "As I said, I got a bit of news today. Sad news." She looked up as if to make sure we were fully clear on that fact. "I'm not sure you remember him, but your father's old partner, Marcus Dean called me last night."

My lasagna-ladened fork froze half-way to my mouth.

"We remember him," Seth said, going stone-faced.

An unhappy frown line formed on Mom's forehead. She reached for a plastic tub of salad. "He called to tell me that Ellen, your *other* grandmother, passed on yesterday."

I manufactured some surprise. "That's terrible. What happened to her?"

"She wasn't a young woman," Mom said, arranging a few lettuce leaves on her plate. "She and Marcus had been staying with his family." She waved her fork vaguely. "Somewhere in the South. Ellen was baking and had a stroke. It was very quick."

Baking cinnamon rolls, I'd bet my black belt.

"When is he coming?" Seth asked.

Mom lifted her gaze to Seth's. "He's not. Why would he?"

If a face of stone could go even harder, Seth's did. She knew exactly why Uncle Marcus should come, and why Seth would ask. But she didn't know *I* knew. I dialed back my frustration. "What did he say exactly?"

"Nothing more. Why would you expect someone who hasn't visited us in years to suddenly show some—"

"Don't pretend they stayed away by choice." Seth's

voice dropped into his flat, pissed-off register.

Mom heard it and red splotches crept up her neck. "You think I could have kept them away if they'd wanted to see you? Your grandmother always did exactly as she pleased. We haven't needed Marcus for a long time, and we certainly don't need him now."

I wish I could have come back sooner, Grams said last night. *Something* kept them away. Seth gave me a smoldering look, and I was sure that he'd break his promise and tell Mom everything.

Instead, he pushed his chair back. "I'm not hungry."

"Don't leave the house," Mom said stiffly.

Why don't you want him to leave? Why don't I? If we weren't playing this, I know she knows, but she doesn't know I know game, I could ask her.

Mom didn't look up as he dumped his full plate into the sink and stalked out of the kitchen. I jumped up and had to grab my chair to keep it from toppling over. "I'll be right back."

"Hey!" I whispered as loudly as I dared. He stopped with one hand white-knuckled on the stair railing. "No way Mom scared Uncle Marcus off. Grams came back from the dead to tell us he was coming. He's coming." On a huff of breath, Seth's shoulders relaxed a little. I hesitated but I had to say it. "And don't leave the house. It sounds crazy, but I've got a feeling and apparently Mom does too."

Slowly, he looked at me over his shoulder. "Like your cat thing?"

I shrugged helplessly. "Maybe something like that."

"Okay."

I waited until his door slammed upstairs before steeling myself to walk back into the kitchen.

"Have you noticed anyone new in Seth's life?" Mom asked as I sat down. She sipped her tomato juice, starring at the little heap of salad on her plate.

I took a bite of lasagna while I had the chance. "Like who? A girl?"

"Not necessarily a girl, just someone special."

"Are you asking me if he's gay?"

That pulled her stare away from the salad. "Will, I'm serious. Does your brother have a new friend? Someone he's suddenly very close to?"

Ohhh, like a Keeper. I could end this game right now. All I had to do was lean over and say, *It's me, Mom. I'm Seth's Keeper.* I almost did it, but the glass of juice was trembling in her hand, and her eyes were bright with a fear that bewildered me. "No. There's nobody new."

Not an outright lie.

"Good. That's good." She let out a long sigh.

"Mom," I began cautiously. "I think it might be good to see Uncle Marcus again. I'd like to know where he's been all this time."

She shook her head. "He isn't welcome here, honey. You're too young to remember, but Marcus was your father's partner, closer to him than a brother, closer to him than I . . ." She pressed her lips into a tight line. "It was his *job* to keep your father safe, but he failed him."

"You mean that night?" I asked frowning. "That wasn't his fault. Uncle Marcus got shot too." I didn't know all the details. Seth didn't know much either, but we understood that Dad died in one of those

70

nightmare scenarios that cops pray they never run into, a domestic disturbance call, a gun in the dark. But now an uncomfortable question occurred to me. Was Mom blaming Uncle Marcus the cop, or Uncle Marcus the Keeper?

She tossed her napkin on the table. "That's enough talk about him. He hasn't been part of our lives for a very long time. I'd prefer to keep it that way." She stood with her empty glass and left the kitchen.

I quickly cleared the table, cramming in a few more bites of lasagna, and then followed the sound of rattling ice cubes. Mom hadn't bothered to flip on a light in her office, so I reached for the table lamp. Sketches and wallpaper samples covered the top of her desk. Mom set a bottle of vodka down on the corner and then bent to the mini fridge to top her glass off with a splash of tomato juice.

"Your father and I met in college. Do you remember that story?"

I struggled to reroute my thoughts away from the vodka and the night Dad died. "Sure. Yeah, uh, Dad crashed your sorority party."

She sank into the corner of her leather sofa. "He was so different from the other boys. Those beautiful, serious eyes. Seth has them too." Mom shifted her gaze to the bookshelves and a familiar photo in a glossy brass frame. On either side of it were small vases where Mom always kept a few fresh flowers. In the picture, Dad was holding baby Seth over his head, both of them wide-eyed and laughing.

I felt a pang of jealousy. "It was love at first sight for

you and Dad, huh," I prodded to keep her talking.

"For me, oh yes," she murmured. "I was impressed that he'd go to the police academy after graduation. He had such gravitas. And yet his mind was open to things that my parents would never accept. I began to see myself the way he did. It was . . ." Her wistful smile turned bitter, and she took another sip. "It was a fantasy."

"Mom," *Careful.* I pulled the desk chair around to sit across from her. "Grams' death has churned up a lot of memories for me. She used to tell stories about—"

Mom's hand shot out to clutch my knee. "Ellen's dangerous beliefs have nothing to do with *you*, Will. Nothing. Did Seth say something?"

"No." *Not before Grams did.*

She searched my face. "I shouldn't have told you boys that Marcus called. I almost didn't." Standing, she turned away from me, her gaze back on that picture. "We've talked about the past too much tonight."

"Mom."

"No, Will. That's enough. Go now, honey. And leave my door open, please."

I could see it go up, the wall she'd held between us and BridgeKeeping all these years. *What happened the night Dad died?* Grams had been adamant about me being ready to protect my brother, but from what exactly? The echoes at Muddy Bend hadn't been so bad. How much of what was making Mom suck down that drink like it was a magic potion did I want to know?

She could be right about the past, at least for tonight. "Goodnight, Mom." Before I was out of the room, she turned off the lamp. Would she sit in the dark all night, listening for Seth to come down the stairs? If she heard him leave, would she try to stop him?

Or would she watch him go and then change the locks?

CHAPTER TEN

Knock-knock-knock. Reen rapped her knuckles on the table at the café.

Will, she said with that bewitching smile, *your aura really turns me on.* Her warm breath tickled my ear as she leaned close. *Will, wake up.* I turned my head, my lips burning for a kiss. She kicked my bed.

"Will!"

"Wha-? Seth? Wha' th' hell, man? It's Saturday." I curled away from him, grabbing for covers to hide the side effect of that dream.

"Huh-uh. Come on. It's almost noon. I've got to get out of here!" He peeked out my door and checked both ways before slipping into the hall. "I made coffee. Hurry up."

"Son of a . . ." I groaned, rolling out of bed.

He met me in the kitchen, my Fender guitar mug and a blueberry Pop-Tart in his outstretched hands. "Mom's gone off the deep end," he whispered, checking the stairs over my shoulder. "I came down this morning and she jumped out of her office like she'd slept there. She's following me around."

"She's worried that you'll go out and find yourself a Keeper," I whispered, feeling guilty again. I didn't want Seth to leave the house either, but staying trapped inside with Mom might be worse. I bit off half the tart and washed it down with coffee. "Where are we going?"

"Nickerson's." Seth grabbed his jacket and my hoodie off the pegs and motioned frantically at the back door for me to hurry up.

I downed the coffee and managed not to choke on the rest of the tart on my way out. As we jogged around to the front of the house, I sniffed the crisp, morning air. "Thank God," I muttered.

"Grams isn't out here?" Seth stuffed my hoodie under my arm, looking disappointed.

"That's a *good* thing."

"Sure. Of course."

The clear, white sunshine made my eyes water, but it helped the caffeine do its magic. My paranoid interpretation of everything Mom had left unsaid last night seemed less dire in the light of day, but I resolved to keep my nose on high alert. Seth and I made the trip to Nickerson's Nature Reserve often. It was walk-therapy time. I waited for Seth to start to vent about Mom, but he was a man on a mission.

"Hey, we just set a speed record," I complained when we reached the park entrance.

"Did we?" Seth jammed his hands into his pockets and kept walking, crunching down the gravel road toward the trailheads. "Let's take the North Loop."

"What's the rush?" I dodged leaves fluttering down from the maple trees like giant, Day-Glo snowflakes. At the trailhead, fresh mulch deadened the sound of our footsteps. The temperature dropped ten degrees in the semi-darkness in the woods. Shivering, I pulled my hoodie over my head, and ahead of me, Seth reached back to turn his collar up.

"Hold on." I grabbed his elbow and pulled him around. "Here we go again."

Seeing the look on my face, he spread his hands open. "Am I . . .?

"Yeah. Everywhere I can see skin." That eerie, milky glow was back.

"I wish I could see it," he said. "It'd be easier to believe."

"Believe it." A whisper of adrenalin started a buzz between my eyes. "Maybe we should turn back."

"You worry too much. It's just a little farther."

"What's a little farther? Where are we going?" Seth ignored me, hustling around a curve in the trail. Mulch gave way to gnarled roots, loose rocks, and a layer of slippery, damp leaves, but it was the sudden hollow in my chest that made me stumble. "Seth, wait. The cat." I looked up and my breath caught. "You asshole!"

The edge of a broad, murky creek marked the park's boundary and beyond it, a manicured lawn dotted with tombstones shone in open sunshine, Walnut Glen Cemetery.

Seth had a sheepish but stubborn frown on his face. "Look, we don't need to wait around for Uncle Marcus to show up. We can figure this out on our own."

I waved a hand. "That's a new cemetery. Real ghosts, not echoes." In Muddy Bend every headstone jutted out of the ground at an angle, soft-edged and weather-worn. The ones across the ravine gleamed, straight and white. The dark mound of a new grave stood out like a fresh scab in the nearest row at the edge of the ravine.

"We're at least a hundred yards away from the closest grave," Seth said. "Come on. We'll stay on this side of the creek."

I knuckled the spot between my eyes where the buzz had grown into what felt like a bumble bee bouncing off the inside of my skull. The still air suddenly grew heavy with the stink of stagnant water. My lip curled as I looked down to the creek. "Seth, this doesn't feel—"

"Wait, I hear something," Seth hissed, jerking his gaze toward the cemetery. He slapped his hands over his ears.

"Seth, what's wrong?"

"Somebody's screaming!" Light burst from his hands and face. Not just a glow. Not this time. He doubled over, grunting like he'd taken a punch and the light collapsed, disappearing into his body. A deep cough gurgled up from his throat.

"What is happening?" I reached for him, but when Seth wrenched himself upright and spun to face me, I stumbled back, gaping.

His features were twisted into unfamiliar lines, his face a rubber Seth mask stretched over somebody else's skull. Through clenched teeth, his breath hissed in and out, and his eyes—I'd never seen rage burn like that in my brother's eyes. With a low snarl, he dove for me, and my head bounced off packed earth as I hit the trail.

"Mmudda . . . basssstt. Murd . . . dering bas . . . bastard!" Seth's face contorted like he couldn't get his mouth to work. He dug his fingers into my shoulders.

"Seth, holy crap! Snap out of it." For a second there was a flicker of recognition tinged with terror in his eyes. "It's me! Your brother!" The glimmer vaporized.

"Brother," he snarled, stretching out the word. "You'll never find her." He cocked a fist back.

Pain, sharp, sickening! I'd never taken a bare-knuckled punch. Something metallic pooled at the back of my throat. I coughed. Crimson spattered Seth's jacket.

"Stop! Seth, kick him out!" I blocked his next punch and then used a palm strike to rock him back. Planting a foot, I twisted my hips, shoved him off into the brush. I didn't have time to get away. On me again, he smashed me onto the rocky trail. I drove an elbow back, but then heard his grunt of pain.

"Seth," I panted, "I don't want to hurt you."

Grabbing a fistful of my hair, he jerked my head back. *Not Seth* pressed his face hard against my temple. "You killed me, but you won't get Megan." His spit trickled down my cheek.

"I didn't kill you. I don't know who Megan is!"

With an ugly snarl, he jerked my chin up higher, hooked his elbow around my neck and squeezed.

Another new experience, choking. I fought, tried for leverage with my knees. Tore jeans and skin on the rocks. Lost it. Full on panic. The harder I struggled, the more I needed air. My lungs caught fire. My heart hammered the dirt trail. The whole time Seth cursed into my ear.

"Murdering pervert, I'll kill you before I let you find her. You're through hurting them."

Black, swirling fog squeezed my vision to a pinpoint. My fight turned into flopping jabs and twitches. All that was left was that voice in my ear. "Murderer. Murderer!"

"Enough!"

My brother's voice, the right voice, reached me down at the bottom of a long, dark tunnel. Relief set me floating.

"Leave! Get out," Seth rasped.

For once, I obeyed him without some smart-ass remark.

And I let myself go.

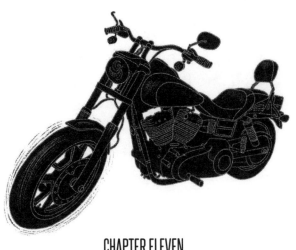

CHAPTER ELEVEN

My lungs relayed a message. BREATHE. But I couldn't remember how all the parts worked. Somebody clamped a vice on my nose then pushed my head back. My lungs filled to the point of popping. The pressure let up—air rushed out.

"Will!"

Light seeped in between my eyelashes.

"Will?"

I drew a breath. Coughed it back out. Remembered the rhythm. In . . . out . . . in . . . out. When I managed to open my eyes, three copies of Seth swam around an inch from my nose. His warm puffs of breath made me blink.

"Get off me!" Panicked, I shoved him and scrabbled backward. We sprawled on opposite sides of the trail until Seth doubled over, barely making it to his hands and knees before he puked in the grass.

I hauled myself over to him, croaking, "Sorry, Seth, sorry. I thought you were still . . ." His skin looked blotchy

80

and pale, a dirty trail of tears streaked his cheeks, but he wasn't glowing. When I pulled him back onto his butt away from the stinking puddle of bile and coffee, he threw himself at me, wrapping his arms tight enough to stop my breath again.

I held on. "S'okay, man," I said through a throat full of gravel. "Ease up. I'm all right."

Seth sagged against my hands, shuddering. "You weren't breathing. I had my arm around your throat. Did I almost—?"

"*He* almost. The ghost, not you," I said, trying to convince myself too.

He scrubbed his face. "Dad never said anything like this could happen. How did he live with it?"

He didn't. I shifted trying to ease the rage in the hollow of my chest. The cat felt far away, but he was still pacing across my grave. I squinted through the trees at the grave scarring the lawn in Walnut Glen, and my heart pounded in my throat. "Come on." Hauling Seth to his feet, I pulled his arm over my shoulder.

"What's wrong?" He clumsily wiped his lower lip.

"We've got to get home. You really need a breath mint, man."

I dragged my semi-conscious brother home, *again.* By the time we staggered up our driveway, I was running on fumes, thinking about nothing but keeping my arm clenched around his waist and our feet moving. By sheer, dumb luck, Mom didn't meet us at the door. For all I knew, she was out searching for us.

I got Seth into a hot shower fully clothed. He ordered me out of the room twice, but I didn't go far. "Jesus."

My mouth tasted like a rusty nail. My t-shirt was ripped. Bloody scratches on my chest stung every time I moved. The voice that wasn't Seth's snarled in my ear, vivid, real, Keeper memories. Sliding slowly down the wall outside the bathroom, I pressed the heels of my hands against my eyes, trying to make the horror movie stop.

Seth's room came into focus. Bed made, dresser, bookshelves library neat, everything orderly, sensible like my brother. Or like he used to be. Normally, he'd be the one I went to when everything was falling apart. Now, the only person with answers was Mom, but after last night, I knew she'd lose it if I told her what happened out on the trail. *Damn it, we need help!*

Steam billowed as the bathroom door opened. Seth stumbled out and dropped to his knees at the foot of his bed. His shirt was plastered to his back, pain radiated off him like toxic gas. "Your little graveyard games aren't cutting it, Dad," he said into a wad of bedspread clenched in his fists. "I could've killed him!"

Sunlight shimmered through his window, dancing over the bed, so I almost couldn't tell how badly he was shaking. Almost. I pushed myself up the wall. "Hey. Dad showed you the Disney version of the McCurty legacy. What else could he do? You were twelve?"

He released the bedspread, stripped off his wet shirt, and pulled another one out of his dresser. "I can't stay here," he told the buttons. "It could happen again. What if the next time I attack you in your sleep?"

Or right now. I couldn't put up much of a fight right now.

"What's going on in here?" Mom's voice rose as she appeared in the doorway, wide-eyed, wearing the same clothes she'd had on last night. "Seth, what's happened?"

"Mom. Mom we . . ." My voice petered out, words didn't exist to break this to her gently, but she wasn't listening to me anyway. Her eyes were fixed on Seth.

"Grams came for a visit," he snarled.

Color drained from Mom's face. "No," she whispered. "No!" Lurching forward, she threw her arms around him. Seth's breaths came in uneven huffs, but his arms stayed at his sides. "Ellen wouldn't do this to you," Mom wept into his shoulder. "You're too young! Oh, Seth." She pulled away just far enough to look up into his face. "What did you tell her? You didn't let her . . ." Unsteady on his feet despite Mom's grip, Seth glared his defiance. A silent *no, no, no* escaped her on a long, shaky breath.

She backed off, staring at the floor, her eyes focused on something dark and far away. I was sure one of them was going to collapse without the other to hold them up, so I reached out to catch whoever dropped. As if it took terrible effort, Mom lifted her gaze. I could tell the moment she really saw me and my torn, bloody shirt. The deep sadness in her eyes turned to horror as she looked back up at Seth. "What have you done?"

He let out a low moan and dove for the bedroom door.

"Mom, stop him!"

She hesitated, but then glanced at me again and stepped aside as he rushed past. The closet door in the hall slammed against the wall. Shoes and boots clunked as Seth fumbled through them. I started after him, but Mom blocked my way.

"Mom! We can't let him leave."

"Will, oh, honey." She could hardly speak. "We don't

have any choice. It's too late! If your grandmother came to him, he must have chosen a Keeper. I can't keep him safe anymore. He's theirs now, baby."

I edged back, but she held on to my wrist, jamming my bracelet against the bone.

"I *prayed* this day would never come. I tried to stop it! I know you don't understand, but you have to trust me. Seth *chose* this. You don't know the things he'll do, baby, dangerous, unnatural things. I can't watch it happen. Not again. And I won't let him put you in danger too. Look at you!"

She reached out to wipe the tears from my face, but I flinched away from her touch. She was wrong. I did understand why BridgeKeeping terrified her now, but I'd never understand how she could think that leaving Seth to face it alone was the right thing to do.

A realization hit me. She *didn't* think we were leaving him alone. She thought Seth had a Keeper out there somewhere, waiting for him.

"Mom . . ." I began slowly, "I was with Seth the night Grams came. She gave me a choice too." I could hear Seth stumbling down the stairs but kept my eyes on Mom's. "*I'm* Seth's Keeper."

About fifty emotions slid across her face. The one she finally settled on made her drop my wrist like I'd burned her. "No. That's not possible. Not both of you!"

Clasping her hands, she closed her eyes, begging or praying, I couldn't tell which and didn't have time to find out. The floor squeaked downstairs, Seth had made it to the living room. I moved Mom out of the doorway and breathed, "I'm sorry."

Teetering in unlaced boots, Seth reached for the front door. "Seth, stop!" I vaulted the couch, hit my shin on the coffee table, and made a desperate grab that missed him by a mile. He jerked the door open but then reared back.

Wearing road-beaten leathers that matched his dark skin perfectly was the biggest frickin' biker I'd ever seen. He looked like a carved wooden statue filling our doorway, one massive fist frozen mid-knock.

With a flash of dazzling teeth, the statue came to life. "Seth? Is that you, boy? You're all grown up!"

My brother blinked a couple times. Then he drew back a fist and with a wild, flailing swing, punched Uncle Marcus in the jaw.

CHAPTER TWELVE

U ncle Marcus didn't notice the impact of Seth's fist as far as I could tell. With bulging, leather saddlebags slung over his shoulder, he held a motorcycle helmet under one arm and my unsteady brother under the other.

"What the hell's going on here?" he asked, confused, but still smiling like this was some warped welcome-home joke.

The Fender guitar mug that I'd gulped coffee out of this morning came from Uncle Marcus on my seventh birthday. I'd spent most of that afternoon riding on his broad shoulders at an outdoor concert. Best seat in the house. The mentor Grams promised was finally here. I should run to him blubbering with relief. So why was my inner guard dog—*I have an inner guard dog?*—baring its teeth and snarling? "Get your hands off my Bridge," I said, my voice unrecognizable even to me.

Uncle Marcus narrowed his eyes. "Will? Little brother,

if I let go, he's gonna fall on his ass. Is he drunk? You don't look too great either." His smile grew uncertain. "Wait. What did you just say?"

The tiny part of my brain not occupied with screaming, *MINE, MINE, MINE,* recognized an alpha male when it saw one. *Uncle Marcus, Rottweiler. Me, scrappy Jack Russell.*

Seth jerked out of his grip and staggered backward. "You're late!" he said, with a wild sweep of his hands. "She's already been here."

Uncle Marcus sucked in a breath and then blew it out. "Damnit. I've been tearin' asphalt since Atlanta, trying to get here before she did."

I unclenched my jaw enough to speak. "Grams showed up two nights ago. This morning we got ambushed by somebody else." I heard a gasp. It was Mom clinging to the banister.

Uncle Marcus narrowed his eyes. "*We* got ambushed? What do you mean, we?"

I pointed to Seth, "Bridge." Tapped my own chest, "Keeper."

His stubbled jaw dropped. Mom sidled around the edge of the room and Uncle Marcus pinned her with a glare.

"Don't look at me like that," she snapped. "I didn't tell you when you called because I didn't know. What was Ellen thinking? They're children!" She collapsed into the wingback chair by the fireplace.

I grabbed Seth's elbow, tucked him behind me, and then walked him back until his calves hit the couch and he slumped into it with a scrunch of leather.

Uncle Marcus shut the front door and then turned on me. "How old are you?"

"What does that have to do with anything?"

"Answer the question."

I jerked my chin up. It didn't make me any taller. "Sixteen."

"Sweet Jesus." He rubbed the back of his neck. "You said that Ellen *showed up*? You're telling me she manifested physically?"

"Yeah. Physical as hell." I felt less glad to see our mentor with each passing second. "But you'll have to take my word for it. Seth didn't remember a damned thing, and Reen, our server, couldn't see her. Which was just . . . oh, not freaky at all."

"Spirits choose who to reveal themselves to, kid. That's why nobody else saw your grandmother." He rubbed a hand over his face. "Tell me what happened this morning."

I didn't feel compelled to *Share* everything with him, but an avalanche of vivid, violent memories made it hard to get even an edited version out. "In the park across from Walnut Glen Cemetery. Seth didn't know me. His voice was . . ."

"Could you see this one too?"

"Yes, I mean, not exactly." I closed my eyes, seeing the other face over Seth's skull. "Not separate like Grams." Uncle Marcus sighed like that was the first good news he'd heard so far, but Mom looked more horrified with every word I said.

"I almost killed him. I've got to leave." Seth pushed himself off the couch.

I pushed him back down.

Heavy, biker boots thumped the hardwood as Uncle Marcus walked over. He laid a hand like a sandbag on my shoulder and gave Seth a reassuring smile. "Seth, calm down. Your brother got a little roughed up, that's all."

"I had my arm around his throat," Seth said. "He stopped breathing."

"Oh my God," Mom moaned.

Shock flashed across Uncle Marcus's face so fast I wasn't sure I'd really seen it. In a millisecond, he rearranged the expression back to that smile.

"Your instincts stopped you. No Bridge would kill his Keeper." He gently shook my shoulder, looking at Mom and then Seth. "Look at him, he's fine."

Seth blinked up at us, tears pooling in his eyelashes. I tried to put an untraumatized expression on my face, which must have looked more convincing than it felt, at least for Seth, because his chin sank as tension flowed out of him like a sink coming unclogged.

The earth grew solid under my feet for the first time since I woke up on the trail. My survival this morning hadn't been random good luck. Seth had control. I sank onto the couch beside him.

As if he understood that the farther he was from Seth, the happier I'd be, Uncle Marcus dropped his helmet and saddlebags into the chair opposite Mom and then leaned both hands against the fireplace mantel. "Sixteen-year-old Keeper," he muttered, shaking his head. "Never heard of such a thing."

"A sixteen-year-old *child*, Marcus." Mom said desperately. "He can't protect *himself*, let alone Seth."

I touched the back of my fingers to Seth's cool, clammy forehead. "He's been out of it since the park. What's wrong with him?"

"It's the languor," Uncle Marcus said over his shoulder.

"The what?"

"Languor. Just call it ghost sickness. Seth's inexperienced, taking on an extra soul so soon after your grandmother was too much." He turned around, arms crossed over his broad chest. "You shouldn't have let him leave the house."

An ache in my throat made me whisper. "What did I do?"

"You didn't do squat," Uncle Marcus snapped.

"I didn't do squat because I don't know squat! Grams said you'll teach me."

Uncle Marcus looked like he'd rather teach a cockroach to scuttle in the dark. "I came back to teach *your brother*. I thought I'd have more time. I thought there was a chance he'd—"

"Choose you for his Keeper!" Mom said, hope bright in her eyes. "That's what should have happened, isn't it? *You* could keep him safe."

Uncle Marcus didn't say a word, but I could see Mom had hit the mark. And wasn't she right? This morning sure as hell proved that I wasn't up to the job. *Your brother chose you as his Keeper the day you were born. The bond between you is strong and clear.* Could Grams have been wrong?

"I'm goin' upstairs," Seth mumbled, putting a hand on my shoulder to push himself up. I stood with him.

"Give him extra blankets," Uncle Marcus said. "His

90

thermostat'll be useless for a while."

He was right, I could feel Seth shivering. I bit my lip. "He'll be okay, won't he?"

"He's burned out. Exhausted."

"And that's my fault. I get it! Will he be okay?"

"Just let him rest."

That wasn't the reassurance I wanted, but I got us moving. Mom's voice followed us up the stairs.

"It's all wrong, Marcus," she said, starting to cry again. "I can't lose both my boys. Kevin promised it would only be our firstborn. Only him."

Seth made a choked, clicking sound in his throat.

I got us out of there.

CHAPTER THIRTEEN

In Seth's room, I leaned the two of us against the closed door, glad that the distance between me and Uncle Marcus quieted my weirdly possessive guard dog. "Now I have a cat and a dog. What's next?"

Seth didn't have an answer. By the time I piled blankets over him, his head looked like it was attached to a manatee under the covers. "What if Grams was wrong?" I whispered. "Uncle Marcus is a better Keeper. No way you could have gotten a choke hold on him."

"Hey." Seth shrugged one arm out from under the covers. His leather bracelet, the twin to mine, was dark, full of water from the shower. The shiny, black friendship rock braided into the leather dangled above the sheet. I took his already sleep-warmed hand.

"He might be better for somebody else," he said. "Not for me. You're my Keeper. Don't let 'em bully you."

My eyes felt hot. "You sure about that? I screwed up big time today."

"*We* screwed up," he whispered. "We'll be ready next time."

Next time. How many next times would there be? We were on a rollercoaster in the pitch dark. Scared as hell. Strapped into our seats with nothing to do but hang on and scream. Was my future a string of mornings like this one? Rubbing a knuckle under my eye, I tucked his arm back into the covers and closed his door softly.

"They deserve a chance at a normal life," Mom was saying as I came into the living room. "Seth has to tell Ellen to take it back. Stop this insanity."

"It doesn't work like that, Barbie," Marcus said.

"Then take Seth with you. Give Will a chance at least."

"That's not happening," I said. Mom did a guilty bounce in the chair.

Marcus strode up, curled both hands over the back of the couch, and leaned toward me.

"If I wanted to take over as Seth's Keeper," The couch creaked under his weight, "you think you could stop me?"

I swallowed, staring into his hard eyes. "Yeah, I'd stop you." There was barely any breath behind my voice, but my body settled into fighting stance.

Marcus loomed. Hours passed. No breathing allowed.

He shoved himself back. The couch rocked, then settled with a thud. "Good Lord, you *both* got your father's stubborn genes! He's bonded all right. Good and proper."

My knees buckled. "What the hell is wrong with you? What's wrong with *me?*"

Marcus spread his arms. "I'm a Keeper without a partner, unbound, horning in on your territory. That kind of thing's going to rub you the wrong way from now on. Mix that with your pubescent hormone stew and you've got a hell of a cocktail." He stuck a hot dog-sized finger in my face. "You're darned lucky I love ya. If I made a serious play for Seth—"

"Do it!" Mom pleaded. "Why don't you do it?"

"No, Mom!" I walked over and knelt in front of her. "Please stop pushing and help us deal with this. Where Seth goes, I go."

For a second, all I saw in her face was hurt and betrayal, but then her eyes went flinty. "You're a minor, Will. Seth's nineteen, legally an adult. I . . . I have no obligation to let him live here."

"Mom, you wouldn't kick him out," I stammered.

She stood, forcing me to stand too. "Seth is first born, lost to me before they ever let me hold him." Her shoulders jerked as she closed her eyes. I didn't think she'd be able to go on, but she drew in a shuddering breath and pulled her gaze back up to mine. "If I can only save one of you, I'll do whatever I have to. Marcus . . ."

"I'll stay a few days to help them get on their feet." Marcus touched Mom's shoulder, but she shrugged him off. "We can't change the way things are, Barbie. Will *is* Seth's Keeper."

Mom's fist clenched around a wad of tissues. "We'll see about that."

When her bedroom door slammed upstairs, I drove my fist at the wall. "Damn it!"

Marcus caught it like a fast ball in a catcher's mitt. "Settle down, boy."

"Why is she doing this? Didn't Dad explain everything

before they got married?"

Marcus dropped resignedly into an armchair and leaned back to watch me pace. "Of course, he did. But there's a big difference between hearing about channeling spirits and actually seeing it happen."

"Believe me, I get that. That's no excuse for treating Seth like a boarder behind on the rent."

"Your mom wasn't cut out to be a cop's wife, let alone a Bridge's."

"But she loved Dad." I'd seen it in her face last night, the way she stared at that picture in her little office shrine. "Seth too."

"She did. She does. But there's always been a war going on inside your mom, between the beliefs she was raised with and the world your dad opened up for her. That's why she's so scared." He leaned forward heavily and propped his elbows on his knees. "Did she reconcile with her family when we left?"

"Who else did she have to turn to? You and Grams bailed on us!" Marcus dropped his gaze to the floor, and my throat tightened as the silence stretched. "Why the hell didn't you stay? None of this would have happened!"

He looked up at me through lidded eyes. "You're not ready to hear that."

"Oh, I'm ready. I've been ready for eight years!"

"Well, I'm not ready to tell you." Pain, raw and deep burned in his eyes.

The force of it turned my righteous anger to ash. I snapped my mouth shut and dropped into the chair opposite him. "Okay." I cleared my throat. "Okay, then at least explain this unbound Keeper thing. Why can't I stand being in the same room with you? All I want to do is . . ." Violent strangling motions finished my sentence.

Marcus wagged a finger back and forth between us. "We have history. You can dredge up a few good memories, can't you?"

I tried not to, but they came. His deep, rumbling laugh at my stupid knock-knock jokes. Gum he gave me on April Fool's Day that turned my teeth black. Uncle Marcus never had to be invited to family holidays. He was expected.

"There's a few," I admitted as my stomach unclenched a little.

"Good. Trust your memories, let your logical mind, not your overactive Keeper instincts, guide you. They'll settle down. And when I tell you I'm no threat, believe it. Your Mom doesn't understand how the bond between Bridge and Keeper works. You're Seth's Keeper for the rest of your life. Nothing can change that now."

For the rest of my life?

"You okay," Marcus asked quietly.

I managed a nod. "Why does the idea of Seth leaving the house scare the crap out of me?"

"The threshold of your home is a barrier against spirits. Until he's totally in control, this house'll be the only place Seth gets any rest."

"How did I know that?"

Marcus tapped his forehead. "All kinds of new things are happening in that brain of yours, kid."

I bumped my knuckles against my bruised jaw. With the twinge of pain came visions that blocked out the living room. I squeezed my eyes shut. Bad idea. That gave my brain a nice, blank screen to run the horror show against. I popped them open wide.

"Flashbacks?" Marcus asked.

Letting out a shaky breath, I nodded.

"We'll fix that when Seth wakes up."

"We know about the Sharing. What'll I do 'til then?"

"You need distractions. But I'll answer the rest of your questions about BridgeKeepers when your brother's conscious. No use going over everything twice." Marcus stood, pressing both fists against the small of his back, and then reached for his helmet and packs. "Is there a kitchen? Food? A man could get lost in this castle."

I ground my teeth to hold in the rest of my ten thousand questions but led him into the kitchen. While we made a dent in the pan of lasagna, Marcus asked about school, my friends, the kind of stuff any uncle who hadn't seen you since you were little would ask. When I told him that Seth was driving Dad's Mustang, his face lit up.

"Where is she?"

Raising an eyebrow at the *she*, I pointed toward the garage. He was up and out before I could push back from the table.

"Well, lookee there," he said, running his fingertips along the polished hood. "Midnight beauty. I can't believe your mom didn't sell her."

"She tried a few years ago. Only time I ever saw Seth throw a fit."

Marcus nodded. "Good boy." He walked around the car. "You kept Kevin's mechanic's bench too, huh? Does Seth tinker with her engine?" I snorted and shook my head. "You?" he asked hopefully.

"Nope." I rubbed my temple where somebody was pounding a tiny hammer. "More distraction, please."

Marcus opened the driver's side door and started a meticulous inspection of the Mustang's interior. "You know how your dad got this car? It's a ghost story."

"Nobody's told me any ghost stories." I said, watching him through the windshield.

"Well, this case was nothing like what's churning around in your head right now. This was an average-Joe spirit, the bread-and-butter of a Keeper's life."

"There must be a lot of bread and butter. People die every day."

"Of course, but you don't think everybody sticks around, do you? The world would be flooded with ectoplasm."

"Is ectoplasm really a thing?"

"Do you want to hear this story or not?"

Crossing my arms, I settled a hip against the car. "Yes. Please give me some good news."

Marcus' gaze went far away as he ran his hand across the dashboard. "Young woman's father died. She was staying in his house to put things in order and heard strange noises coming from the garage. Dispatch sent us out." He patted the Mustang's steering wheel. "Turned out this baby was haunted. Your dad bridged the veil and let the spirit cross. The guy wanted to tell his daughter about her biological mother. He'd had an affair. Mistress got pregnant. He forced her to give the baby up to him and his wife. Lots of ugly resentment all around. So, he was stuck In Between because he wanted his daughter to know the truth."

"Did he kill his mistress? Or his wife?" *And then come across the veil in a berserker rage?*

Marcus gave me a look. "No. Eagle Shoal's not the crime capital of the Midwest. He just wanted to settle things."

"Hmph. So, you walked in and told the daughter all that?"

"Ah, no. We got creative. Typed a letter from her dad, slipped it in among the papers she was going through. She got the message. His soul passed on."

A little bit of weight left my shoulders. He was right about Eagle Shoal, jaywalkers were headline news around here. Our spirit this morning had to be a fluke, bad luck. "How'd Dad end up with the car?"

"He happened to mention how much he admired this beauty, and the daughter called him first when she was ready to sell it. See, the spirit was at peace, and your dad scored a classic. All in a day's work." Marcus stood in the Mustang's open door, sobering. "Will, there *is* one more thing you need to understand."

"Yeah? Just one?"

He ignored my sarcasm. "You're Seth's Keeper for now. But you're replaceable. Your mom's right about that."

I blinked. "You said we were stuck with each other for the rest of our lives."

"I said for the rest of *your* life."

I frowned, not sure I got the distinction until a couple of seconds went by. "Oh," I said very quietly. "So, if I die first?"

"Seth can choose another Keeper."

"You're not planning to off me, are you?" Marcus rolled his eyes wearily, and I managed a smile.

The doorbell chimed. "What time is it?" I pulled out my phone. Saturday afternoon had turned into Saturday evening. "Crap. It's got to be Nico. Should I answer it?"

"If you can think of an excuse for the way you look." He waved a hand at my torn, blood-smeared clothes.

"There's a costume thing tonight. The Fall Fling."

Marcus narrowed his eyes. "You might be able to pull it off, but you can't tell whoever's out there the truth."

"He's my best friend!"

"Doesn't matter." The doorbell rang again, and Marcus put a hand on my shoulder. "Will, you think your life's turned upside down now? You'd never breathe another free breath if people knew what you and Seth can do?"

My skin grew warm under a sudden, cold sweat. "But Nico . . ."

"There's no way to predict how people will react to the supernatural. Even the ones you know well. Your mother ought to be proof of that."

"You haven't told your family? Mom said you were staying with them when Grams died."

"No. I haven't."

"Didn't they wonder why you were travelling with a white lady old enough to be your mother?"

Marcus shifted uncomfortably. "Of course, they had questions, but they trusted me enough not to ask. Most of them."

Right. Secrets never turn toxic. "But I can't leave the

house, can I?"

"Why not? Seth's safe here." I narrowed my eyes at him, and Marcus raised both hands. "I'm not going anywhere near your Bridge. You need distractions." He made shooing motions. "Go. Be normal for a while. Just promise me you'll keep your mouth shut about BridgeKeeping. I'm telling you, things can go sideways real fast."

"Fine."

"Not anybody."

"Okay!" I grabbed my hoodie in the kitchen. "Hey, there's a guest room downstairs." Marcus nodded and made more shooing motions.

Staring at the front door, feeling like an alien invader was ringing the bell, I wiped sweaty palms against my thighs. Was the real world still out there spinning? Could I step over the threshold and shed this BridgeKeeper insanity for a few hours?

Nico rapped, tap-tap-a-ty-tap-tap. I snorted and gave him two taps back. Normal? Hell, yeah, I could do normal.

All I had to do was keep a secret.

CHAPTER FOURTEEN

Normal wasn't exactly what waited for me on the porch. Nico looked like a casualty from a smoothie explosion.

"Hey, man. About time," he said, "What's going on in there?" He craned his neck to look into the house as I closed the door. "You got company? Whose Harley is that?"

My mouth opened, then closed. There were exactly eleven words left in my vocabulary, *Dude, you will not believe what happened to me this morning!*

Just keep the secret. I snorted inwardly. Had I ever *met* Nico?

"Wait." A smile grew on his face. "You made a costume sort of! I can't believe it! Let's see, are you a . . . Fight Club guy?"

"Uhm, yeah. Yeah, you got it in one."

"The scrapes are a little under done. But nice first effort. Next Halloween we'll go nuts with the fake blood.

I've got a recipe."

"Of course, you do." I pushed Nico off the porch ahead of me. "What are you supposed to be?"

"Can't you tell?" He held his arms out, walking backwards. "I'm a salad." He pointed to the wilting lettuce leaves that he'd twist-tied into his black hair, and then down to a wide belt with a bottle of Ranch dressing duct taped to it like a gun in a holster. "With dressing on the side, get it?" He waggled his eyebrows.

I groaned. "Man, I don't even know what to say."

"Say it's great." He chucked me on the shoulder. "So, that giant Harley have something to do with why you didn't show up at the dojang last night?"

Marcus's grit-spattered motorcycle took up a chunk of the driveway. "Yeah. That's Marcus Dean's. He was my dad's," *Keeper, he and Dad talked to dead people,* "old partner." Every word that left my mouth stumbled over fifty I had to keep in. If he kept asking questions, I'd have to lie. To Nico. I might as well develop a taste for soap.

"Ah, that explains the family dinner."

A screech echoed off the house as Dr. Muro opened the truck's door. "Hola."

"Hey, Dr. Muro."

"That fine Harley belongs to Mr. McCurty's old partner," Nico said as his dad backed out of the driveway.

"I thought I recognized it. Been a while. What's he doing back in town?"

Something in Dr. Muro's softly accented voice said he wasn't too excited about Marcus being back. "He came to, uh, tell us that our grandmother passed away." *Not a lie.*

"Aw, man," Nico said. "That sucks. I'm really sorry."

I'd felt a lot of things since we found out Grams died, grief wasn't one of them, but there it was, making my eyes burn. "Thanks."

"You must have family business at home tonight," Dr. Muro said gently. "Text me if you need to cut this outing short."

"Thanks." I wondered if I should read anything into the way he'd said, *family business*, but decided not to let Marcus' paranoia infect me tonight. We got to school and jumped out of the truck slapping dog hair off our butts.

"Hijo," Dr. Muro called. Nico leaned in the open window talking quietly with his dad while I waited at the sidewalk.

"What'd he say?" I asked as Dr. Muro drove away.

Nico shook his head. "All these years we've been friends and you haven't learned a word of Spanish." He was only half kidding.

"That's not true," I said sheepishly. "I'm working on a solid B in Spanish *and* I'm fluent in dinner conversation."

"Uh huh, pase las tortillas, por favor." Nico threw an arm over my shoulders as we headed toward the parking lot behind the school. "Dad said you're a delicate flower and I need to look after you tonight."

"Oh." That felt disturbingly accurate.

"So, where's your abuela been all these years?"

"Could we not talk about her? I could use a couple hours of distraction, you know?"

"Sure, I get it, sorry." Nico squeezed my shoulder and then spread his hands wide as we came around the corner of the building. "Here's distraction with a big, red bow around it."

Portable lights blazed above the parking lot burning out the night sky. Music blasted from speakers on a flatbed truck, but it was little more than a thrumming bass buzzing through me out here on the fringe. In the open space created by the booths that rimmed the lot, a hundred kids milled around. We showed our student ID's and then walked between two booths, one sizzling with the sound of popping grease and the other clattering as a roulette wheel spun.

Nico elbowed me. "Stop that."

"Stop what?"

"That caveman hunch you do. You're scary enough lookin' all Fight Club. Relax. Have fun!"

Fun. Could I still do fun? I inhaled. Popcorn, the sweet, greasy scent of funnel cakes. No cinnamon rolls, no stagnant water. *Relax.*

"There, that's what you need." Nico pointed to the flatbed where a DJ stood behind a console jamming to the music. In front of it, most of the pep squad, wearing uniforms that included high-collared vampire capes tonight, dragged people out of the crowd to get the dancing started.

"You want me to dance?"

"Sure, but that's not what I mean. Karaoke, man!"

A hand-painted sign beside the makeshift stage read, Karaoke Contest! 8:00 tonight!! Sign up NOW!!! I rolled my eyes.

"Dude, you can sing! You've been practicing guitar since third grade."

"Sure. In my basement."

He gripped my shoulders. "You can do this, primo. Who convinced you to start Hapkido?"

I sighed. "You did."

"Uh-huh. I dragged you to that first practice kicking and screaming and look where it's gotten you."

"Here. Kicking and screaming."

"Exactly." He grinned. "You'll love karaoke too. This could change your life."

"I've had enough life changes in the last couple days, thanks."

"Dude, trust me. There's the sign-up table." He gave me a push.

"This is a terrible idea," I mumbled, but my feet kept moving. I could feel my focus shifting away from what waited back home like the Titanic turning from the iceberg. As distractions went, karaoke could work.

"We'll pick out an awesome tune. Girls will go wild. I bet . . ." Nico stopped talking, stopped moving. He'd spotted someone in the crowd.

I followed his gaze. "Wowww," I said. "She's so sparkly." Nico's crush de jour, Tiffany, captain of the debate team, was rocking a costume that made her look like Lady Gaga on her first spacewalk. "Got some drool on your chin there, buddy," I said. "Let me get that for you."

He batted my hand away. "She's the key to me winning the election for Snow Ball dance committee president. Got to shine up my college resume if I want to get into med school. If . . . *when* I get her vote, her posse will follow. The election's Monday noon. You'll nominate me."

"Wait a minute. Since when am *I* volunteering for the dance committee?"

He finally turned away from Tiffany to look me straight in the eyes. "Hey, I need your help. I'll make a good president."

I sighed. "I know, I know. I'll do it."

"That's the spirit. You go sign up for karaoke. I'll be back in a couple minutes." He turned to jab a finger in my face. "Don't chicken out while I'm campaigning."

"Yeah, yeah." As he hurried off, adjusting the lettuce in his hair, I reluctantly joined the end of the line.

"Dance committee? Karaoke? What is happening?" I must have been muttering louder than I thought because the girl ahead of me turned to stare over her shoulder. "Sorry," I said, feeling my cheeks warm. "Just talking to myself."

In a face painted entirely red, the girl's lips rounded into a little, oh. Her eyes shone with that same aching combination of desperation and confusion that I'd seen around the lunch table yesterday. *Crap, another one.* I'd forgotten about my shiny, new aura.

The girl had sandwiched her torso between two circles of glossy, red cardboard that had a capital M stenciled in the middle. "Hey, that's a great, uh, M&M costume," I guessed, trying to get her to stop staring.

"I'm worried about my girlfriend," she blurted. "She hasn't come to school in a week, and I don't even think her mom knows where she is. Nobody's looking for her! She's not answering my texts or . . ." With a little gasp, she slapped both hands over her mouth to stop the flow of words.

"Well, that's a bummer," I said, trying for enough sympathy to be polite but not enough to invite her to keep talking. "I hope she shows up." I pointed behind her. "You're next."

"Oh, right." She turned to the tired looking parent working the table. "Um, I'm a duet, but I'm not totally sure my friend will make it tonight. Can I still sign us up?"

"Sure, honey. Just put their name down with yours. We'll cross you off if we need to."

The M&M signed up. After a confused, lingering look at me, she walked off scanning the crowd for her girlfriend. I blew out a sigh as I leaned down to the entry sheet. The last two names written there, barely legible under smeared red paint, were Missy Miller and Megan Smalley.

Megan. My vision blurred as vivid Keeper memories flood in. *You'll never find her, brother. You killed me but you won't get Megan!*

"You okay, son?"

I caught the edge of the table and gasped to remind myself that Seth's arm wasn't locked around my throat.

"Karaoke's kind of scary, huh? You'll have fun once you're on stage." He turned the playlist around so I could pick a song.

Too bad I couldn't get my eyes to focus on anything but those two names. "Sorry. This was a bad idea." Heart pounding, I reeled away from the table, fumbling out my phone to text Nico's dad.

"Will! Did you enter the contest? Tonight's the perfect night for karaoke."

The dancing crowd and flashing booths were

jumbled in my vision with a rocky trail and tombstones in the sun, but Reen's smiling face cut through the chaos. My heartbeat slowed. The Keeper replay faded, and I felt myself return her smile.

"What's perfect about tonight? Other than you showing up." *Oh my God. Did I just say that?*

"Ohhh, I've got a feeling."

Reen fell into step beside me. Our shoulders bumped, leaving me a warm, happy patch of skin. She was wearing a deep green shirt, belted at the waist with fringe around the bottom, black jeans, and black boots. Her only costume was a headband that had a glittery witch's hat attached to it. Her eyes swept me through dark lashes, and I went all warm and tingly until I realized that what I was interpreting as a flirty gaze was actually more of an inspection. *Damn.* "You're reading my aura again, aren't you?"

"It's hard not to," she said. "It's crazy powerful tonight. But also . . ." A red crystal in her charm bracelet glinted as she reached up, almost brushing my jaw. "Are you okay?"

My hand moved to cover the bruise, but I forced it back down. "I'm fine. It's fake, makeup. Just my costume." *Great, start the conversation with a lie.*

"Very realistic," she said with a doubtful arch of one perfect eyebrow.

Change the subject. Say something. Anything.

"You remember my grandma, don't you?" Reen changed the subject for me.

"Sure, a little," I said, relieved that she'd brought up *her* grandma, not my dead one. Kids in the old neighborhood thought Reen's grandma was a witch, cauldrons and potions, the whole bit. I glanced at the miniature witch's hat. She must have seen the memory on my face.

She smiled. "Yeah, Grandma's still unusual. But she knows things."

"Like?" We stopped next to an unmanned table covered in school flyers.

"Like, the veil is a slice of Swiss cheese this weekend. Around All Hallows Eve, you know. It's easier for spirits to communicate." She drew air quotes around communicate. "Not a phone call or a sit-down chat or anything."

Yeah, because a sit-down chat would just be crazy. I managed a sick, breathy chuckle as my hopes for a bit of romance drained away.

"I asked Grandma about you and your brother after you came into the café." Her hands swept up in a circle around me. "People's auras don't change overnight like this. Grandma knew something, I could tell, but she went all quiet and told me not to pester you about it. So, in advance, I'm sorry for snooping, but what's going on?"

She was a little breathless at the end of that speech, eyes sparkling, cheeks flushed. *Beautiful.* The truth tapped at the backs of my teeth like a fly against a screen. I wanted to tell her. I needed to tell somebody. But Marcus' warning kept my lips sealed and the silence must have gone on too long.

"You're right," she said, breaking eye contact with a shake of her head. "It's none of my business."

"I want to tell you, but . . ."

"Just tell her, man! Hey, Reen."

I jumped like a guilty five-year-old as Nico walked up behind us.

"Hi," Reen looked at Nico's wilting lettuce, then down at his duct-taped dressing. "Salad, with dressing on the side. I love it!"

He swept her a bow. "Unlike some, you're a person with a keen eye and quick wit." His cocky grin softened as he turned to me. "Will's grandma died."

"Ohhh." Reen said. "I'm so sorry. When did she pass?"

A disturbingly speculative tone mixed with the sympathy on her face. I hedged. "Not sure exactly. Couple days ago."

"Halloween night? The night you guys came in?"

Nico shivered. "Maybe that's why you had the cat tramping over your grave all day."

Reen's eyes widened with even more speculation. "You feel that too?"

"Since he was a little kid," Nico answered for me. "What do you think it is, aura reader? Did his abuela come to tell him goodbye?"

"Look, I don't want to sound like a jerk," I interrupted, sounding like a jerk, "but I really don't want to talk about it." Nico slanted Reen a look. He knew me too well not to suspect that there was more going on tonight than sad news about Grams. For all I knew, Reen could pick up the truth from my aura. "Hey," I began a little desperately. "Reen was right earlier. It's the perfect night for karaoke." I turned to Nico. "You were right too. I chickened out and didn't sign up, but I'm going back. I'll enter the damn contest."

"Really?" Nico said slowly.

It took every bit of chill I could dredge up not to look away as his eyes bored into mine. I swallowed hard and forced a smile onto my face. "Yeah, yeah. It'll be . . . fun."

Nico gave me a pat between the shoulder blades that made me wince. "Well then, I'm proud of you." Pulling me around, he got us headed back toward the sign-up table. "Reen, you'll love this. Our guy's got talent."

"Can't wait."

She fell into step with us, her continued presence the only thing that put a dent in how much I regretted this move. At the table, I picked the first tune that looked familiar.

Nico nodded. "This one's kinda low-key but a good choice for your first time on stage. Can't believe you're really going up there, dude!"

I looked up at the bright lights on that flatbed truck. My body and the stage repelled each other like matched magnets. I gritted my teeth.

Are we having fun yet?

CHAPTER FIFTEEN

My brain spewed catastrophes as I stared at the karaoke jockey grooving behind his console. I'd drop the mic, sweat like a pig, swallow a bug, adjust my balls, fall into a flashback in front of a couple hundred people. Way to keep a secret.

"Just a second," I croaked, pulling out of Nico's grip. Puking wouldn't be my first choice as distractions went, but it seemed like a distinct possibility. I spotted the line of porta-johns at the edge of the parking lot and made for them. Their smell hit me from ten feet out. Was I desperate enough to force myself into one of those things?

I stumbled.

The cat, light-footed like it was a long way away, hollowed out my chest. An echo of the hot rage I'd felt coming from Seth this morning flowed in. The stink of stagnant water mingled with the porta-john funk and a wave of goosebumps rose across my shoulders. Barely

113

breathing, I turned full circle searching the crowd.

"What is it?" Reen asked, hugging herself as she walked up.

"I don't know."

Nico looked back and forth between us. "Is it the cat thing? Both of you? Awesome," he whispered.

I felt a tug in my chest, like a compass needle bouncing around unable to settle on North. I scanned the crowd past Nico and Reen's increasingly worried faces. Fifty yards away, talking to the security guard I'd tangled with by the message board, was the red M&M. I couldn't hear what they were saying, but when the guard put a beefy hand on her shoulder, M&M girl winced and backed away. He said something else, stern-faced, and she bolted. The scent of stagnant water intensified with the rage in my chest. Was she Megan or Missy? I lunged after her.

Nico stepped in front of me. "Hold it. What's happening?"

Craning my neck to see around him, I watched the girl pull out a cell phone and head for the front of the school. The guard didn't follow her. Should I?

Stay. It wasn't a voice, not exactly, but a clear intention rode in on another scent. Cinnamon rolls.

"Do you guys smell that?" I asked, shivering.

"I smell the popcorn booth," Reen said.

"And eau-de-toilet," Nico said. "What the heck is going on with you?"

Two ghosts, neither of which could talk to me without Seth, were trying to push me around with weirdly communicative odors. Grams was better at it than the

114

other guy. Cinnamon overpowered the pond scum and the hollow filled with her grandmotherly directive. *Stay.*

"Just give me a second." Waving Nico off, I jumped into the closest unoccupied john, but discovered when I threw the latch, that corrugated plastic doors did not count as thresholds. Grams had no trouble crowding inside with me.

"I got the message. I won't go after her," I hissed. With the edge of my sleeve, I closed the toilet lid and sat on it. The air grew less complicated, and Grams gave me some privacy. She got what she wanted, but what about the other guy? Had he been nudging me toward the girl or the guard? Or neither? Were they witnesses? Suspects? I groaned and squeezed my head between my hands as the Keeper memories boiled up.

"Iiiiit's karaoke tiiiime!" A voice boomed outside.

Nico rapped on the door. "You okay in there?"

"Fine." I felt weirdly reluctant to leave. Out there, Reen and Nico would ask a thousand questions, but in here I had sewage scented air and murder on a loop in my brain. I opened the door.

"Are you okay," Reen asked, still hugging herself. "Let's go somewhere else and talk."

"That's cool with me," Nico said. "I'll text my dad."

"No, don't." The last thing I needed was someplace private where these two could worm the truth out of me. "Look, I just got cold feet. I'm over it."

Nico's eyes narrowed. "You know you can tell me anything."

"I know," I said. And God, I wanted to, but I jammed my fists into my pockets while a silent conversation passed between Reen and Nico. She gave him a little shrug.

He swept his arm out, gesturing for me to walk ahead of them. "If this is the way you want to play it, we're right behind you."

This was the only way I *could* play it. When the DJ called the contestants to line up, I dragged my feet to the bumper of the flatbed. The trailer's lights blinked like they were stuck in hazard mode.

Nico yanked my hoodie down from one shoulder and stuck my entry number onto my t-shirt sleeve. "Thirteen. Your lucky number! And you're up last. You can watch everybody else and learn a trick or two."

"Right. Good idea." I nodded. There had to be more to karaoke than, *Sing the words. Don't pick your nose. Don't suck.*

"You'll be the big finale. That's perfect!" Reen gave me a smile full of encouragement and promise.

I had to smile too. Literally, had to. If I could get through one song and *not* totally suck up there, maybe Reen would get over her fascination with my aura. Maybe she'd see *me*.

"All riiiiiight! Let's get this party started," the DJ boomed. "First up, a delightful duet performing, *The Tiiiiime of My Life!*"

"Theater kids," Reen whispered as a couple bounded onto the stage.

They'd obviously sung together before, danced too. My palms started to sweat. "Do I have to dance?"

"Wing it. You got moves," Nico said. "Not like *those* two, but nobody expects choreography from a regular guy."

"Oh. Good." I felt no relief at all watching them twirl their way to a great finish. "They're bowing. Should I bow?"

"Only if people clap," Reen whispered.

If? Before the next kid went up, he tipped his head back so his buddy could squirt ketchup under his eyes. Wearing a pair of glasses with eyeballs dangling on springs, he belted out, *I'm Watching You.* The crowd howled.

"I don't have a schtick." I shed my hoodie and felt the unmistakable chill of damp pits. "I could borrow some ketchup."

Nico kneaded my shoulders. "Nope, been done now. You'd just look desperate."

There was a good chance of that whether I resorted to ketchup or not. For a second, I wished I had my guitar, but then the thought of singing *and* playing in front of all these people made a superball ricochet around my stomach.

The line got shorter, and I came closer to those blinking hazard lights. My palms were so sweaty, I doubted I could hold the mic. Applause for a girl bowing and throwing kisses died to silence as the next singer trudged up the wooden steps. It was Unibomber Junior.

"What's that kid's name again," Nico asked out of the side his mouth.

"Anthony," Reen and I said together.

He hadn't changed clothes since yesterday. The same beat-up army jacket made his neck look too thin to hold up his mop of hair. He seemed as excited to be up there as I was about to be, but he took the mic from the

DJ and walked to center stage.

Eyes glistening out of dark hollows, he lifted his chin and cleared his throat. "This was my little brother's favorite song."

"All righty then," the DJ said, looking doubtfully at the playlist. "Let's give it up for a guy who's . . . *Happy*." He jabbed a button and five opening chords bounced out of the speakers.

"Shouldn't he be smiling?" Nico whispered. Reen put a hand over her mouth and nodded.

Anthony came in right on the beat. He even moved a little. But his voice was raw. Nothing coming off this kid remotely resembled happiness. I couldn't take my eyes off him. Neither could anybody else.

"Why is this song so long?" Nico groaned after about fifteen seconds.

As if the silent, gaping audience was sucking the energy out of him, Anthony's voice cracked. He missed a beat. He hiccupped every other word but didn't stop. Nervous muttering rippled through the crowd.

"He's crying." Reen sounded like she was about to too.

"Awwww. Crap." I cut out of line. Nobody objected to me taking my turn early as I headed for the stage. The DJ picked up a mic and thrust it out like he was tossing me a life preserver as I lurched to Anthony's side and faced the monitor.

A hundred pairs of eyes in unsmiling faces froze the blood in my veins. My lungs shrank to teabags. Reen and Nico elbowed their way down front and Reen gave me a desperate thumbs up. Nico mouthed, *Sing, Sing!*

Dan-the-man, Sanna, and Pocket Protector Kid,

118

coming from different directions, made their way up front too. Dan crossed his arms and glowered like if somebody didn't start singing in the next two seconds, he was going to come up there and kick my ass. The other two stared, silently pleading.

Sweat trickled down my temple and I nudged Anthony. He sniffed, wiped his face with the sleeve of his coat, and finally nodded. We caught the beat, got a little groove going, and Anthony found his voice again. Pocket Protector Kid thrust a huge plastic sword into the air and yelled at the top of his lungs. "Happy! Happy! Happy!" Laughter bubbled up from the crowd.

That glimmer of positive energy squared our shoulders. As Anthony sang, I said into the mic, "You gotta dance to this song, right?" The crowd agreed, and a grin started on Anthony's face. He busted out some hip-hop moves that made his army jacket fly around him like Batman's cape. Cheers went up. Catching his breath, Anthony waved at me to take the song from there.

The lump of terror clogging my throat was forcibly ejected from my body by Reen's excited scream. There must have been a bunch of girls screaming, she couldn't make that much noise on her own, but it was *her* voice that made mine fly. I sang. I crooned. I moved! Anthony and I passed the lyric back and forth. The whole crowd took up the chorus. Their cheers rolled over us like a warm ocean wave as a bouncing mosh pit grew down front.

On the last chord, Anthony whipped off his jacket and flung it into the crowd. Spreading his feet at the edge of the flatbed, he tossed his head back, and shouted to the night sky, "That was for you, Jamie!"

Panting, laughing, I braced my hands on my knees and hung back to let him soak up the cheers. God, he needed them. He was a shriveled balloon pulling helium right out of the air to float again. His little brother had died, that was obvious. How and when I didn't know, but the cat was quiet. No out-of-this-world scents stained the air. The only troubled soul was out there taking a bow.

Nico megaphoned his hands. "Told you so!"

He was right, I loved karaoke. Who knew? Grinning like an idiot, I shook my head, knowing I'd never hear the end of it, and gave him a hapkido style bow acknowledging his great wisdom. When I straightened, I found Reen's astonished gaze locked on mine. The crowd, the cheers, faded away. She was out of breath too. Her little witch's hat had slipped sideways. The smile, not on her lips, but in her eyes, sent carbonation fizzing through my veins.

It wasn't my aura those beautiful brown eyes were fixed on this time. It was me. Just me.

CHAPTER SIXTEEN

I walked off the stage, anticipating the warmth of her body against mine, the sweet taste of her lips.

But Reen didn't jump into my arms. That was Nico. Reen stayed close, but as the three of us wandered around the Fling, I failed to capitalize on the look I'd seen in her eyes from the stage. She always seemed a little too far away for me to take her hand and pull her close.

Ten o'clock came too soon. Dr. Muro texted us that he was at the curb.

"Oh look, there's Dad," Nico said, faking surprise as he pointed at the truck. "I'll just go over there and get in. You two take your time." He backed away. "I won't see or hear anything from there."

"He's," I hitched a thumb in Nico's direction, "he just wanted to, uh . . ." Look up *awkward* in the dictionary. See my picture.

After the crowd in back, the sidewalk seemed hushed and intimate. Reen nibbled the corner of her lip, looking even more beautiful by moonlight. She'd lost her witchy headband. Dark curls sprung out around her hairline.

"Are you cold?" I asked. Taking my hoodie from where it was slung against my hip, I held it out to her.

"I am. Thanks."

She turned to show me her back, and I draped my hoodie over her green fringed shirt letting my fingers linger, barely touching her. Warmth filled the narrow space between our bodies. A lemon cookie scent wafted from her hair, and I breathed it in.

"I'd forgotten what you're like," she said, with her back still to me. "What *we* were like. When we were little, you know."

She turned and her eyes brushed mine, not lingering. The clinical, Wiccan curiosity I'd seen in them since my aura blew up was gone. But now, she seemed uncertain, even worried as she pulled my hoodie closer around her.

If her uncertainty was caused by me not making my feelings absolutely clear, I wanted to correct the situation. With my eyes on her lips, I leaned down.

Reen stepped back. It was a tiny step, slow, reluctant, but it felt like a slap.

A deep flush bloomed on her cheeks. "I'm sorry. It's your aura. Anthony, and some others too, they're troubled. They're drawn to you. I think it might be working on . . ." She pressed her lips into a line, frowning. "I'll give this back to you on Monday, if that's okay."

"Sure. Reen—"

"I've got to say goodnight to a couple of people." She turned to walk away but paused. "You did a really nice thing tonight."

"Thanks." She hurried off before I could think of anything to keep her from leaving.

Stunned, disappointed, confused, I wandered to the truck, shut the door, and sat in the cab, letting my thudding heart slow down.

"How'd it go?" Nico asked.

"It didn't. I thought we had . . . She had a look, you know?"

"Absolutely, dude. She's totally into you."

I shrugged helplessly.

Nico let out a long, disgusted sigh. "Women."

Chuckling to himself, Dr. Muro pulled the truck away from the curb.

Nico filled the silence as we drove, giving his dad an enthusiastic recap of the contest. I wished I could call up Keeper-sharp memories of those last confusing minutes with Reen so I could figure out what the hell I'd done wrong. She'd kept my hoodie. Did that mean anything? Had she wanted me to make a move? Had I blown my chance by being too dumb and slow? Clearly, whatever she saw in me on stage had changed from awesome, to disturbing.

I worried the problem until our headlights flashed against the Harley's chrome fender in the driveway. The night's distractions had worked too well. Everything waiting for me at home came crashing back, and I couldn't make myself get out of the truck.

"You could text Seth," Nico said quietly, after we'd sat for a while. "Tell him you're spending the night at our place."

"No. It's okay," I said, still not moving. Was Seth

still asleep in his room? Or had Mom dragged him downstairs and thrown him out? My guard dog bristled at the thought of Marcus. I should get in there.

"Thanks for the ride, Dr. Muro." Zero motion toward the door.

"De nada," Dr. Muro said. And then, very gently, "Go on in now, Will." He nodded toward my house. "It'll be all right."

It was a dad thing, spouting a cliché like that with so much sincerity that a person believed it. Seth had the knack too. The truck door gave a loud squeak as I pushed it open.

"See you tomorrow for Ultimate Frisbee," Nico said.

I nodded but didn't dare turn my head as the truck drove off for fear the rest of me would chase it down the street and hop back in. I put my ear against the front door. No sound. The keys weighed a ton when I pulled them out of my pocket, but after the third try I got one in the lock and cracked the door open.

"Is that you, Will?" A shaft of light from Mom's office slashed the carpet. She stepped into the living room and leaned against a chair beside the fireplace. Ice tinkled in her highball glass. "Are you alright, honey?"

I winced as a buzz started between my eyes. It spread down my neck, across my shoulders. I recognized that buzz now. Somewhere in the house, Seth was glowing.

"Will?" Mom wailed, stumbling behind me as I leapt for the stairs. "What's the matter?"

I shouldered Seth's bedroom door open. "Seth! Holy crap!"

My brother lay flat on his back in the pitch dark.

124

A supernova version of his glow pulsed in a beam that erupted from his chest, illuminating nothing in the room. "Turn it off!" Panic shoved my voice up an octave.

He lifted his head off the pillow with a sleepy smile, but then he blinked at me. "Am I—Oh no." Grabbing for the tangled covers, Seth clutched them like he could staunch the flow of light. It erupted from his bare back. "How . . . how can I stop it?"

"Don't know! Just imagine your skin is armored. Liquid metal. You're a . . . a terminator. Terminator 2, the old one, not—"

"Shut up. I get it." Seth squeezed his eyes shut.

"Long, slow breaths, man."

His claw-like grip on the covers loosened as he breathed. The light sank away from the ceiling just a little. "You got it," I whispered. "Reeeel it in." Light sputtered along the fine hairs on his shoulders until finally, the darkness collapsed over him. Seth dropped his head into his hands as I sank onto the bed next to him.

"Nice work." A deep voice said from the darkness in the hall.

"Marcus!" I jumped back up, one fist clenched, my other hand pushing Seth behind me. "What are you doing here? Can you sense it when he's open? Did you see that?"

"No. I heard you run upstairs. *You're* his Keeper. Nobody else can see or sense anything from your Bridge. Calm down."

"Is that *thing* coming for Seth?" From somewhere behind Marcus, Mom sounded close to hysteria. "Did he call it here?"

"It's all right, Barbara. He's got it under control."

"Do I? Can I control it?" Seth asked, still hunched behind me.

"You were half asleep just now," Marcus said. "You let it slip."

"But it was . . ." I made useless gestures at the ceiling in the dark trying to convey the scope of what I'd seen. "Bright, really bright."

Marcus' silent pause lasted a heartbeat too long. "Even if he got some attention, spirits can't get past your threshold. I'm sure it's fine."

"It's not fine," Mom's voice was bitter. "None of this is fine, Marcus! Don't *lie* to them."

As her quick, uneven footsteps pounded down the hall, Marcus switched on the light.

"Hey, a little warning," I said, squinting against the sudden glare.

Seth blinked up at me, and then his eyes widened in shock. "Will, are you alright? Did I do all that?"

"Do what?" *Oh.* I almost told him it was my Fight Club costume. I'd repeated the lie so many times tonight I half believed it.

Marcus grabbed my forearm and pulled me with him out into the hall. "Seth, get dressed. I'll meet you in the kitchen."

"But is he alright?" Seth called.

"He's fine." Marcus called back and then jabbed a finger toward my room.

Right, calming down. Show the damn guard dog who's boss. I let out a long, slow breath, *mind over instinct,* and forced myself down the hall, away from my Bridge.

126

"Did you bother to look in the mirror before you ran in there?" Marcus asked after he'd closed my bedroom door.

"No." I pointed to my forehead. "I was dealing with a killer bee situation."

"You can't let Seth see you looking," Marcus wrinkled his broad nose, "like some junkie who just got rolled in an alley. Change your clothes. Splash some water on your face." He shook his head and his voice gentled. "Will, you've got to unlearn everything you know about being the little brother. If you can't make Seth believe that there's no chance he'll hurt you while he's channeling, he won't be able to do his job."

"What do you mean, make him believe? There's no chance he'd do any real damage, right? That's what you said."

"I lied."

"You lied? You son of a bitch!"

Marcus grabbed a couple fistfuls of my t-shirt and pushed me backward till my shoulders bumped the wall. "Seth was about to bolt when I got here. I told him what he needed to hear." No apologetic tone. Statement of fact. "Let me explain something," he went on, spearing me with a hard gaze. "No matter how good people are before they die, they're desperate by the time they find you two. Desperate and ruthless."

"Was your warm, fuzzy ghost story about the Mustang a lie too?"

"No," he said, closing his eyes for second. "But there are dark things out there too, kid. Things looking for a Bridge as strong as Seth. When he's channeling, no matter who it is, he can't spare a millisecond worrying about you."

I pressed my lips together, fighting the urge to puke for the second time tonight.

"Clean up." Marcus stepped back, straightened my t-shirt. "Meet us in the kitchen."

I wasn't sure what would come out if I unclenched my teeth, so I just nodded down at my shoes. My bedroom door closed with a soft click.

After a two-minute shower that woke up a million aches and stings, I leaned my hands on either side of a stranger's reflection in the mirror. The mark on the side of my throat had gone purple. My bruised jaw clashed with the bloodshot whites of my eyes. A long stinging scrape, not deep, but messy, went across my chest and down my ribs.

He could have killed me. The thought wormed its way among the Keeper memories.

"Screw Marcus," I told the Fight Club loser in the mirror. "Seth had control. He didn't let it happen."

He did. He almost did.

"I won't get caught off guard like that again." I finger-combed my hair into submission with one hand and carefully brushed my teeth with the other. The inside of my cheek felt like hamburger. Digging to the bottom of my dresser drawer, I pulled out a turtleneck the grandmonsters gave me last Christmas. It half choked me but covered up a bruise or two. I pulled on clean jeans and looked longingly at the pile of rumpled, green blankets beckoning from my bed.

"There's Tylenol in the kitchen cabinet." That promise got me moving.

CHAPTER SEVENTEEN

Seth, dressed in a university sweatshirt, and jeans, stood up from where he sat across from Marcus at the kitchen table. Coming straight to me, his gaze hit every sore spot like he had x-ray vision. The damn turtleneck had been a waste of time. I leaned around him to glare at Marcus. Seth was the one who needed to un-learn the whole *big* brother thing.

"So, I can shut out the next screaming spirit?" Seth asked Marcus, without turning away from me.

"Bridge the veil or don't. You'll learn to control it," Marcus said. "But I'll tell you this. The ones who came screaming? Those were the ones your dad wanted to let in the most."

Seth's forehead wrinkled. I kept my eyes glued to it because the guilt mangling the rest of his face was too intense to deal with. He cupped my chin and turned my tie-dyed cheek.

"Your brother's fine," Marcus sighed. "He just has a

lot to learn."

Seth's frown deepened. "We both do."

"Okay, enough!" I pulled my chin out of his hand and started for the cabinet. Seth stopped me and pointed to a glass of milk and two red Tylenols. "Thanks." I downed the tablets and then leaned against the counter. "So, what else did I miss?"

"Marcus is trying to convince me that I won't be trapped in the house forever," Seth said.

"Mm-hm. How's that going?" I asked.

"Still going."

Marcus leaned his elbows on the table. "How do you feel when you're fully open to the veil?"

Seth crossed his arms and looked away like the question embarrassed him. Thinking of the smile on his face this morning and just now when he was half asleep, I said quietly, "You feel like Captain America."

Marcus gave a decisive nod. "You're your father's son. Bridging the veil is what you were born to do."

"What *is* the veil?" I asked. "And In Between is in between what and what?"

Marcus frowned down at the kitchen table. "That's a tough question. *I* picture the veil as an ethereal kind of membrane." Grimacing at our raised eyebrows, he waved his hands searching for a better description. "It's not made of anything physical, of course, and doesn't lead to a physical place. When most people die, their souls pass right through the veil, through In Between, and keep moving on."

"Moving on to Heaven? Hell? Valhalla?" I asked.

"Let's just say, afterlife," Marcus said. "Nobody

knows for sure until they go, and there's no coming back to drop hints. Passing beyond In Between is a one-way trip. Now, spirits that are confused or reluctant might linger near the veil, staying In Between for a time, but most eventually find their own way to their afterlife. A few, very few, can't stop looking back. They get stuck. In Between's not a good place to stay for long."

"But you said it's not a place at all," Seth said, arching a skeptical eyebrow.

With a defeated sigh, Marcus hung his head. "Get some experience. You'll make sense of it in your own way." Taking in our less than satisfied looks, he threw up his hands. "This is mystery-of-the-universe stuff, boys! That's the best I can do."

My brain didn't have room for mysteries of the universe. I pushed my thumb between my eyes, massaging the spot that was steadily leaking Keeper memories. "When are we doing the Sharing?"

Marcus's chair scraped the floor, relief was clear on his face. "Right now. I saw a sparring mat downstairs. Does it get any use?"

Eyeing him warily, I said, "Yeeeah."

"Come on then."

When I didn't immediately follow Marcus down the steps, Seth reached over and tapped my shoulder. "Let's get this over with. I know this morning had to be bad, but don't hold anything back. The truth can't be as rough as what I'm imagining, believe me." He started for the basement.

"Yeah, I'll make sure of it," I said to the empty kitchen, determined to edit the hell out of the Sharing this time.

Or not. Standing in the middle of the mat, Seth asked me to tell him a ghost story. Despite the growing horror on his face, I spewed it all, every detail, just like with Grams. Leaving anything out just wasn't an option. Afterwards, I saw the wisdom of starting on the mat and stayed flat on my back enjoying pulling air in and out of my lungs. Seth, kneeling beside me, turned to Marcus.

"Why does it have to happen like that? He relived the whole thing!"

"They won't all be that dramatic," Marcus said, rubbing his temple.

"Dramatic!" Seth bolted to his feet. "Why can't I just ask him a simple question and get a simple answer?"

Despite the drama, once I was breathing again, I felt pretty good. For the first time in hours, my skull didn't feel a couple sizes too small. I reached over and slapped Seth's leg. "Down boy. I'm fine. But that *is* a good question."

"Did those feel like *normal* memories to you?" Marcus asked me. I snorted and rolled up onto one elbow. "You have one shot at getting a soul to tell you everything you need to know to free it from In Between. Every single detail, every nuance of the conversation, is vital. Especially when the visit goes down like that one did."

"Why only one shot?" I asked. "He's still around. I've sensed him."

Marcus glared at me. "Your Bridge must never channel the same spirit twice." He turned the glare on Seth too. "Every time you're possessed, the soul leaves something of itself behind. You'll hardly notice one brief visit, but—"

"More than once starts to leave a mark?" I asked, eyeing my brother.

"I don't feel different." Seth patted himself vaguely.

"Good. Keep it that way." Marcus turned to me. "Until you Share them, Keeper memories sharpen and re-sharpen themselves in your head. Every detail stays vivid. You've felt the pressure."

"Yeah," I said. "Not fun."

Marcus's eyebrows came together like two muscular, black caterpillars. He rubbed the dent in his forehead and kept his eyes closed long enough that I started to wonder what god-awful Keeper memories he had playing across the backs of his lids. "Marcus?" When he opened his eyes, the raw pain I'd seen in them this afternoon blazed for a heartbeat, but then he blinked, and the only thing left was something diamond hard glinting in my direction.

"Stand up, Keeper." Marcus pulled off his thick-soled biker boots, then his socks as I slowly stood. Shrugging off his denim shirt, he tossed it over the back of our old couch where the rest of his gear was piled. I wouldn't say he had the sculpted torso of a guy with a gym membership, but his plain, white muscle tee had reached its XL limit around his shoulders. The edge of a puckered scar was visible on his left side. A bullet wound, Marcus' souvenir from the night Dad died.

"What are you doing?" Seth asked nervously. Marcus stepped onto the mat and gently pushed Seth off with the sweep of one long arm. Even without the extra height of his boots, I was looking up into his nostrils.

He tapped his chest with a finger. "I'm Seth carrying an agitated spirit," he said, and then began circling me loose and heavy as a bear. "We'll talk while we move because that's the way it'll be. You must keep your head in the game no matter what's going on. I'll tell you the fifty ways you screwed up this morning while you show me your moves." His eyes narrowed. "You got any moves, little brother?"

Five years of training with a triple black-belt Hapkido mistress, Jet Li's mini-me. Yeah, I had moves. None I'd ever tried outside the dojang. I doubted that Marcus knew Ms. Beverly's safety rules for sparring, and he didn't give me a chance to explain them. His palm smacked my chest like he'd tossed me a bowling ball. Air coughed from my lungs. I landed on my butt, hard, three feet back.

"Son of a bitch." I wheezed.

"He wasn't ready!"

Seth reached to help me up, but I was already on my feet. Time to let the guard dog off the leash. I gave Marcus a smile that was mostly curled lip. "I got moves." *Elbow strike to the nose. Sidekick to the knee, around his back for a kidney strike.* I rolled my shoulders.

"These moves of yours, are they painful?" Marcus sidestepped, mirroring my circle around the mat.

"Oh yeah," I said.

He shrugged. "Fine. Won't disturb the spirit a bit. It doesn't care what you do to the body it's using. But are you planning to send your brother to the hospital?"

As his meaning sank in, I stopped moving. Marcus's thin smile widened, he lunged for me again. I blocked,

135

pushed his hands off-target. Momentum carried him past me, but before I could drop him with a relatively painless kick to the back of the knee, he spun, and locked an arm like an oak log around my neck.

"Here's your first lesson," Marcus murmured low in my ear. "Never let your Bridge get close enough to hurt you." He huffed out a breath that was almost a moan. "Consequences could be much worse than the little guilt-trip Seth's on right now." I smelled leather and asphalt, sweat. Marcus's voice went lower. "You were stupid-lucky this morning." He shifted his hold until his forearm pressed one side of my neck, his bicep the other. He squeezed.

Sleeper hold! I'd pass out in seconds if I didn't do something. I drove an elbow into his ribs. Stomped my heel hard into the top of his foot. No effect. None at all. The guy was impervious to pain.

"I told you. Pain won't work," Marcus whispered. "You'd have to cripple or blind Seth to slow the spirit down."

My pulse pounded in my temples. A hum of pressure climbed in my skull. I lifted both feet off the mat hoping to throw him off balance. I might as well have been hanging from a tree branch. "You worried about passing out?" He gave a breathy chuckle. "Think about this. You did pass out this morning. What if you'd woken up on that trail and Seth was gone—still possessed!?"

His voice was hot breath in my ear, but I shivered like he'd soaked me in icy water. "You let him hurt you, disable you, and you could really lose him. Do you understand what I'm saying?"

136

"Marcus!"

Seth's voice cut through my foggy panic. Marcus loosened his arm. He didn't let go, just held me up while blood pounded back into my brain and my vision cleared.

"The only way to get out of that hold is not to get into it," he said, loud enough so Seth could hear. "Keep your distance from your Bridge."

He shoved me away. I waved Seth off when I got my balance. Marcus's warning rang in my ears. I shook my head, trying not to imagine Seth possessed by that berserker spirit, out in the world somewhere alone. I wouldn't be calling on my guard dog again. He was whimpering in a corner.

Marcus waited for me to pull it together. The pain I'd seen in his eyes was gone. He seemed calm, like he knew he'd made his point. There was even a little sympathy in his look when I slowly straightened up. The sympathy didn't stay there long.

"Ready for lesson two?" he asked.

CHAPTER EIGHTEEN

With blood still pounding through the kinked veins in my neck, it wasn't easy to start moving again. Seth paced the edges of the mat looking like he'd fought the sleeper hold right along with me.

"When you realize someone's crossed, talk to them, not to Seth," Marcus said as we started a slow dance of attack and evade. "The spirit this morning was mad as hell. You two did everything short of an exorcism to stop him from telling you why." Marcus cuffed me hard on the shoulder. I stumbled sideways. He stepped behind me smooth as silk and gave me an elbow tap between the shoulder blades that knocked me flat on my face. I rolled, got to my feet.

He nodded approvingly. "You forced the spirit into that fight. They don't drop by to chat, for God's sake." Marcus took a swing. I arched back. Felt a cool breeze brush past my nose as I staggered. "Don't step off the mat!" He roared. "Never leave your Bridge!"

Heart in my throat, I twisted like a falling cat and somehow stayed on the mat and out of his reach. There was another glimmer of approval in Marcus's eyes. It lasted about half a second.

"Seth," Marcus jabbed a finger at my brother, startling him. "Let spirits in, one hundred percent." He pointed at me. "Listen to them instead of baiting them. Figure out why they're stuck In Between. You're promising to put things right. That's all they want."

"What if we can't put things right?" Seth asked from the sidelines.

Marcus ignored him and grabbed for me again, but this time I dropped, swung my leg in an arc, and knocked his feet out from under him. He rolled, but I flung myself onto his back and barely managed to lock my hands behind his head in a full nelson. Digging my toes into the mat, I threw my weight forward.

"Too much?" I asked through gritted teeth. "Can you talk?"

"Excellent question," Marcus said, his voice strained from having his chin shoved against his chest. He gave the mat beside him two hard slaps.

He did know Ms. Beverly's safety rules. I unlocked my fingers and slumped back on my heels, breathing hard. Maybe Grams was right about destiny. Black belts don't come easy. The hours I'd spent at the dojang practicing had more of a purpose than I knew.

Marcus tipped his head back and forth, cracking his neck to get his vertebrae all lined up again. "Use a restraint like that as a last resort. Some spirits aren't so good with words. They have to be able to show you what they need. Best not to bind them up."

"Oh sure. That doesn't sound impossible at all." I offered him a hand up, but he waved me off. "This would be a lot easier if you could show us. If we could actually watch somebody else do it right."

"I'll give that some thought." Marcus stood, stretching his arms up until he pressed his fingertips against the basement ceiling. "Sparring's over. What time is it?"

Seth pulled his phone out of his pocket. "Not quite midnight."

Marcus nodded. "Good. We've got time to debrief while it's fresh. Then sleep."

I stripped off the sweaty turtleneck and dumped it in the trash can by the washing machine. Good riddance. Pulling a clean shirt out of the dryer, I took the glass of water Seth offered me. Marcus, walking a little stiffly, picked up his denim shirt and put it back on, accepted a glass of water too, and then led us over to the plaid couch and worn recliners that faced the fireplace.

The furniture came from the living room in our old house. As Seth and I clicked on lamps and then claimed recliners, I could hear Dad's laugh, imagine him and Marcus watching ballgames, talking cop shop while Seth and I played UNO on the floor. The faint smile on Marcus's face made me wonder if he was hearing it all too. He moved his saddlebags and helmet into a neat pile and then slumped onto the couch, and spread his arms across the back, looking every bit as comfortable there as he had back in the day.

"That your dad's guitar?" he asked, pointing to me.

I looked down and saw that I'd picked up the acoustic

on my way to the chair without even realizing it. Habit. "Yeah. Mine now."

"Play something. Your dad used to strum while we sorted things out. Don't worry. The music lubricates the synapses, we won't really be listening."

"Oh great. Thanks a lot." I set my glass of water beside me on the floor. Karaoke air guitar hadn't warmed me up, my fingers felt stiff and clumsy on the strings. But I tuned up a little and then wandered through some picking patterns until I found my thoughts settling.

"Okay," Marcus said, eyes half closed. "Tell me what you know."

I nodded for Seth to start.

"Well, first, I think somebody drowned our man."

"What makes you think that?" Marcus asked.

"That gurgly cough right at the start," I answered for him. "And I smelled scummy water. What's up with the smell-o-vision? It's cinnamon rolls when Grams shows up."

"Do you still sense her presence?" Marcus asked, opening one eye wider to look at me. He sounded surprised but not totally unhappy about that possibility.

"Off and on. When she feels the need to boss me around."

He smiled a little. "Souls bring their last moments of life with them. We were in Georgia. My aunt has a hell of a kitchen, and your grandmother couldn't resist the chance to use it. I got her to the hospital after the stroke, but there wasn't anything they could do." Marcus nodded to himself. "Good way to go."

"But if Will's still sensing her, Grams stayed In

141

Between. Why?"

Marcus took a long sip of water before he answered. "She has her reasons. Let's stay on topic here."

Seth looked ready to argue, but I was feeling every minute of a rough two days. I wanted nothing more than my bed and a long, dreamless sleep. "He's worried about some girl named Megan." I shifted to another quiet riff on the guitar. "I might have a lead on her. When I signed-up for the karaoke contest tonight, the girl in front of me . . ."

Seth sat up. "Wait a second. You sang in front of people?"

I shrugged. "Yeah. That's not the point. The girl in front of me—"

"Can't believe I missed that." With a surprised smile, he reached across the space between us to smack me on the knee.

Marcus made a keep-rolling gesture. "Can we get back to this supposed lead?"

"I'm trying," I said, stifling a grin. "This girl in line was worried. She said her girlfriend had been missing for a week and nobody was looking for her. One of the names she wrote on the sign-up sheet was Megan."

Seth sobered right away. "Two girls. That fits. Our guy said, *you're done hurting both of them.*"

"Megan's a common name," Marcus said.

"That's what I told myself too, but . . ." I hadn't mentioned our ghost hanging around the porta-johns with Grams and felt too tired to open that can of worms. "Just call it a hunch."

"Listen to your hunches," Marcus said. "Now, why'd

142

your visitor try to kill you this morning?"

My fingers stumbled on the strings. "We've been over this. I pissed him off."

"I think there's more to it," Seth said slowly. "He took you for somebody else, Will." Marcus nodded for us go on.

"Right," I said nodding. "You'll never find her, *brother*. That word . . ." I grimaced. "There was poison in it. But if he didn't mean *me*, he must have meant—" *Oh shit.* I pressed a hand over the guitar strings and the basement went silent. "His brother drowned him?"

"Murdered him." Seth's voice sounded too hard for this homey corner of the basement. "Our ghost wants payback. He deserves it."

"What he deserves is justice," Marcus corrected. Suddenly no longer half asleep, he leaned forward, elbows on his knees. "You're not in the revenge business, boys. Follow a spirit down that dark path and all three of you are lost." His voice dropped lower, as if his thoughts weighed it down. "Here's how I see the murder happening. The killer was strong enough, vicious enough to hold his own brother in scummy water fighting for his last breath. Takes a good five minutes to drown a man. Your spirit called him a pervert. He's hurt at least two girls. Now he may be hunting them."

I swallowed, my throat gone dry, and reached for my glass of water.

Marcus looked at Seth. "You attracted this spirit without even trying, just walking down the trail. You're a stronger Bridge than you ought to be. Maybe stronger than you can handle." When he turned to me, I got the distinct impression he thought I was the weak link in our short chain, but all he said was, "You drew a bad one for your first time out, boys."

CHAPTER NINETEEN

So much for a long, dreamless sleep. The only way I knew that I'd slept at all was waking up to the bees drilling a hole between my eyes again. Adrenalin launched me off the bed. I rounded the corner into Seth's room just in time to see his light collapse. "Craaaap," I moaned, drooping against the door frame.

He turned a sheepish smile my direction. "Sorry. But I'm getting the hang of it."

I shook my head. "Man, you're going to kill me." I staggered back to my room, smiling a little. Better.

In the kitchen, achy and muzzy-headed, I squinted as I flicked on the lights and then poked my head into the garage. Mom's car was gone. If she'd gotten up and out this early, she must not have been drinking as much as I thought last night. She'd probably met up with the grandmonsters for Sunday services. The thought of their old, creaky church and its old, creaky pastor made me shudder, but I hoped she'd find some comfort, for all our sakes.

Marcus cooked breakfast, flatly refusing to eat one of the prepackaged Showy Chef meals stacked in our freezer. "Your spirit's remains will be close to where he made first contact," he said as he slid scrambled eggs onto my plate and sat down. "We need to work on ID'ing him."

I worried about how old the carton of eggs Marcus found in the fridge must be but decided to risk it, and tucked in. "There was a fresh grave across the ravine in the cemetery," I said, after giving due diligence to those hot, fluffy eggs and warm toast. "I saw it right before our guy showed up."

"That's the ID we need," Seth said, straightening from his nearly spotless plate. "His name will be on the grave marker. We've got to go over there."

"We? You speakin' French?" I asked. "Walnut Glen'll be a beyond-the-grave paparazzi frenzy!" The thought of my brother and his beacon anywhere near a modern cemetery with all those fresh bodies made my breakfast churn in my stomach.

"Will's right," Marcus agreed quickly. "You'll stay inside, behind the threshold." He ignored Seth's mutinous look. "If your spirit's been dead long enough to have had a proper burial, then his murder made the papers. You can do some research here at home."

"A drowning might look accidental," Seth said sullenly.

"Why can't we go to the police right now? We know it was no accident." The sooner we handed this off to the cops, the better. Popping the last corner of toast into my

146

mouth, I stood with my plate.

Marcus stood too, shaking his head. "It's too soon. If there's not already an investigation going on, they'll need hard evidence to start one. Our first step is Walnut Glen."

Seth, frowning down at a spot in the middle of the table, wadded his napkin with a quiet fierceness that made me nervous. He pushed his chair back. "Before you two leave, I have to try something." Marcus realized he was headed for the front door about three seconds after I did. With both of us on his heels, Seth threw a defiant look over his shoulder. "You said I control it."

"You do," Marcus said. "Or you will. You need a few more days—"

Seth cut him off with a shake of his head. "Now." Desperate and determined, he squared his shoulders. "Are you coming?"

"Aw, crap," I said.

Seth took that for a *yes* and flung the door open. The morning air, sharp and cold, smelled clean, uncomplicated by ghosts. I looked Seth over. No glow, not yet. "Armor up," I whispered. "Nothing gets in, nothing gets out." He nodded once, closed his eyes, and stepped onto the porch like he was stepping off a cliff. Keeping my weight on the balls of my feet, my hands loose at my sides, I followed him, trying to convince myself that I was ready if he morphed into someone else.

Seth opened his eyes and cautiously walked over to lean on the porch railing. "Nothing?" I asked, rubbing my chest.

One side of his mouth turned up. "All quiet. I don't hear anything. What about your—" Seth flinched. "Wait."

Light flickered under his skin as suddenly as far-off lightning, and a buzz started between my eyes. I pulled him back from the railing and shoved him against the house. "Close down! Right now." The stench of stagnant water prickled my nostrils.

Seth hunched, trembling. "He's not angry anymore, Will. He's desperate."

I felt it too. Bleak desperation filled the hollow in my chest, so strong that my eyes burned.

Marcus leaned around me, and I barely caught myself before I jammed an elbow into his ribs.

"Listen to me, Seth," he said. "I know every instinct's telling you to let this spirit cross. But you must not bridge the veil for him again. Do not let him in. Do you hear me?"

"Tell him, Will!" Seth grabbed my shoulders. "Tell him we understand what he wants."

"How?" I had no idea how to get a message through if Seth couldn't bridge the veil. Grams seemed to understand me without him, but she was Grams, not some stranger.

Seth gave a frustrated snarl and then dug his fingers into my shoulders. The glow left his face and coalesced, shining through his shirt above his heart. Mesmerized, I watched it divide, move across his shoulders, flow down his arms. His fingers twitched, and I gasped.

Pure one-hundred-percent joy sizzled into my veins. How did Seth keep from exploding when he was full of *this*? He was shaking, right on the edge of throwing himself open to the veil. But hell, if it meant more bliss, I wanted him to do it!

We had to end this.

I could hardly catch my breath, had no idea if anything I was about to say would get through to our ghost, but I made my voice steady. "We hear you, man. You died rough. We get that." Seth's fingers dug in tighter. "Your girl's in trouble. Megan. We'll look for her, and I *promise* you we'll find a way to help her. It's our job to put things right for you."

With bliss still flowing through me, I had to force myself to say, "Seth. That's all I can do. My promise'll have to be enough for him. Shut down."

Seth's hands sprang open hovering over my shoulders. I almost whimpered when the light slid away. It flickered in his eyes for the span of a breath, then dimmed and disappeared. I collapsed against the house next to him. "Damn, Seth. I mean . . . just *damn.*" I rubbed the stinging spot where the bees had tried to drill me a new nostril, and squelched the urge to ask my brother to do it again.

"What the hell just happened!" Marcus shouted into our faces, and we both jumped. This time he was too loud, too close. My inner guard dog growled. I didn't realize that I'd stepped in front of Seth until he took a firm hold of my elbow and pulled me back beside him.

"You told me not to bridge the veil so I . . ." Seth shrugged and made a little push gesture. "I gave Will a little light, so he'd attract our guy's attention instead of me, improve his chances of communicating, you know."

"No. I don't know!"

I frowned. "What's the big deal?"

"What's the big deal? This . . ." Marcus waved a hand

back and forth between Seth and me, "doesn't happen. The Bridge, and only the Bridge, channels the light. There is no sharing!"

"But the Sharing—" I began.

"You know what I mean! The Keeper communicates *only* while the Bridge is possessed." He enunciated every word.

I wasn't sure I'd call what passed between our ghost and me at the Fall Fling communication, not compared to what happened with Seth's help just now, but Grams was a different story. "Grams isn't a typical spirit, right? She's a blood relative and she was a Bridge. I mean she sat with us at the café."

"Oh right, that's another thing," Marcus said. "You know how many times your dad managed to let a spirit manifest physically? Twice! Twice! And that was after we'd been partners for five years!" He scratched his short, black hair like he was trying to rearrange the tangled thoughts in his head. Huffing disapprovingly, he stomped into the house. "Seth, get back inside."

Seth and I looked at each other, eyebrows raised. "Sheesh," I said. "You'd think he'd never seen anybody do whatever the hell we just did." I couldn't explain what we'd done any more than I could explain a sneeze. It just happened.

"Yeah. You're okay, right?"

Awestruck. Scared shitless. I'd be chasing ambulances and hanging out at funeral homes if running into dead people let me tap into that bliss again. How did Seth keep it bottled up? "Yeah, you?"

He shrugged. "Hey, I know that wasn't the sanest thing

150

I've ever done. Thanks for coming out here with me."

I patted his shoulder. "You did good. You're outside! Feel better?" He nodded soberly. "Come on in then." I tried not to actually push Seth back over the threshold into the ghost-free zone, but when I closed the door, I stood for a second, my forehead pressed against it, wishing there was a quick way to brick it up from the inside.

Marcus looked older and more tired than he had a few minutes ago. "I'm out of my depth here, boys and I don't like it. Tell me exactly what your grandmother said at the cafe. Start at the beginning."

Between the two of us, we gave him a thorough recounting of Halloween night. "So," I asked cautiously, "Is that all you need to know?"

Marcus snorted and then looked up like he'd made a decision. "Change of plans. There's a pair of BridgeKeepers down in Kansas City. They've been at this for a long time. The sooner you watch a *normal* team at work, the better."

"When do we go?" Seth asked.

"We!" I said, ready to repeat my crack about speaking French, but Marcus held up a warning finger and turned to Seth.

"Out there," he nodded toward the front door and the big, wide world, "You won't have to be near a cemetery to get waylaid by voices. The only way to protect yourself—the only way to live a normal life—is to have iron-fisted self-control every second of every day. You're not there yet. I'll take Will on this little field trip."

Seth crossed his arms, looking stubborn, but thoughtful.

"Kansas City's forty miles away." As curious as I was to watch an experienced team do their thing, putting that many miles between me and my Bridge made my palms sweat.

"We'll be there and back in a couple of hours," Marcus reassured me. "Afterward, we'll check out that new grave at Walnut Glen."

"I can handle some alone time," Seth said. "Go learn something."

I rubbed my palms on my jeans. "You can practice while we're gone. Open up for business, then close down, open, close. Flex that Bridge muscle. He'll be alright practicing inside, right?"

Marcus looked doubtful, but Seth jumped in before he could object. "I can do it."

"Do not try it outside," Marcus said. Seth glared at him. Marcus glared right back.

"Right, good. Glad we got that settled," I said. It was a good thing that Mom wasn't around. Seth was a tiger in a cage already. Her poking him with a stick would have guaranteed that he'd claw his way out, ready or not. "And if you get bored, clean the kitchen, it's a mess. My room needs dusting too. Do your homework."

"And see what you can find out about a drowning, accidental or otherwise. Let's go so we can get back." Marcus opened the front door and Seth shoved me through it. I gave him a finger-wave as the door closed, but then my smile faded. "He can do this, right?"

"If he can't, it's better we find out now," Marcus stepped off the porch then looked back. "The range for a Bridge's signal is about ten miles. Pay attention. It won't feel nearly as strong when he's behind your threshold."

"Ahh! Shhi . . ." I spun back around and pounded on the door.

Seth poked his head out. "What!? I was practicing. Did it work?"

"Yeah, I felt *a tingle*." I knuckled the burning spot between my eyes and turned to Marcus. "Can he tone it down?"

Marcus blinked away a startled look. "He can tone it down, turn it up, aim it, call to a specific spirit . . . with practice."

I shooed Seth back inside. "Give us a few minutes before you do that again. And tone it down at first. Crank it up when we're a few miles out of town!"

Seth watched us walk away through the little beveled window in the door. I couldn't shake the feeling that we were leaving him locked in a padded room. The sooner we got back from our field trip the better.

CHAPTER TWENTY

"Here, wear this." Marcus shoved a helmet into my hands. "It was a little too big for your grandmother so it should fit you fine."

"Grams rode on the back of your bike?" I worked the helmet on and instantly felt claustrophobic. Only the thought of getting bugs in my teeth made me slide the visor down.

"Thousands of miles. You should have seen her in her leathers." A sad smile briefly appeared on Marcus' lips as he swung his leg over the bike and raised the kickstand. "Get on."

I eyed the big machine. "I've never ridden a motorcycle. How do I . . ."

"Put your left foot on the peg and swing your other leg over like you're getting on a horse."

"Never ridden a horse either," I muttered. But apparently, I'd seen enough Westerns. I found the only object on the Harley that looked like a peg, stepped up and swung into the saddle. *Yee-haw!*

Marcus revved the motor. With a desperate grab, I clutched him around the waist, and we took off. Two minutes later, Seth zapped me, and my reaction made the bike wobble. *No flinching!* As we accelerated up the ramp onto the highway and merged into traffic, I decided that keeping my eyes closed didn't make me a wuss.

We finally got where we were going, and I jumped off before Marcus cut the engine. Struggling out of Grams' helmet, I gasped, "Any chance we could walk home?" He just chuckled. "Where are we?" The parking lot was attached to a single-story building that looked like an office with an all-vampire staff. There were no windows.

"County Medical Examiner's headquarters," Marcus said.

"The morgue?"

A woman jumped out of a light blue hatchback parked at the other end of the lot and waved. "Hellooo, Marcus!"

Marcus waved back as the woman hurried over. She wore blue jeans and a pink sweatshirt with a crowd of Pokemon on the front. Her short, brown hair was sprinkled with gray at the temples, and though she didn't exactly look athletic, she had too much energy to be a couch potato.

"Is she part of the demonstration?" I asked him.

"Half of it."

"Ooohhhh, it's been too long!" The woman's eyes crinkled when she smiled, reaching up to hug Marcus. "I'm so sorry about Ellen."

"Thanks, Maria. Is Angela . . ."

"She's here. She stayed in her car so I could give you a proper greeting."

Marcus nodded unsmiling, and then turned to me. "Maria, this is Will, Kevin and Barb's youngest."

I started to offer her my hand, but her fading smile stopped me.

"Our youngest Keeper," she muttered. I shoved my hands into my pockets, and she seemed to realize that it wasn't polite to stare. She cleared her throat. "How's your mom dealing with all this?"

Marcus' expression gave me no clues about how honest I should be with this woman. "She's . . . adjusting."

Maria gave a short laugh. "Well, I'm sure you don't want to be away from your Bridge for long, and today's my daughter's tenth birthday, I've got a cake to bake. I'll go get Angela. Meet us by the buses."

Marcus locked both helmets on the bike and then started for the medical building while Maria trotted off.

"Which one was she?" I asked.

He raised an eyebrow. "Can't you figure it out?"

It took a second, but then I realized the answer was obvious. "She's the Bridge. The one who stayed in her car's the Keeper. Is she going to react to you like I did?"

Marcus turned his gaze on the distance, frowning. "Yeah. But we've known each other for a long time. She'll keep it together." He didn't look as sure as he sounded.

"Maria has a kid," I said to move this conversation along. "Are she and Angela a couple?"

"Definitely not."

"Do they even like each other?" My question was only half serious, but he paused, thinking it over.

156

"They're committed. They trust each other. That's all it takes."

That's all it takes? Grams and my grandfather were Bridge and Keeper, and husband and wife. Marcus and Dad were like brothers. Seth and I *are*. If these two were a more typical BridgeKeeper team, then the McCurty clan must be a whole different breed. *Freaks among freaks?*

The *buses* turned out to be shiny, black vans with *Jackson County Coroner* stenciled on their sides. The sign on the wide, sliding glass doors that led into the building read, Employees Only.

"Are we going inside?" I tried to keep the heebie-jeebies out of my voice.

"Don't worry. I doubt we'll have to. Maria will call someone out."

"Call them how?"

"The same way Seth will eventually. The morgue doesn't form a threshold like a home does. When Maria lights up, if there's anybody in need, they'll come out to her. I wasn't just trying to make Seth feel better when I said he'd have control."

"That's good news." Seth was still at home working on that. At this distance, all I got was a tickle between my eyes when he opened up, but it was a comfort to know we were still connected. I looked around the nearly empty lot. "Is Maria going to let herself get possessed right out in the open?"

Marcus shrugged. "Those two could probably host a visitor in a crowded grocery store, and nobody would know it was happening. You'll see."

After yesterday morning, it was hard not to

be skeptical.

As the two women joined us on the sidewalk, Angela, the Keeper, positioned herself between Maria and Marcus, watching his every move. She was taller than her Bridge, and older, but her black leggings showed off runner's legs. The way she carried herself, I wondered if she practiced martial arts too. There was no doubt how she felt about Marcus. The woman radiated hostility.

He took a slow step backwards as he introduced me. "Will, this is Angela. She's a hell of a Keeper. You'll learn a lot today."

His words made Angela dip her chin, looking a little embarrassed. "Well, we'll show you how *we* do it anyway. Marcus said you already have a case."

The tops of my ears went hot. "Yeah, and I already screwed it up."

Maria gave me a sympathetic look. "It's tough when they catch you unawares." She pointed to the corner of the building, and we started down the sidewalk. "I stop by the morgue every day after I drop the kids at school. The nice thing about encountering souls here, besides not getting surprised, is we can usually get the name and cause of death from the coroner if we need to."

We stepped off the end of the sidewalk and went around the corner of the building. The sun was bright on this side, the highway close enough that whatever happened would be visible to people speeding by. I felt even more exposed, but nobody else seemed bothered.

"Give us some space," Angela said, tersely.

Marcus nodded, unphased by her rudeness, or hiding it well. He touched my elbow. Our shoes crunched the dry, weedy grass until we were a good twenty feet from where Angela and Maria stood facing each other.

"Marcus," I whispered.

He shook his head and put a finger to his lips. "Shh. Just watch."

Angela stepped back, waiting patiently while Maria cocked her head like Seth had at Muddy Bend, tuning into ghost radio. After a few seconds her eyebrows lifted. She nodded once. "Male voice. Ready?"

"Bring him," Angela said.

I expected to see light burst from Maria's skin, but of course, I didn't. She wasn't my Bridge. But the hairs on my arms prickled under my shirt. My chest hollowed out. Anxiety and deep sadness seeped in. I may not have been the Keeper on duty, but my cat still knew when a soul was around. Maria's breathing turned fast and shallow, but her face didn't morph into a double image, not that I could see.

Angela's hands dropped loosely to her sides, and she shifted her weight onto the balls of her feet. Ready stance. Maria looked wildly around and gently, Angela said, "You're alright. I'm here." She moved to block Maria's view of us and held a finger up in front of her Bridge's face. "Stay with *me*. What's your name?"

Maria's lips trembled. "F . . . F . . . Fred," she said, her voice deeper and less steady than when it had been her own. "Please, help me."

"Yes, sir, I will." Angela gave him a reassuring smile. "Take your time. Tell me what you need."

The man slowly raised Maria's trembling left hand. "She won't be able to find it."

"Find what, Fred?"

"Been years since she could wear it. I took it to get resized last week. Anniversary surprise." On the last word, the man covered Maria's face and sobbed.

"Fred," Angela said. "Everything's going to work out. Where did you take the wedding ring? We'll make sure your wife gets it."

Maria's hands slipped away from her face and her eyes shone. "Ticket stub's in my sock drawer but . . ." He clenched Maria's fists. His voice grew anguished. "I won't leave her all alone."

He's gonna lose it! Should I try to help? Would that make it worse? While my heart raced, Marcus stayed propped against the building, arms crossed, watching calmly. I forced myself to copy his cool.

"Your wife will find the help she needs, Fred, just like you found us." Angela's tone left no room for doubt. "Tell me the name of the jeweler, we'll get her ring." She held his gaze with absolute assurance until finally, Maria's shoulders slumped.

"Deming's Diamonds," Fred said in a raspy whisper.

Angela smiled. "Thank you, Fred. You've done a good thing for your wife. Go now and be at peace till you're together again."

I could tell as the tension melted from Maria's face that that was exactly what Fred needed to hear. On a long exhale, her knees buckled, and she leaned against the side of the morgue. Only then did her Keeper come close enough to catch hold of her arm.

Marcus looked pleased. "Now that's the way you do it."

"That was a coherent conversation," I said, awed.

160

"How'd Angela know exactly what to say?" *Oozing trustworthiness is Seth's thing.* "No way I could pull that off."

Marcus scratched the stubble on his chin. "You'll learn."

"Okay?" Angela asked her Bridge.

Maria nodded and brushed her hair back from her face wearily. "Ready for the Sharing?"

"Sure," Angela said.

My mouth dropped open. I whipped my head around to Marcus again, but he shrugged like this was exactly what he'd expected. And just like that, Maria asked, and Angela calmly shared every second of Fred's visit. To anybody who noticed them from the highway, this would look like a couple of women having an intense conversation, not a supernatural encounter.

When she finished, Angela squared her shoulders. "Okay, how do you want to handle getting the ring?"

They had it all worked out in about five minutes. The ring would be where it belonged before Maria's daughter's birthday party.

"It's surprising how little the way a person dies predicts whether or not they linger In Between," Maria said as she walked with me past the coroner's buses, heading to her hatchback.

Angela and Marcus hung back, having what looked like a heated discussion. From the occasional gestures flung in my direction, I guessed it was about me.

Maria took my elbow and kept walking. "Even murder victims and suicides usually pass on without a hitch. Most souls' problems seem huge to them, but they're easily fixed from our side of the veil." She covered my hand with both of hers. "You got thrown into the deep end, Will, but you'll surface. The rest of your career will be spent helping souls like Fred."

Her smile said she was trying, but I remembered the worry and doubt on her face when we first met.

"Good luck," she said, and giving my hand one more squeeze, Maria went off to bake her daughter's cake. I wondered if Angela was invited to the party.

CHAPTER TWENTY-ONE

M arcus met me at the Harley looking pissed. I waved, but Angela, hands on hips, just glared as we roared out of the parking lot. I tried not to let that worry me. I wanted to savor what I'd just witnessed. Not every troubled soul was homicidal. BridgeKeepers had room to live normal, *separate* lives. All we needed was practice.

I yelped and threw Grams' helmet at Marcus when we stopped in our driveway. Seth flung the front door open before I got to it.

"Dude!" I said. "You are *not* getting better at toning it down!"

"You should have texted me when you started back. I would have tried. How was the demonstration?"

I smiled and gripped his shoulders. "Turns out even if you're hanging out with the dead, there are still birthday parties."

Seth gave me a slow grin. "Yeah? Tell me everything."

163

"Will," Marcus interrupted before I could follow Seth inside, "we've still got a grave to check. Seth, keep practicing while we're at Walnut Glen."

Seth let out a discouraged groan, but I knocked his shoulder. "We'll be back soon. Hang in there. And tone it *down*."

Marcus had legs like circus tent poles, so I had to do an annoying jog-skip-walk thing to stay alongside him as he headed down the driveway. "We're not taking the bike?" I didn't know whether I felt relieved or annoyed. Walnut Glen shared a boundary with the nature reserve, but we'd have to walk an extra quarter mile to get around to the cemetery gates.

"You wanted to know why your grandmother and I left after your dad's funeral."

I blinked up at him. Sure, I wanted to know, but why bring this up now, out of Seth's earshot? Marcus' profile could have been carved in the side of a tree. I had a feeling that whatever he was about to tell me was going to seriously mess with my newfound optimism. "Uhm, is this what you and Angela were arguing about?"

He stopped and grabbed my arm. "Look up." When I just stared at him, he rapped me under the chin. "Look up." I did, squinting into a bright, crayon-blue sky. "Hear those birds? Feel that fresh wind on your face? God's earth is a beautiful place."

Marcus's rumbling voice sounded tattered around the edges. Goosebumps rose across my shoulders and down my arms. "Okay, that's the scariest damned thing anybody ever said to me."

"Just remember it's the truth while you listen to what

164

I'm about to tell you." He let go and started off again. After a long silence, four words drifted back over his shoulder like little toxic clouds. "Your dad killed himself."

"What?"

"He shot himself. To keep from killing me."

"He . . . That's not what . . ." Making a coherent sentence wasn't possible. *He shot himself to keep from killing me.* The words bounced around my head like a ball of rusty barbed wire.

"Keep walking," Marcus said.

How? My feet were bricks.

Marcus pulled me gently by the elbow. "Look around. Don't tunnel down. You hear me?"

"Yeah," I managed a sloppy jog.

"We got a domestic disturbance call that night. The house was dark, dog was barking its head off inside. I went to the front door. Your dad went around back. I'd barely knocked and announced myself when I heard your dad kick the backdoor in. There was a gunshot and the barking stopped. I called for backup and ran."

Marcus' voice dropped so that I bumped his shoulder getting close enough to hear. "He must have sensed the entity, but something was very wrong. I felt him open up, pierce the veil. He wouldn't have done that, not without me beside him. Not willingly."

He was breathing fast, his eyes fixed straight ahead, boots pounding down the sidewalk like he was trying to outrun me, or the story. "The place reeked. Every room was trashed. I yelled for your dad but couldn't hear anything except glass crunching under my boots. I found the dog and the homeowner dead in the kitchen.

The drawers and cabinets looked like they'd exploded. The guy'd been dead for a while, hit with every can of food and dish in the place. Beaten to a pulp."

"Where was Dad?" I wasn't sure whether Marcus heard me or just kept talking, locked in the memory.

"I didn't see Kevin till he moved. He stumbled out from a dark corner and . . . the darkness came with him. Shadows tangled around him, twisted into his chest. He yelled for me to get the hell out. It was your dad's voice. Not the thing that had come through the veil. But it had control of his body."

"How did you know that?"

His mouth turned down in a quick, sharp grimace. "He shot me."

I just about tripped off the curb. Marcus grabbed my elbow again, dragging me with him.

"I didn't see his gun come up until too late. Bullet hit my shoulder, slammed me into the counter. He yelled, *Get up, damn it. I can't stop it,* but he had the barrel pressed against my forehead, thumbed the hammer back. Just as his finger tightened on the trigger, he jerked the gun up to the middle of his chest where that thing had—"

"Gotta sit down," I choked out.

We staggered to a stop and Marcus let go of my elbow. I dropped onto a grassy rise beside a driveway, breathing like we'd run a marathon. Somehow, we'd ended up just inside the stone and wrought iron gate to Walnut Glen Cemetery.

"The shadows left him as he died. Just blew away like a stiff breeze had caught them." Marcus looked down at me, his face nothing but a dark silhouette against blue

166

sky. "It shouldn't have happened that way." He knelt, his eyes feverish, and tapped my cheek to make sure he had my attention. "Keepers are expendable. Never forget that. Alive, I wasn't strong enough to help my Bridge, but if he'd let it kill me . . . Will, I might have been able to fight it from the other side."

"Jesus, Marcus."

He clamped a hand on my knee. "When your grandparents bonded as Bridge and Keeper, they passed the notion on to your dad that the team is sacred. Hell, I believed it too." Marcus leaned in. "Your dad and I were arrogant. We didn't think anything could break our bond. We were wrong. He should have let me die. If I'd killed that thing from the other side and he'd lived, he'd have trained Seth the right way. Your brother might have bonded with someone—"

"Stronger? Older?" I asked, my voice raw.

"Someone less important to him."

I dropped my forehead onto my arms. "Shit." My mind rolled out visuals—Seth wrapped in black shadows, fighting for control, having to make that choice. I tried to imagine having the guts to put a bullet in my own chest. I just didn't have an imagination that big.

"The last thing your dad said was, *Protect my boys.*"

I knew that'd be a direct quote, a Keeper memory. "You Shared all that with Grams, right? Got it out of your head?"

"No." He turned away to stare down the road that curved up to the cemetery chapel. "Doesn't work that way."

Bile filled my throat. Marcus had that nightmare seared into his brain in super hi-def. Forever. He pushed me because he knew exactly what kind of hell I'd live with for the rest of my life if I screwed up.

"Now's the time to feel the wind on your face, kid. Run your hands through the grass."

I pressed my palms into the cool, bristly lawn. Some of the weight crushing me bled down into the dirt as a breeze dried the clammy sweat on my face.

Marcus sighed like he was pulling himself back from far away and sat down next to me. He plucked a few blades of grass, crushed them between his fingers, and held them up to his nose. "Do you remember what happened the day your grandmother and I left?"

I thought about it for a second, happy to have something to pull my mind away from what I'd just heard. My most vivid memory from the week of Dad's funeral was food, stacked in the fridge, cluttering the counters. Our tiny, old house seemed weighted down by it. For days I'd run to the door every time some hushed, casserole-laden person came in, expecting Dad to show up for the party.

"I think the day you left was the day Seth told me Dad was dead." Marcus frowned at me. I shrugged. "Mom thought I was too young to go to the funeral. Everybody kept saying, sorry. Sorry your dad's gone. What's that mean to a little kid? I thought he was on a trip."

Marcus blew a quiet breath out his nose. "Good Lord. I had no idea."

"That afternoon, I asked Seth when Dad would be back. That's when we went for a walk."

Marcus concentrated on the blade of grass between his fingers. "You weren't outside more than fifteen minutes when Seth dragged you back in. All either of you could tell us was something bad was out there."

I'd told Seth that somebody was sucking out my insides and filling me up with bad dreams. That was the first time I got the cat-walking-on-my-grave feeling. "It was that thing, wasn't it?" I whispered, remembering the cold, jagged touch of it. "Dad died, and it came looking for Seth."

"Ellen suspected it. She'd given up BridgeKeeping when your grandfather died, but she took me as her Keeper and opened herself to the veil that afternoon. She managed to draw the entity's focus to her. I was barely fit to travel, but we left an hour later."

"That's why you ditched us." There was a weird lack of comfort in finally understanding that they hadn't abandoned us willingly. "So, now that Grams isn't distracting it, what's keeping that thing from finding its way back here?"

Marcus' silence raised the hairs on the back of my neck again. Seth was at home practicing with that damned searchlight of his. I scrambled up. "Seth's got to stop. He has to suck it up and close himself off. Permanently." I started back through the wrought iron gates.

"Hey!" Marcus called before I got twenty feet. "There's a spirit out there that you two have to deal with. It's not going away."

After several muttered breaths, I forced my feet in the opposite direction from where they wanted to go. A hearse was parked in front of the cemetery's main building. Marcus' funhouse reflection joined mine in its polished side as I stormed past.

"I know this is a lot to take in," he said.

That was such a massive understatement that I had to laugh. It wasn't a funny sound. I sped up, intent on getting the name off the grave and handing it over to the police so we could wash our hands of BridgeKeeping.

Marcus easily matched my pace. "Ellen and I didn't just wander while we lured that thing away. We tracked down other teams, talked to every legit psychic, crystal gazer, and voodoo priest we could find. It took us years to pull together enough lore to come up with some theories. In Between's not a good place to stay for long."

"Yeah, you told us."

Marcus nodded. "Over time souls lose what made them human. All that's left is the essence of the *need* that got them stuck in the first place. They decay together, grow stronger, and become the thing that attacked your dad. We still don't understand how or why it manifested here, but every time you and Seth help a spirit pass on you save it from that fate. And Will, your Dad's still there, In Between, holding the entity off."

"Well, shit, Marcus!" A mess of panic and anger set me shaking. "Dad's been there for years? Years! How's he not part of that thing already?"

"He's not looking for a way back like the others." Marcus's voice was as calm as mine was raw. "He has a purpose there, protecting you. But if Seth stops channeling troubled spirits now, and the entity grows even stronger, everything your dad sacrificed, staying In Between, not passing on, will be for nothing."

Crap, crap, crap! Once Seth understood what was at stake, there wasn't a snow cone's chance in hell he'd stop channeling. My eyes pooled, blurring my vision, and I stopped my race to the new grave.

"Dark entities manifest in different ways, that's why it's so hard to pin down the lore," Marcus went on quietly. "They have many names. Poltergeists, shades, wraiths."

"Werewolves? Vampires?" I asked, spewing semi-hysterical sarcasm, but Marcus's face stayed stone serious, and my chin sank. "You have *got* to be kidding me."

"There are other hunters for those things. They're not your problem."

"No wooden stakes in my future? Damn." More sarcasm, but there wasn't any energy behind it. My body felt like a sponge, heavy and drooping with everything I'd just soaked up.

"Come on." Marcus put an arm around my shoulder and got us moving. "Your dad's kept the entity at bay all these years, and I'd bet a lot of money that Ellen's with him now. They won't let it find Seth until you're both ready to deal with it. Like Angela and Maria showed you, ninety-nine percent of the time Seth will channel ordinary people with ordinary problems like Fred's."

Marcus was trying to offer me some comfort, but I thought that even if Seth channeled the Easter Bunny next, it'd be rabid and likely to chew my foot off to get what it wanted. "Are you lying to me now because it's what I need to hear?"

He took a deep breath and let it out. "No. No more lies. Although, I think we could hold off telling your brother until he's got his ability under control."

171

I looked at him sideways. "By, *deal with the entity,* you mean destroy it, right?" He nodded. "How?"

There was a long pause. "I'm still working on that."

We followed a curve in the road, passing into a section of the cemetery where the trees were young and spindly, the tombstones new. An angel knelt on a marble pedestal, wings folded heavily across her back, her polished surface gleaming white above the sunny lawn. A few yards away lay the fresh grave that had snagged my attention Saturday morning. Alone, unadorned, our ghost's resting place marked the very edge of the cemetery property.

I stepped into the grass.

Crap, crap, crap! Once Seth understood what was at stake, there wasn't a snow cone's chance in hell he'd stop channeling.

Marcus was trying to offer me some comfort, but I thought that even if Seth channeled the Easter Bunny next, it'd be rabid and likely to chew my foot off to get what it wanted.

CHAPTER TWENTY-TWO

"Martha Janine Pearson, born 1949." I reread the temporary marker, a plastic cross that stuck out above the dirt clods. "What the hell?"

Marcus knelt beside me, a thoughtful frown on his face. "Unless you got your ass kicked by a little old lady, this grave doesn't belong to the spirit we're looking for."

"Maybe there's another one." I raised up and twisted around in the grass. Cold soaked through the knees of my jeans. There were fifty graves within sight, but no other new gashes in the lawn. This had to be the one I'd seen from the trail in the park. "I can't believe it. I was so sure. Could he be in one of these older graves? What if he got killed years ago and hasn't had a way through the veil until now?"

"Is that what your gut's telling you?" Marcus asked, studying the ground around the grave.

I remembered how Seth had bowled into me on

the trail, his desperate rush of words. "No. His feelings were too raw."

Marcus pressed his palm against the mound and then, staring at it like Mrs. Pearson might call from six feet down and tell us what was going on, he crumbled a clod. "The body's nearby. Most souls can't travel far the first time they make contact." He scanned the forested hillside across the ravine. "Did you smell anything besides stagnant water Saturday morning?"

"Like what? Oh, you mean . . ." My mouth went dry. I'd smelled the sickly scent of rotting flesh a couple times in my life, a dead possum in the road, an unlucky mouse in the garage at the old house. It's not a smell you ever forget. "No, I didn't smell anything dead." A heavy chain strung along a row of marble posts marked the edge of the ravine. I walked over and leaned out searching the rocky cliff thirty feet down to the creek bank. No dead bodies.

Marcus stood. "We can't do any more from here. Let's go back and see what Seth found online."

Marcus and Dad had had the whole police department and all its resources at their beck and call. We weren't cops, what did he expect Seth to find? And why had Seth stopped zapping me? He seemed to have gotten fed up with practicing back home.

But a block from our house, Seth finally hit me with the bees, or one bee. His signal was disturbingly faint and showed no sign of stopping. He wasn't shutting down.

"Something's wrong." I sprinted down the sidewalk, Marcus pounding behind me.

Our garage door was open with Mom's BMW parked

174

half inside and half out on the driveway. She'd barely missed hitting the Harley. Her shrill voice rose from inside the house before I'd rounded the big car's bumper.

"You can stay at home with us if you'll only stop! Say you'll stop!" she shouted, standing over Seth as I burst into the kitchen. "I can't watch you get killed! I won't!"

Mom clutched a large glass of her favorite juice. Her hair was a little mashed on one side, her straight black skirt, twisted so the zipper snaked across her stomach. If she'd gone to church, she'd hit the liquor store after the last amen. Seth, defiant and furious, looked up from where he was perched on the edge of a kitchen chair, light flickering over his skin.

"What's going on?" I asked, trying not to add my panic to the supercharged air in the room. Their heads swiveled toward me at the same time.

"Mom's trying to convince me to give up my gift." Seth immediately turned back like he expected her to pounce.

"Gift," Mom sneered, shifting her focus blearily to Marcus. "I believed your lies too. I turned my back on my family! You and Kevin told me you helped good people get to heaven, but there's nothing *good* In Between. Those aren't poor, lost souls. They're evil! They don't deserve Heaven." She jabbed a finger at him. "It's a sin to help them!"

Seth flinched, and his glow brightened. Trying to ignore the drilling bees, I knelt in front of him. "Chill out, Seth. Shut down."

"He's calling one of those things again, isn't' he?" Mom flung out her arm, sending an arc of tomato juice

175

across the floor like blood spatter. "Get out! Get your things and go!"

"Mom, don't do this," I pleaded.

Seth pushed me behind him and stood. "Stay out of this, Will."

"He *was* out of it," Mom shrieked. "I kept him out of it! And *you*! But you won't listen." A squeaky sob escaped her. "Oh Seth, do you want Will to die too?"

Every muscle in Seth's body went rigid. I grabbed his arm before he could bolt out of the house glowing like a flare. Mom snagged my sleeve, trying to pull me over to her. It was a three-way tug-of-war. I would have laughed out loud if she hadn't looked so desperate, and if the situation hadn't been so damned awful.

"That's enough." Marcus' deep voice rumbled through the kitchen. He hadn't shouted, but all three of us froze. Opening his hands slowly, he held them out to Mom. "Barbie, this is my fault, showing up out of the blue like this. I know it was a shock. I handled it badly."

Letting go, Mom snarled and rounded on Marcus. "You handled it badly? Like you handled my husband badly? Like you handled Ellen badly?" She stumbled toward him. "Well, you can't have my babies. Do you hear me?!"

Marcus nodded, agreeing with every cutting word. "You're right. They're your boys. They need to stay here with you where they'll be safe."

"That's right!" Mom said, and then frowned, blinking.

I could almost see her vodka-soaked wheels grind. *Don't think too hard, Mom.*

Crossing her arms again, she sipped the tiny bit of

tomato juice left in the bottom of the glass. "My sons stay home." She nodded like that had been her decision all along. "But *you're* leaving."

"I am," Marcus agreed. "Didn't mean to cause so much trouble."

"Today, Marcus. Leave today."

Marcus' chin sagged in a nod. "Today."

With one final glare, Mom turned unsteadily and walked out of the kitchen.

"Seth, it's over," I said, relief making my voice weak. "You're staying. You've got to rein it in now."

With his eyes shining with tears as bright as his glowing skin, Seth had a lifetime of hurt etched on his face. He managed one slow breath, then another, and the light slowly sank back under his skin. He dropped his forehead into his hand. "She's just—"

"Terrified," Marcus said.

"Drunk. She's not good with vodka, it brings out the asshole in her." Despite the lingering hurt, Seth arched a disapproving eyebrow at me. If things ever got so bad that I heard a cuss word cross *his* lips . . . I shuddered and pulled a towel out of the drawer by the sink to wipe up Mom's bloody vodka. "You're not really leaving, are you Marcus? You'll get a hotel or something, right?"

Marcus pulled out another towel. He got to work on the other edge of the splatter but didn't answer my question.

"You *are* leaving," Seth said quietly.

I balled up the smelly towel. "We need you here. We've hit a dead end."

Seth's eyebrows rose. "There wasn't a name on

the grave?"

"Oh, there was a name, Martha Janine Pearson. It wasn't our guy's grave. We got nothin'."

Marcus walked to the sink. "I take it you didn't have time to do a lot of research."

Seth ducked his head. "Barely got started."

"This town's still got a local paper, right? Look for anything out of the ordinary that's happened in the past month. Search missing persons' sites. You don't need my help for that." He turned on the faucet and looked over his shoulder at Seth. "Stay busy, *in* the house."

"Tomorrow's Monday, I have class on campus," Seth said.

"Get notes from somebody." He turned to me. "You go back to school. Follow up on the girl in the M&M costume."

"Where are you going to go?" Seth asked.

"I want to talk to your grandmother. And, no, you can't channel her again. I'll find another team."

"Grams must still need something from us," Seth said. "If she's still around, find out what it is."

Marcus nodded, and he and I exchanged a look. I didn't like keeping the truth from Seth, but he had enough on his plate. Once we knew for sure that Dad and Grams had figured out a way to stop the entity, I'd tell him the whole story. But for now, it seemed wise to have only one of us terrified out of his mind.

"Can't you go to Angela and Maria again?" I asked Marcus.

He wrung out his towel and then took mine and held it under the water. "We've asked enough of them. I know a pair outside Des Moines." He hesitated, frowning. "If they can't help, there are others. I'll be back in a week at the most."

If he was lucky. Marcus had never travelled the BridgeKeeper circuit unbound. He'd be on the road until he found a Keeper who'd hear him out and not throw a punch when he got within a mile of their Bridge.

Marcus laid out a plan for our junior detective work while he packed his saddlebags. Too soon, he threw a leg over the Harley and rode off into the sunset.

CHAPTER TWENTY-THREE

I *hate Mondays.* Yesterday's blue sky was gone. The sun was a dim bulb shining through a soot-smudged window. My cheeks had frozen a mile back. Numb-lipped, I hunched over the handlebars of my bike with cold wind gusting down my jacket collar.

"At least it's not the Harley." I switched to granny-gear to pedal up the half-mile rise to the high school. I'd woken to Seth's voice this morning instead of the bee stampede. He was getting control of the light fast. Highly motivated. Without Marcus, we were back to cold Pop-Tarts for breakfast. I'd gotten used to the constant irritation of my inner guard dog, but having it finally stand down was a small, bright spot in the gloom of knowing that Seth and I were on our own.

"Marcus said to skip classes for a couple days," I'd reminded Seth as he shoved me out the door this morning.

"He was talking to me," he said, determined to get one

of us back to a normal routine. "Go find your red M&M."

Would I even recognize the girl from the Fling? It was doubtful she'd come to school with her face painted red. She was either Megan or Missy. Knowing their last names might help, but I'd still have to pick the right girl out of the crowd. I thought of one promising course of action, enlist help from Reen. She knew a lot of people, zero ulterior motive there. All I had to do was come up with a smooth way to ask her about the girls without explaining why I was so interested. Had to work on that.

The usual suspects roared through the parking lot in their muffler-challenged cars as I shoved my front tire into the bike rack. Standing for a minute, watching kids funnel through the doors, I felt myself settle. Nobody here had a final message to brand on my brain. None of the teachers were likely to drag me onto a sparring mat and kick my ass. I took my helmet off and clawed my tangled hair.

"Hey, dude, where the heck have you been? You missed Frisbee yesterday. I texted you a thousand times."

Nico and a hundred other people had texted me. Apparently, a video of Anthony and me on stage had gone viral. I could still feel the weight of all those strangers' texts dragging on my pocket. "Sorry, man. I forgot all about it."

"You forgot?" He glared. "How bad are things at home? Is Marcus still there?"

"No, he left. I'm sorry. I . . ." Pretending the zipper on my backpack was stuck, I desperately sifted through the truth trying to find enough to make up an explanation. Before inspiration could strike me, Seth did. I flinched, curling over my pack. Seth's signal only lasted a couple of seconds, but my eyes were watering when I straighten up. "Look, I'm sorry. I missed one Frisbee game. So what?"

"We barely pulled out a win without you, that's what. Hold on," Nico grabbed my arm. His eyes flicked to my jaw. "Fight Club costume, huh? What really happened?"

Crap. The bruise had spread, adding yellow and green to the black and blue. I'd worn another one of the grandmonsters' turtleneck sweaters which, evidently, worked about as well on Nico as it had on Seth. I squeezed through the doors with the crowd. Nico stayed at my shoulder. "Seth and I did some sparring,"

"And he landed a punch? I don't believe it."

At my locker, I tossed in my helmet and spun the lock. Nico grabbed my elbow again and swung me across the hall into the guys' john. The door closed and the hallway noise sank to a muffled roar.

"Okay, what's really going on? Did Marcus do that? Did he pick a fight?"

Nico wasn't mad, he was worried. A pang of guilt made me drop my gaze to my feet. "No. You don't have to worry about Marcus."

"Okay, good. But come on, primo, talk to me."

The truth muscled its way to the tip of my tongue. I turned to the sink where a traumatized freak looked back at me from the mirror. No help there. I didn't know that guy. Right then, lying to Nico, I didn't much like him.

I raised my eyes to Nico's reflection. The worry on his face made me sick, but I forced myself to change the subject. "Why are you so dressed up today?" He'd ditched his usual ravaged hoodie and instead, wore the leather sport coat he'd scored at the thrift store a month ago. "Did you actually comb your hair?"

Nico stared at me for a second, and then his expression changed from worry to shock as he realized I wasn't going to fess up. He set his lips in a thin line and stepped up to the sink beside me.

"I'm campaigning," he said, finger-combing his strangely civilized hair, not looking at me. "You're supposed to nominate me for president of the Snow Ball committee this afternoon. Did you forget about that too?"

"I remember." Not until that second, but I remembered. "You've got to get elected so Tiffany will fall in love with you, right?" Nico narrowed his eyes, not smiling at my lame joke. "Look, Nico," I whispered. "I'm dealing with something."

He crossed his arms again. "No kidding. Want to talk about it?"

I opened my mouth. Closed it. Looked away.

Nico huffed out a disgusted breath. "See you at the meeting."

He left, and I didn't stop him. It was an alien feeling having no idea what to say to my best friend. I didn't like it and hated the idea that I might have to get used to it.

In the halls, I hadn't been smiled at, nodded to, or chatted up between classes so much since Friendly Fridays in fourth grade. *Damned karaoke contest.* Ms. Piebottle called on me in Poli-sci before I raised my hand and seemed devastated when I told her that I hadn't done the reading. By the time lunch rolled around, I had neither a plausible explanation nor a diversion figured out for Nico. I grabbed a carton of milk and started for our table under the giant eagle.

Nico wasn't there. Neither was my strange fan club. The table was full of kids I barely recognized. Clenching my teeth, I fought down sickly panic. Was Nico mad enough to ditch me? I set the milk carton down on the table mumbling, "Here you go. Enjoy."

"Thanks," one of the kids said. "Hey, you're Will McCurty! Loved your song Saturday night."

I raised a hand but didn't bother to turn around. Where would Nico go? He couldn't bring food into the library so that was out. Dreary weather nixed a picnic lunch. The gym? I pushed through the cafeteria door.

"There you are! Come on." Nico dragged me down the hall.

"Here *I* am?" I said, lightheaded with relief. "Where were you? Hey man, we need to talk. I should have told you what was . . ." My voice petered out as Nico pulled open a classroom door. "Where are we going?"

"The dance committee meeting," he hissed. "Elections? Hello."

Crap. I hesitated in the doorway, struggling to redirect my thoughts from full confession mode to wingman duties. *Okay, this is good. Nominate Nico now. Confess later. I can salvage this friendship.*

The room smelled of pizza and peanut butter. People had pulled the desks out of their rows making mini versions of the cliques in the lunchroom. Dan-the-Man, definitely not the dance committee type, gave me a solemn nod from the back row. What was he doing here? Stranger still, Pocket Protector Kid stood across

184

the room in a yellow plaid shirt. It took me a second to find Sanna, the girl from the pep squad, but there she was, sitting with Tiffany and her crew. I barely recognized Anthony because he greeted me with a happy smile and a wave. Did I have a fan club, or stalkers?

Nico adjusted his leather coat, and as he worked the room, I spotted the only person I truly wanted to see. Reen stood out from the other kids like a bluebird slumming it with a flock of sparrows. My heart started a little happy dance until she caught sight of me and quickly looked away. Whatever I'd done wrong Saturday night, had not been forgiven.

When Nico waved me over to an empty desk up front, I cringed at the sight of our faculty sponsor. Ms. Piebottle pushed her chair away from her desk with a loud scrunch that quieted the room.

"Now that everyone's here," She gave a little nod in my direction, and I slumped lower in my seat, "let's get started." Uncapping a marker, she walked to the board. "The floor's open for nominations for dance committee president."

Before I could shoot my hand up to nominate Nico, a flaming-hot poker jabbed me between the eyes. *Seth!* Stifling a groan, I doubled over and dug in my backpack like I'd lost a hundred-dollar bill in there. Heat flowed over my face and down my arms, a full-body-bee-sting, before Seth finally snapped it off. Gasping, I pulled my phone out and texted him, *TURN IT THE F@!*$ DWN!* I silenced the phone.

"Mr. McCurty, any objections to being nominated?"

"Huh?" I sprang upright. "Me?"

185

"Yeah, buddy." Nico's mouth was the only part of his face smiling until he noticed my panicked look, then his grin got a lot more sincere. "Put his name up there, Ms. Piebottle. This is all part of his diabolical plan for world domination."

Laughter bubbled up. I glanced around, looking for the joker who'd put my name in the hat. Everybody in the room smiled encouraging smiles. *Damned karaoke contest.* Nico's name was on the board too. Somebody besides his best friend had nominated him. His face was stony, eyes straight ahead. This was bad, very bad.

Fortunately, Reen and a couple other people had been nominated too. My chance of winning against her or Nico were a billion to one. I relaxed a little.

"Well, Mr. McCurty?"

"Uh, sure. Fine," I heard myself say. Ms. Piebottle added my name in her kindergarten-perfect block print then passed out stacks of blue cards.

"Write your candidate's name on a card, then pass it to the front, please," Ms. Piebottle instructed. I snatched up the card and scribbled Nico's name. When the kid behind me tapped my shoulder passing in the filled-out ballots, I had a wild urge to stuff any with my name on them into my mouth and chew them to a pulp.

Ms. Piebottle took her time counting out five little piles. I watched one of the stacks on her desk grow twice as tall as the others. *Nico or Reen. Gotta be Nico or Reen!*

Finally, she sat back smiling. At me. "Congratulations, Will, you're our dance committee president. Reen, as runner-up, you'll be vice president."

The room erupted with applause. Nico reached

186

out to pump my limp hand. The grin on his face was as brittle as a sheet of ice. He didn't react when I yelled, "It should be you!" I don't think I was breathing at the time. Maybe I just moved my lips.

Ms. Piebottle asked Reen and me to go out into the hall in the few minutes before classes started to figure out when to have our first, *executive dance committee* meeting. As the door closed on twenty people talking and texting at the same time, I dropped my backpack on the floor, then flopped against the lockers. A hollow sound, like the one inside my skull, echoed down the empty hallway.

Reen pulled my hoodie out of her bag and held it out to me. "Thanks for the loan."

This should have been a beautiful moment, alone with her, the promise of many such meetings to come, but she wouldn't look me in the eye and hugged her backpack in front of her like a life preserver.

"Look, Reen, this . . ." I gestured toward the classroom door. "This is a huge mistake. Nico's the one who wanted to be president. I should have refused the nomination. Ever since that damned karaoke contest everybody's acting like I'm some kind of rock star."

Eyes serious, she glanced up at me. "You know it's not just the contest."

I let out a frustrated groan. "The aura thing. I wish I could turn it off."

She hugged her backpack a little tighter. "When you walk into a room everybody knows it. They know when you leave. For most people it's no big deal, but others like Anthony really need your help."

"Helping Anthony was an accident. I had no idea

187

that going up on that stage would do him any good."

Her lips curved softly. "But you did it anyway." For a few seconds, her face was open the way it had been when I looked at her from the stage, but then she caught herself and turned determinedly to look down the long hall. "We'll all get used to your aura," she said. "Things will go back to normal."

"How can you be so sure?"

Reen glanced towards my hands, which sometime during this awkward conversation, I'd rolled up inside my hoodie. "I could try to get more information," she said as if the prospect didn't make her happy. She held one hand out to me. "May I read your palm?"

"First my aura now my palm?"

Reen let out an impatient breath. "I'm trying to help both of us . . . all of us. I mean everybody who's being affected. Do you want to know if it'll go away or not?"

How many family secrets could I possibly spill through the lines in my palm? And our hands would be touching, my skin to hers. It was worth the risk. I unwrapped my hand and rubbed it against my jeans.

Biting her lip, Reen seemed to brace herself before we touched. She smoothed my sweaty fingers open with a brush of her soft, tawny ones and leaned over my palm.

"Hmmm. This is weird."

"What?"

"Just a second. Your lifeline, it's really . . ."

"Really what?" *Short? Faint? Veering into the Twilight Zone?*

Before Reen could elaborate on the state of my lifeline, the fourth-hour bell rang.

And Seth zapped me.

"Ahh!" I slapped my free hand against my forehead and tried to snatch my other hand back, but Reen's grip petrified. Her head popped up, eyes round, lips curved into a pink, glossy, *oh* as if she'd been zapped too. The bell went silent, and doors opened up and down the hall. Pink spots bloomed on Reen's cheeks as she let my hand drop.

"Are you alright?" I shouted over the noise.

"You . . . you have sixth period study hall, right?" she said, a little breathlessly.

"Yeah."

"Meet me in the library. We *have to* talk."

CHAPTER TWENTY-FOUR

N ews of my election spread through the school. Nico was the only person in the student body who *didn't* want a piece of me. By sixth period, I was a wreck from avoiding friendly strangers and speculating about what Reen had learned from my palm. Completely off my game, I froze at the door to the library when she appeared by the checkout desk.

"Hey, Will, I saved us a table." She curled a finger, motioning for me to follow. Taking that step into the library was like forcing myself out of an airplane. Parachute? Was I wearing one?

We passed the long bank of computer stations, whispering groups of kids huddled around tablets, and finally reached the most remote corner of the library, the reference section. When Reen sat at a table in front of windows that looked out over the parking lot, I stood there, shifting my feet, dreading, and dying to know what she was about to say.

"So," she began, tapping her pen on a spiral notebook already open in front of her. "I made a list of people for subcommittees."

I scowled down at the neat column of names. "You want to talk about the dance?"

"Mm-hm. We've got a few weeks to go, but we can't do this by ourselves." Reen drew little stars beside three names with a bright yellow gel pen. "Serena, Alex, and Maia all said they'd be interested in the decorating committee. Which one do you think should head it?"

"Which one do I think should head it?" I sounded moronic, but the idea that we might talk about the dance committee at our executive dance committee meeting hadn't occurred to me.

"Yeah. Alex, Maia, or Serena?"

Had I totally hallucinated her reaction in the hall? Maybe she'd already satisfied her curiosity about BridgeKeeping when she read my palm. I dropped my backpack and lowered myself into a chair. Reaching over slowly, I turned her notebook toward me. "You've got Maia at the top. She's a pretty good painter."

"Yeah, and she's organized." Reen scooted her chair closer. "Nico should head the entertainment committee. That's a given, right?"

"Right," I said daring to believe this might turn out to be a normal conversation. Nico would love auditioning DJs so hopefully he'd hate me a little less. Despite Reen occasionally tossing worried, sidelong glances my way, we got the rest of the subcommittee list done in ten minutes. Ten minutes without telling a lie, flunking anything, or Seth zapping me. "Delegation, it's a wonderful thing." I took my first deep breath all day.

Reen closed her notebook and then sat, eyes down, nibbling the corner of her lip. I didn't mind watching her, she looked beautiful nibbling her lip, but the silence lengthened. I didn't want to risk her speaking up first and moving us into a topic that would ruin my buzz.

"So," I said, "I guess we need to find these people and ask them to volunteer for the jobs." Reen didn't respond. "Uh, it might be better if you find Nico." I waited. "Because he's not happy with me right now."

Without looking up, Reen blurted, "I know that your dad was a medium."

My lips parted with a little smack.

She finally tilted her eyes up to mine and grimaced. "Sorry. I'm freaking you out again, aren't I?"

"How could you possibly know that? *I* didn't know until a couple days ago."

"Well," with her gaze back on the table, Reen tucked a curl behind her ear, "my parents died when I was four. Don't know if you knew that. Our house in the country caught fire because of a faulty space heater. That's when I came to live with Grandma and Grandpa."

"Damn," I breathed. How had I *not* known that? I guess it never occurred to my four-year-old self to ask why she lived with her grandparents. "That's horrible. I'm really sorry. But what does that have to do with my dad?"

"The night of the fire, I woke up with my room full of smoke. I don't know how I got outside, but I remember taking off running. My bare feet felt like blocks of ice, but I didn't stop. Grandpa said it was a whole day before anybody realized I hadn't died with my folks." She

192

looked up at me, her gaze deep and serious. "If your dad hadn't given my dad a way across the veil, it might have been longer before anybody figured out that I was lost in the woods. They got a search party together, dogs and everything."

"Dogs?"

"Yeah. Big, floppy-eared ones."

A slow grin spread on my face. "Dr. Muro's bloodhounds, I'd bet anything."

"Kinda cool, huh?" She asked cautiously. "Your dad and his partner saved my life."

"Definitely cool," I assured her. Finally, one of those simple, Fred-like jobs Marcus had talked about that made sense of why BridgeKeepers existed. The incredible person across the table might have ended up a little pile of bones in the woods without my dad and Marcus. They'd done their job and saved a life.

I twitched in my chair. *I* had a job to do now too, a job that I'd completely punted so far today. There was a ghost and a real live Megan out there somewhere who were counting on me.

"Reen," I said. "This is coming out of left field, but do you remember the girl in the red M&M costume at the mixer? Her name's either Missy Miller or Megan Smalley." Reen's dark brows made a vee, and I was sure she'd object to me changing the subject. But, if I'd frustrated her, she seemed to shake it off.

"Uhm, sure, I know both of them. They've been together for a year or so. Missy was dressed as the red M&M Saturday night."

I nodded. "She, Missy, was worried about

her girlfriend."

"Hmm." Reen tapped her pen. "I haven't seen Megan at school lately, but I just saw . . ." She stretched up from her chair, looking over the tops of the bookshelves. "There's Missy over in the nonfiction section. Let's go talk to her."

Without waiting for me to agree, or take a breath, she took off, ponytail bouncing like a fistful of Slinkies. "Wait!" I library yelled. "I didn't want to talk to her right—Oh, okay then." I hauled myself out of the chair and hurried to catch up.

A girl, *not* encased in a giant red cardboard circle, but dressed in black cargo pants and at least three layers of shirts in shades of gray, stood in one of the aisles with her shoulders hunched over a book. Her sleek, dark hair fell forward in a sheet that hid everything but a pale chin and lower lip that she pinched and pulled as she read.

Reen called to her in a hushed voice. "Missy?"

The girl jumped, snapped the book closed and tried to shove it back onto the shelf, but dropped it instead. All of us followed it down to the floor, squatting around it like a campfire. The cover read, *Invisible Girls: Speaking the Truth about Sexual Abuse.*

"Oh, darn it," Missy whispered. Clutching the book against her as she stood.

"Sorry, we didn't mean to startle you," I said.

"It's okay," she said. "Hi, Reen."

"Hey, Missy. This is Will McCurty."

"I know." She glanced at me from under thick, black lashes. "We sort of met in line at the Fling. I missed your song, but I saw the post. That was nice." Her smile was a blip of black lipstick and braces.

"Thanks." I cleared my throat. "Um, Missy, the reason we came over here . . ." *Was to ask you if you're checking out that book because your girlfriend is being abused by a psycho who murdered his brother.* I desperately needed a not-so-creepy approach. "You know, Reen and I are working on the Snow Ball?"

"Uh-huh."

I gave Reen a look, praying she'd play along.

She smiled at Missy. "We're hoping that Nico Muro heads the entertainment committee. He'll need help and you and Megan are musical types."

Relief made my words come a lot easier. "Would the two of you like to help out?"

Missy's eyes filled with the desperation that had set her babbling at the mixer. "I would. But Megan's not . . . I don't think she'll be able to help." Only her thick bottom lashes kept a flash flood of tears from spilling onto her cheeks.

Reen gently rested her hand on Missy's arm. "Did you guys break up?"

She shook her head. "No. It's her mom's creepy boyfriend. He's one of the security guards here."

"The one you were talking to the other night?" It wasn't really a question. How many creepy security guards could one high school have? It was the guy I'd *tangled* with in the hall.

Nodding, Missy pulled one of her gray shirts tighter around her. "His name's Vic. I think he used to play football here. When he first hooked up with her mom, we thought he was really nice. He bought Megan a bunch of stuff, took her places like he was trying to get her to like him, you know?"

I knew. My mom had brought home a few of those guys over the years.

Missy kept her eyes fixed on me. "But then last Christmas he moved into their house and got super strict with her like he was her new dad or something. When he found out that we were together, he took away her phone, wouldn't let her come to my house anymore. I hardly saw her all summer." A tear escaped the eyelash dam. "I thought we'd be able to talk again when school started, but she . . . she was different. Last week she stopped showing up at all. Her mom's acting totally weird about it too. She won't admit there's anything wrong."

Reen dug a tissue out of her pocket and handed it to Missy.

"Oh, darn it," Missy said again, dabbing her eyes. "I don't know why I keep dumping this on you."

"Don't worry about it," I said.

"It's his aura," Reen said, reassuringly. "It draws in certain people. But pretty soon we'll get used to it and it won't affect us at all."

"Oh good." Missy nodded as if she thought that was a perfectly logical explanation.

Reen sounded very sure, hopeful even, that my aura's effect would fade. Was she desperate to get back to normal so she could start ignoring me again? I gave myself an imaginary slap to the back of the head. *Focus!* "Missy. Where does Megan live? I could go by her house and check on her. See what's up."

"Would you? That'd be so great."

Her relieved, you're-my-hero look made me squirm.

"I've been too scared to go there by myself. It's 430 Richmond Avenue. You know where that is?"

"My phone does," I said, typing in the address.

"Well, thanks. I'll be on any committee you want."

"Good. Great. Reen'll put you down."

Reen and I stood side by side watching Missy hurry to the check-out desk with her ten-ton book. What had I just gotten myself into? If Megan turned out to have nothing to do with our ghost, I'd just offered to check on a girl who was ditching school, maybe trying to dump her girlfriend, and probably wouldn't appreciate me butting in.

But I didn't believe that.

"I want to help," Reen said quietly. "I don't have to work at the café tonight. You're going to Megan's house after school, aren't you?"

I didn't answer as we headed back to our table, but by the time we'd packed up our stuff, I realized she was right. The sooner I found out if this was our Megan, the better. Although my heart had leapt at the words *I want to help*, the rest of me cringed. Marcus, Seth, *and* Nico would each take a chunk of my ass if I let Reen come along. Nico, because he'd think I had told her everything before I told him. And the other two because Reen having history with Dad was no excuse for letting her get involved now.

"Reen, thanks for the offer, but this could be a wild goose chase and not the safest field trip in the world."

"All the more reason for you to have backup," she said, sounding determined but not particularly happy about it. She lifted her chin. "I'll meet you at the bike racks after school."

Watching her yellow backpack weave through the crowded hall, I muttered, "This is such a bad idea." But I couldn't stop my lips from smiling.

CHAPTER TWENTY-FIVE

T hinking in any kind of a straight line was impossible with Reen sitting on the back of my bike. She had one arm wrapped around my waist and the warmth of her body seeped through my hoodie and set my skin on fire.

"So, that's pretty much it," I said, glad to stop babbling. Given how much she already knew, Reen was in a gray area where Marcus's tell-no-one rule was concerned. So, hoping that a little information would make her comfortable with me again, I'd decided to give her BridgeKeeping 101. I left out our current ghost. His death and afterlife were traumatic enough without spilling the details to a stranger.

"Turn right at the next street," Reen said, using her phone to navigate us to Megan Smalley's.

I made the turn, hoping that Reen's long silence was because of deep thoughts, not because of a deep regret for coming with me. At the next intersection, I asked,

"Which way now?" The instant I put my foot down in the road to stop, Reen hopped off the bike and skipped up onto the sidewalk.

"I lost all of my bars a little way back," she said, holding her phone up over her head. "But this is Richmond Avenue. Four-thirty should be at the bottom of the hill."

Ancient trees hung heavy and dark over the road. Reen tucked her phone into her pocket and adjusted her backpack as we fell into step, me in the road walking the bike, her on the sidewalk. She kept her head down, navigating cracks and gaps where gnarled roots had buckled the sidewalk. I couldn't tell what she was thinking.

"So, was it my turn?" I asked.

Her profile frowned. "Your turn to what?"

"To freak *you* out. BridgeKeeping's not a normal extracurricular activity."

She hooked her thumbs in the pack straps. "I'm not freaking out. Not exactly. It's just complicated for me, you know?"

I didn't know but didn't have the nerve to ask. I hadn't told her any of the really complicated stuff like evil entities and inner guard dogs. What complications had her wanting to stay as far away from me as possible?

Richmond Avenue curved around a massive pine tree and then dead-ended at a steep, rocky embankment. I leaned my bike against the guardrail, scoping out Megan's house cowering in the pine's dark shadow. The neighbor's mossy roof was barely visible above a long, tangled hedge across the street.

"Nobody around to hear you scream," I muttered,

wishing I could blame my shivers on the shadows. But a faint crackle of familiar rage danced in the hollow of my chest.

Hugging herself, Reen rubbed her hands up to her shoulders, looking around.

"Ah," I said, watching her reaction. "Your cat's walking on your grave too."

She gave me a short, worried smile, but after thirty seconds went by, she blew out a sigh. "Whew. It's gone now. Yours?"

"Sticking around." Our ghost didn't like this house or somebody in it, and my stomach sizzled with nerves. What were we walking into? Best-case scenario, Missy had an overactive imagination. Her girlfriend would come to the door and laugh at us for believing her. Seth and I would be back to square one with our ghost.

I would have spent a while standing at the end of the driveway trying to convince myself that that was a likely scenario, but Reen dropped her backpack by the Smalley's' mailbox.

"I don't see any lights on in the house," she said. "But it looks like somebody's home." A muddy, black truck sat in the driveway next to a messy pile of garage-sale-reject junk. "We're going to have to go down there."

"You should stay here," I said, not believing for a second, that that was an actual possibility. Reen gave a soft snort, and we started down the driveway together.

CHAPTER TWENTY-SIX

Gravel crunched under our shoes, loud in the shadowy hush. I hopped into the grass and pulled Reen with me to pass the truck. *Relax, there's nobody in the big, bad pickup*, I told myself. But the hairs on the back of my neck stood up to take a look as we walked by, and the cat gave a silent yowl.

There wasn't much room on the narrow concrete porch, but we both stepped up, Reen just a little behind me as I pushed the rusty doorbell.

"I can't hear the chime," she whispered. "Do you think it's broken?"

I shrugged, wiped my sweaty palms on my jeans, and had just reached for the button again when the deadbolt ka-chunked and the front door squeaked open.

"Yes?" A woman peeked around the edge.

"Hi. Mrs. Smalley? My name's Will McCurty, this is Reen Gardener." The woman had skin so pale, and blond hair pulled back so tightly, that through the screen door she looked bald.

"We're friends of Megan's."

Mrs. Smalley edged the front door back and sidled around it till she'd sandwiched herself between it and the screen. "You're friends? Do you know where Megan is?" She shot a nervous glance back over her shoulder.

I had to look too but couldn't see anything behind her but a gloomy hallway. "No ma'am, we don't. I'm sorry."

"Don't *you* know?" Reen asked. "Is she missing?"

Mrs. Smalley's gaze darted between Reen and me like a debate was going on in her head.

"Who's at the door?" A male voice boomed from the dark.

Megan's mom squeaked and pulled the door even closer behind her. She looked ready to jump out onto the porch with us. I reached for the door handle wanting to help her out of the trap, but she kept the screen firmly closed.

"It's nobody, Vic," she called over her shoulder. "Just some friends of Megan's."

Vic. Mom's not-so-nice boyfriend.

"You have to go," Mrs. Smalley hissed.

"But is Megan in some kind of trouble?" I asked.

"Of course, she's not," she said, biting her lip. "Not exactly. She just hasn't checked in for a few days."

A bald-faced lie. What was I supposed to do with that?

"Mrs. Smalley?" Reen whispered, sounding as unsure as I was about what we should ask or offer this terrified woman. "We want to help."

Beefy fingers appeared around the edge of the front door, pulling it back. I smelled the man before I saw him. A fog of tobacco smoke oozed through the screen as Vic shouldered Mrs. Smalley aside and took her place. A shiny badge hung on the left side of his uniform shirt.

The security guard from school looked me up and down, a cigarette dangling at the corner of his mouth. "I've seen you at the high school. I'm off duty, son. What are you doing here?"

"We're looking for Megan," Reen said. Vic shifted his eyes to her, and it was all I could do not to pull her behind me.

"Why?" Vic asked.

"Nobody's seen her at school lately," I said, trying to keep eye contact with Megan's mom hovering at the guard's shoulder. "Her friends are worried about her. We came by to see if there was any way we could help."

"Don't put yourselves out," Vic said with a sharp-edged smile. "She ran off. Kids do that sometimes. We're not worried."

"Vic, maybe this boy could . . ." Mrs. Smalley began.

"Beth. You're going to be late for work."

I caught Mrs. Smalley's eye just before she turned away. "Ma'am, you're obviously worried. Can't we—"

"Just get going, kid." The guard took a short, angry drag off his cigarette and puffed smoke through the screen. "This is none of your business."

When I didn't move fast enough, he clamped the cigarette between his lips and smacked the screen door with the heel of his hand. I barely missed having it bounce off my forehead. Reen hopped off the porch as Vic stepped outside and gave me a quick, hard shove. If she hadn't been right behind me, I would have fallen on my ass.

Vic stood with his shoulders back like he wanted us to get a good look at the badge. Men like my dad and Marcus wore their uniforms like a second skin. Vic wore his like a costume. He had on a wide, leather belt with cuffs, Taser, a canister of pepper spray . . . and a gun.

He jabbed the cigarette at me. "You need to mind your own business, son. Megan doesn't need your help. I'll find her."

"Look, we just want to let her friends know that she's—"

"Boy! Are you deaf?" Vic took one giant step off the porch and grabbed a fistful of my hoodie to jerk me up nose to nose.

"Hey!" Reen yelled.

Maybe it was all the ass whoopin's I'd taken on the sparring mat lately. Maybe I had a lot of pent-up anger. Whatever it was, my body went into black belt mode without consulting my brain. I took a quick step back, knocked his hands away, then twisted his arm straight out behind him. The cigarette shot out of his mouth. He doubled over and let out a high-pitched yelp.

Years of Ms. Beverly's sparring etiquette kicked in. "Oh crap." I dropped his arm. "I didn't mean to hurt you. You surprised me."

"Son of a bitch," Vic snarled. "You little son of a bitch!"

"You started it," Reen said, her voice high, edged with anger.

Vic's fingers twitched over the shiny, black butt of his gun. "Turn around and put your hands on the truck."

I stared at him. "Look, I'm sorry. You grabbed me

and I just reacted."

Vic flicked the catch off the holster. "Put your hands . . . on the truck."

"I'm calling 911," Reen said, jerking her phone out of her pocket.

"No signal, honey," Vic told her without taking his eyes off me. "You need a land line. I'm the only 911 around here."

My heart started to pound. One of Nico's favorite study hall games was throwing out scenarios crazy enough to push me into using my "wasted" Hapkido skills outside the dojang. Somehow—*What if a school security guard turned psychopath on you?*—had never occurred to him. "We'll just go. I'm really sorry." I looked away for a second to hold my hand out to Reen. A second was all Vic needed.

My face hit the hood of the truck with a hollow bong that vibrated my skull. I tasted blood, tried to push myself up. Pain exploded in my side. Couldn't breathe. Couldn't move. It felt like he'd stabbed me. I prayed it was just a vicious punch.

"Mrs. Smalley!" Reen screamed. I heard the screen screech open. Reen's fists pounding on the front door. "Mrs. Smalley!"

"You're trespassing on private property!" Vic shouted. "I have the legal right to use any force I deem necessary. Don't make things worse for your boyfriend, honey."

"Let him up," Reen said. "We'll go!" There were angry tears in her voice. I wrenched one shoulder off the car, but Vic leaned all his weight on the elbow he had stuck in my spine. Pain tears slicked the gritty hood.

Vic's free hand started a leisurely search of my pockets. "You two frightened my lady friend."

"She wasn't scared of *us*," Reen yelled.

He jerked my wallet out of my back pocket. "Are you stalking Beth's daughter? William Ian McCurty."

"I'm not stalking her. I just . . . agh."

Vic dug his elbow in, leaned close. "If you have any clue where Megan is, you'd better tell me right now."

"Don't . . . know."

"We don't know," Reen shouted, beside me. "Let him up! Right now!"

Vic hesitated just long enough to let Reen know he'd made his own decision to let me up. I rolled off the hood and Reen grabbed my arm. I couldn't tell which of us was shaking harder.

Tossing my wallet at my feet with a lazy gesture, Vic said, "Get out of my yard. If I see you two anywhere besides the high school, you'll wish you'd never been born."

My hands balled into fists. *Bastard!* I'd had enough of getting the crap beat out of me lately, enough of tasting blood in my mouth. I could take Vic in a fair fight.

Vic narrowed his eyes, stroking the row of toys on his belt.

But this wouldn't be a fair fight.

CHAPTER TWENTY-SEVEN

Vic turned his back, making it clear I was no more threat than a kindergartener. As the front door slammed, his chuckle lingered like the stink of old cigarettes.

"Asshole," I said between clenched teeth.

"Such a psycho! Are you alright?"

I swiped my wallet out of the grass and bit back a yelp as my heartbeat sent synchronized pangs into my cheek and side. In case Vic was watching, I forced myself to straighten up without wincing. "I'm okay. Let's get out of here."

Halfway up the driveway we heard the Smalley's garage door rumble and a rectangle of hazy light spread toward us across the ground. I grabbed Reen's hand, ready to run, but it wasn't Vic, just Mrs. Smalley going to work. Her car rolled to a stop next to us.

Through her closed window, she tipped her head toward the open garage. "What?" I mouthed. Eyes pleading, she tipped her head again.

Junk filled most of the garage except for the hole Mrs. Smalley's car had left. A bit of a muddy tire and the corner of a fender showed from under a canvas tarp on the other side. There was a car wedged in there. I wondered if the space had recently been occupied by the pile of junk we'd noticed in the driveway earlier.

"Is that car what you're trying to show us?" Reen leaned toward the frightened woman's window.

Mrs. Smalley jerked her gaze to the house where the bright end of a cigarette glowed red in a gap in the curtain. Spraying gravel, she backed out, gunned her engine, and disappeared around the giant pine. She was terrified. We needed to take the hint.

"Come on," I said, trying not to imagine targets painted on our backs. "You ride the bike."

By the time I jogged into to the empty high school parking lot beside Reen, the pain in my side was bad enough to keep me cursing under my breath. She hopped off the bike and I leaned on the handlebars to pull out my phone.

"Are you calling 911?" Reen started pacing around me.

"No. Just typing in the license number on that truck." The number tumbled around in my head. Apparently, my super hi-def Keeper memory only worked when Seth was possessed.

"That jerk hurt you!" Reen used both hands to push sweaty curls away from her face. "We should call the police!"

Nothing that happened just now tied Vic to our

ghost, or our ghost to this particular Megan, except my cat, which had gone quiet and wasn't likely to get the police excited anyway. I shook my head. "Megan's mom hasn't reported her missing, and Vic might be right about the trespassing. I don't think the police can help yet. There's more going on here."

Reen let out a little shriek when my ringtone erupted from my phone. When my feet touched pavement again, I checked the caller ID and groaned. "Hi, Seth."

"Where are you?" he shouted.

I held the phone away from my ear. "At school, in the parking lot. Sorry I'm so late. I got a lead on our Megan. We stopped by her house."

"You what? Don't move. I'll be there in a second!"

"What are you going to do, teleport? You're not supposed to leave the house!" Dead air. "Crap!"

"What's wrong?"

I slapped my forehead and left my hand there waiting for the moment Seth stepped across our threshold, wondering how fast I could get home if his signal burned a hole between my eyes and didn't shut off. The roar of an engine snapped my attention to the end of the parking lot.

"Will!" Reen grabbed my arm. "It's Vic!"

I held my bike in front of us like a shield, a useless shield. "Run!" Smart girl, she did. Headlights hit me as a car roared up and screeched to a stop. Overwhelmed with déjà vu from Halloween night, I cringed but this wasn't an SUV or Vic's truck. It was the Mustang.

"I've got a signal!" Reen yelled from several yards away. "I'll call 911!"

210

"No, don't!" I sagged against the bike. "It's my brother."

The driver's door slammed. Seth stalked around the car and grabbed me by the shoulders. "Are you alright?"

"Are you? That was like, thirty seconds!" I gave him the same once-over he was giving me. No glow, not a flicker between my eyes. He looked Eagle Scoutish, solid, like his old self.

"Do you realize that if that was the right Megan's house, the killer could have been there too?!"

"Oh, I'm pretty sure he was." I let my shoulders sag against his hands. Every drop of adrenalin charging through my veins ran out onto the pavement. With the bike sandwiched between us, Seth wrapped me in a hard hug. I was five years old again. Thankfully, the moment passed before I reverted completely and started bawling.

"What happened?" Seth asked.

"The school security guard attacked Will." Reen darted into the headlights. "I'm so glad it was you."

"Maureen Gardener," Seth said after he shook off his surprise. "What are you doing here?"

"She goes by Reen now. And . . . she knows."

"Knows?" His eyebrows climbed in disbelief. "You told her?"

"She read my aura. She's a witch."

"A practitioner," Reen corrected. "It's Wicca mostly, with a little voodoo."

"Right, sorry." I noticed Seth's blank look and changed tracks. "Remember her grandmother? The kids used to say she danced naked in her yard during the full moon?"

"Well, that's not true," Reen said indignantly. "I mean, never inside the city limits. Too much light pollution."

Seth and I turned to her, momentarily struck silent. "Uhh, Reen has history with Dad and Marcus."

"I owe your dad my life." She turned those golden brown, earnest eyes on my brother, and I could see him melting.

Taking the handlebars, he pushed me away from the bike. "I need a second to process."

I'd been leaning pretty hard on that bike. As Seth rolled it away, I shifted over to let the hood of his car prop me up. Heavenly engine warmth soaked through my jeans. Reen, shoulders hunched and shivering, looked like she could use some hood time too. I scooted over and patted the spot beside me.

Her face lit for a second, but quickly shut down as she stepped back. "I'm fine."

She was clearly freezing. I slid off the car. "Here, you take the hood."

"No, you're cold too." She waved a hand in front of her face impatiently. "Oh, for gosh sake, I'm just being stupid. We can both sit here."

I couldn't tell if she was disgusted with herself, or me, or still rattled in general, but I was careful to give her plenty of space when she sat beside me.

After she'd soaked up a little warmth she said, "Your aura spiked yesterday out in the hall when I was reading your palm. It looked painful."

"I was practicing," Seth said, with a guilty grimace as he came around the car.

Reen nodded like that filled in a piece of the puzzle for her. "So, you send out a pretty harsh signal when you make the bridge?"

"We say he opens to the veil," I corrected. "But yeah, harsh is a good way to put it."

"I have a suggestion, if you don't mind me offering."

Seth gave a resigned shrug. "Why not?"

"I think it would be helpful if you both had talismans."

My mind went straight to every fantasy novel I'd ever read. Jeweled swords, rings of power, golden amulets. "*Magic* talismans?"

She frowned. "Not hocus pocus magic like you're probably thinking."

"Isn't all magic hocus pocus?" Seth asked.

Reen's eyes flashed, and if my muscles hadn't been stiffening up, I would have cuffed my brother on the shoulder.

"Given what Will's told me about your family," Reen said evenly, "don't you think you could crack your mind open a little bit about what *my* family does?"

Seth jammed his hands into his pockets and had the decency to look sheepish. "Good point."

"Excellent point," I agreed quickly. "Where, or how does a person acquire a talisman?"

"Any small object that you wear, or carry will work," Reen said. "It should be something that's important to you, that's the main thing."

"Something important to us, huh?" I looked at Seth and then pushed back my right sleeve. "Something like this?" He pushed his sleeve up too. Our bracelets were almost identical. Thin strands of black leather tied into patterned knots and strung through the holes in two small river rocks. Seth's stone shone like a blob of black glass. Mine looked like a tiny gray arrowhead.

"I found these friendship rocks in a shoebox of Dad's stuff," I explained. "Right after his funeral." I'd hidden in the back of his closet in the old house. Breathing the smell of his clothes helped blot out the sound of Mom's crying jags. "The Christmas after Dad died, we got a ridiculous number of presents, but nobody thought to help us shop for each other. Brainiac here went shopping at the library."

Seth shrugged. "I got a book on Celtic knots. We made the first bracelets out of shoestrings."

"There've been three or four new models since then," I said. "Same rocks, but my knot-tying skills have improved."

"Maybe a little," Seth said with a half-smile.

Reen slipped a finger under the soft leather of Seth's bracelet, her own bracelet tinkled with crystals and charms as she moved. "These are perfect. With a little tuning, your stone should act like a lightning rod, Will. It'll turn warm or cold to let you know that Seth's open to the veil. It should feel a lot less painful than his unfocused blasts do now." She looked thoughtful "The way you've made them for each other all these years, using your dad's natural stones, they're practically primed as talismans already. It's almost like you knew what you were doing."

"Clueless, we swear," I said.

"Come on." Seth pulled me off his car. "We'll give you a ride home, Reen. On the way, keep talking so I can get my head around this talisman thing."

We got into the car, me in the front, Reen alone in the Mustang's tiny back seat. As she explained how to turn our homemade bracelets into psychic lightning rods, I nodded along. *Sure, that makes sense. God, she's brilliant. Of course, we can do that. So beautiful.*

My worldview had gone through the looking glass since Grams dropped back into our lives.

More and more, it was my old life that didn't seem real.

CHAPTER TWENTY-EIGHT

W hen we dropped Reen off, I tried to keep the lingering gaze to a minimum as she walked to her door, but as usual, Seth read me like a cheap comic book.

"What's up between you two?" he asked, as we pulled away.

"Why? Did *you* think something was up? Because honestly, I get conflicting signals." My brain and body were too sore to tease out any subtle clues Reen might have dropped tonight that would clarify her feelings. She seemed more than willing to help us out with BridgeKeeper stuff, but reluctant, or even repulsed by the idea of getting closer to *me*. Seth smiled sympathetically but had no helpful advice.

I held up my bracelet as we pulled into our driveway. "We've got to try the talisman thing. If we wait until tomorrow, we'll talk ourselves out of believing this could work." It had to work. I needed a win tonight.

"Now? You need a break, some food."

My stomach was all for eating, but I shook my head. "Later. Go inside and light up. I'll stay out here in the garage."

Across our threshold, with the door to the kitchen between us, Seth turned on the glow. I cringed as the swarm buzzed between my eyes but concentrated on Reen's terse instructions. *Just trust the stones. They'll know what to do. Use your imagination and focus the signal.*

"Concentrate on the signal," Seth yelled, his voice muffled.

"As if I have a choice." Clenching my fist, I held my wrist up, prepared to sweat it out until whatever was supposed to happen happened and the massive power coming from my brother got jammed into a tiny friendship rock.

All it took was a thought. The buzz flowing under my skin swooped down from my skull and up from my feet, heading for the stone like it was magnetized.

"It's working," I hissed through my teeth. The bracelet started to vibrate. "Wow, the rock's getting hot. Hot! Ow!" I flung my fist against the door. "Seth!" The stone went cold.

Seth eased the door open. "It worked?" he asked, looking skeptical.

I blew on a little pink spot darkening my wrist and held it out to him. "Reen's a genius! Magic is real." Could my heart take her getting any more perfect?

"Weeelll, I wouldn't call this magic."

"No?" Grinning, I nudged him back and followed him inside.

217

"Just because you don't understand something *yet*, doesn't mean it's magic," Seth said.

"You just keep telling yourself that." I whipped out my phone, and texted, *It worked! I love you!*

My thumb stalled over, *send.* I deleted, *I love you* and dropped in a heart, deleted that, dropped in five thumbs-up, hit send. Reen's reply came almost immediately.

Another thumbs-up. Just one. Not even a happy face emoji or clapping hands. An exclamation point would have been nice. My moment of triumph wilted and the aches and pains from tonight seeped in. Tylenol beckoned from the cabinet.

"Let me take a look at you," Seth said as I downed the pills.

Imitating his *big brother* voice, I said. "Damn it, Will. If you ever do anything that stupid again . . ." I grabbed the kitchen counter when he found the tender spot.

Muttering, he gently pulled my shirt back down. "*Don't* curse for me."

"Somebody has to." I grabbed a fork and closed the silverware drawer hard enough to make it jangle. "That asshole belongs in jail. Mrs. Smalley was terrified. Megan is missing and her girlfriend was checking out a book about sexual abuse!"

"You're right, the Smalley girl's probably in trouble." Seth sat at the kitchen table where his laptop and a couple of open notebooks were spread out. "But none of that adds up to murder. We need evidence to get the police involved."

I cursed under my breath some more and opened the refrigerator. Letting the cold, soothing air brush my aching cheek, I dug the last bite of leftover lasagna out of the corner of the pan and chewed it carefully.

"I spent the day skimming missing persons sites," Seth said. "Checking news feeds for drownings."

"Wow. Sounds fun."

He waved a hand at the screen. "*Nobody* named Megan's been reported missing anywhere within 200 miles. And nobody's drowned accidentally or otherwise in the past month." He slumped back in the chair and rubbed the back of his neck. "Mom's gone, by the way. The grandmonst—her parents—picked her up at about noon. They packed her a suitcase. There's a note on the fridge."

The cold lasagna lost its flavor as I pulled the empty aluminum pan out and let the refrigerator door close. The Post-it note was high on the left-hand corner. I had to squint to read Grandfather's tiny print, *Pure Faith Recovery Ranch, Leave messages for emergencies only,* and then Mom's cell number.

"As if we don't know our own mother's number," I grumbled as I propped the pan in the sink and then, scraping the last bits of hard cheese off the fork with my teeth, eased myself into a chair beside Seth. "She probably just needs some me-time." Seth nodded. He'd slipped on his nothing-gets-to-me mask. I'd almost forgotten he wore that one.

"At least she won't be stalking you around the house." *Or threatening to kick you out.* "How'd you get to me so fast tonight anyway?" I asked, ready to leave that disturbing train of thought.

He shrugged. "I was sitting here going through all

this stuff when I got a bad feeling. It was four-thirtyish."

"That was about the time my face hit the hood of Vic's truck."

Seth's jaw muscle bunched. "I jumped in the car to drive around looking for you, and something kept steering me toward the high school." He rubbed the spot between his eyes in a gesture I was very familiar with. "It was kind of uncomfortable."

"Like a swarm of bees under your skin?" I asked.

"Maybe one bee."

"Push the little sucker into your talisman." I held up my bracelet. "Our signal goes both ways! We can add that, and these, to the list of things to surprise Marcus with when he gets back." I remembered something and pulled out my phone. "Hey, I got Vic's license plate number."

Seth straightened, letting his fingers hover over the keyboard. "Give it to me. I paid for a couple of background services." I showed him the note. He filled in a form on the screen and then sat back. "I had an idea before I got interrupted by the bee. Do you think Nico could barrow one of the bloodhounds before school tomorrow without his dad finding out?"

It took me a second to figure out where Seth was going with this, but then I nodded. "Finding a dead body in the park would definitely force the police to open the case."

"That's what I thought. If that new grave doesn't belong to our spirit, his body has to be somewhere near Forest Loop trail. We could put one of the dogs on it."

Nico and I had spent more than a few weekends

playing idiot-hikers-lost-in-the-woods to help train the pups. Though they preferred tracking, both dogs had cadaver training too. I had no doubt Che or Lola could find our guy's body if it was anywhere in the park. But my stomach went quivery at the thought of calling Nico.

"We could ask Dr. Muro. I'm pretty sure he's got history with Dad too." I filled Seth in on Reen's rescue when she was a little girl.

He sat quietly for a minute. "I don't think that's a good idea. Even if the dogs she remembers were Dr. Muro's, it doesn't mean Dad and Marcus told him anything. Nico doesn't know. Does he?"

"No, and I feel like shit lying to him." I stood up and tossed the fork into the sink with a clatter. "How can I ask Nico to kidnap a hound without telling him why?"

"He'll trust you. You're his best friend."

I hadn't told Seth about the Snow Ball election. Couldn't begin to explain the effect of my new magnetic aura. How could I whine about making a phone call when he'd spent all day trapped in the house, trolling depressing websites? This plan was the best and only one we had. I collapsed back into the chair and stared at my phone.

"This is Nico," Seth said. "He'll be okay with it."

"Sure." As if I was hammering nails into my coffin, I punched in Nico's number not sure he'd answer when he saw it was me. The phone rang, once, twice.

"What's wrong?" Nico demanded.

"What?"

"Why are you calling? You never call. Did somebody else die? What's the emergency?"

"No. This isn't . . ." I was about to say that it wasn't an emergency, but if finding a dead body wasn't an emergency, what was? "Look, Nico, I have a huge favor to ask you. But you have to promise not to ask me any questions."

There was a long, heavy silence.

"Hey, you still there?"

"I'm here. That's two favors."

"Right, sorry, two. So, can I ask?"

"You can't *not* ask me now, dude," he said, sounding royally pissed.

My mouth went dry. Seth made a get-on-with-it gesture. "Okay, for reasons I can't explain to you right now I, Seth and I, need to borrow Che and maybe Lola tomorrow morning before school to hunt for . . . something."

Another long silence. "Our dogs hunt *for people.* Are you hunting for people?"

I squeezed my eyes shut and massaged my temple. "A person."

"Somebody's lost?"

"Sssssort of." God, this sucked!

"Who is it? A little kid? Did some old person wander off?"

"I don't know much about him."

"Ooooh-kay. But you have a scent object, right? Something the dogs can sniff that belongs to this mystery person?"

"No." I said, my voice so low it was almost a whisper.

"You want our *scent* tracking dogs to track without a *scent?*"

"Uhm, they're trained to find cadavers too, right?"

"You're looking for a *dead* person?!"

"Shh, Nico, this didn't make the six o'clock news, and . . . you can't tell your dad."

Heavy breathing. I couldn't see it, but I knew that a vein in Nico's forehead had popped out. Muffled impacts came from the phone. I hoped he was punching something soft. "Look," I said. "I'm asking you to trust me here. This is important. Can they do it?" The noises subsided, and I held my breath through the next long pause.

"Yes. Where?"

"Nico, man, I'll owe you big time."

"Where!"

"Nickerson's Reserve. The main parking lot by the trailheads, at first light. Bro, thank you so—"

He hung up on me.

Seth raised his eyebrows when I slowly turned around. I nodded, feeling like Nico had landed every one of his long-distance punches on me. "He'll do it." I gave my brother a hard look. "I'm not lying to him tomorrow. He gets the truth."

"You're willing to take the risk?"

"Yeah, screw what Marcus said. It'll be fine. This is Nico."

It had to be fine.

CHAPTER TWENTY-NINE

T he next morning at dawn, there was just enough light to see a bank of gray clouds piling up on the horizon. I'd wanted to walk all the way to avoid facing Nico for as long as possible, but Seth and I had compromised on riding the bikes. My handlebars twitched and jerked rolling over the gravel road. A familiar truck was parked up ahead in the lot, but it wasn't Nico who walked around to open the back.

"What's Dr. Muro doing here?" I asked uneasily. "You think he caught Nico trying to sneak out with Che and blew a gasket?" The idea of Nico's dad blowing a gasket scared the crap out of me. He was the most easy-going adult I knew.

"At least he brought the dogs," Seth said. "Looks like they're ready to work."

Dr. Muro had on the Day-Glo orange cap and matching vest he wore to work the dogs. Che bounded around him as he let Lola out of the second kennel.

Jumping to the ground, she shook herself and I could hear her skin flapping from thirty yards away. There was no sign of Nico.

"Doesn't make sense that Dr. Muro would be here if he was angry," Seth said, chewing his lip. Nico's dad caught sight of us and waved. "He doesn't look angry." Seth got back up on his bike. "Might as well find out."

I stayed where I was as he rolled on. Che, seventy-five-pounds of puppy, caught sight, or more likely, a whiff of me and galloped up, jowls swinging. "Hey there, boy." I knelt and let his long, plush-toy ears warm my fingers. Dr. Muro shook Seth's hand and their voices drifted to me on the cold, morning air. Lola's tail wagged. She, at least, didn't seem uncomfortable.

"So, what's goin' on over there, big guy?" I asked the dog. "Where's Nico?" Che blinked his sad, saggy eyes at me and laid a kiss on my chin. I stuck my nose in his fur, letting his clean-dog scent settle my nerves.

With one hand on the handlebars, I hooked my fingers under Che's harness and walked slowly toward the group. Seth shrugged when I met his eyes, apparently still clueless as to why Nico's dad was here. Dr. Muro nodded a terse greeting and then jerked his head toward the cab. Silent warning received. Nico was stewing in the truck. Che nuzzled my hand, looking worried now too.

I waited until Dr. Muro had snapped on Che's leash and then sidled cautiously over to the passenger side of the truck. I coughed to get Nico's attention. "Hey, man. Who knew there were two six o'clocks, right?"

The door swung open with a loud creak. Nico got out with his hands crammed into the pockets of a set of coveralls, and a vest that matched his dad's. He'd combed his hair with his pillow again so there should have been a wisecrack on the tip of my tongue, but the grim look on Nico's face made the smart-ass part of my brain shut down.

He studied me like he was checking to see if I'd grown an extra arm. "Should I call you Haley Joel from now on?" he asked.

"What? Who's—"

"The classic movie. Sixth Sense." He let out an impatient breath when I still didn't get it. "You see *dead* people?"

"Well, just the one time," I stammered. "How did you know about that? Who told you?"

Nico nodded like I'd spoken a coherent sentence. "I had a little meltdown after you called last night. Dad wondered why I'd stopped studying and started punching the sofa pillow. When I told him what a total ass-wipe you've been for the past week, he gave me a few theories as to why my best friend might have an urgent need for dogs trained to find human remains."

Seth and I turned to Dr. Muro, who slid his hands into his coverall pockets and studied his boots.

Nico jabbed a finger at his father. "He used to work with your dad back in the day, and never bothered to tell me. The dogs helped rescued some little girl and he's pretty sure that your dad got a tip from a ghost to find her."

"Reen. She was the girl," I said. "She told me about it yesterday."

"Yesterday?" Nico said, his voice rising. "So, she

226

already knows about this too?"

"Nico," I said, opening my hands to him. "I wanted to tell you."

"So, tell me now! Who are we looking for? What's going on?"

"Settle down, hijo." Dr. Muro laid a hand on Nico shoulder. "I never heard Kevin or Marcus toss around ghost stories. We'll respect the privacy of the dead, boys." He knuckled the light stubble on his cheek. "I didn't know how they knew what they knew, but after working with them a few times, I had my theories. Over the years, I convinced myself that I'd made it all up, but then you called last night." He looked up at Seth and me. "I was happy to help your dad, happy to help you boys too. No questions asked." Dr. Muro gave Nico a pointed look.

I held my breath, waiting, but finally Nico muttered something and then said, "Fine. Let's get the dogs rigged up before they take off after some racoon."

Dr. Muro took Che's leash from Seth and pressed it into Nico's hand. "Where exactly did the, uh, incident take place?" Seth described how far we'd walked down Forest Loop trail, and Dr. Muro nodded. "Seth and I will start up at the meadow with Lola and work our way back here. You two boys take Che down the trail and work your way out to the park boundary."

"I'll go with Seth," Nico said, reaching for Lola's leash.

Dr. Muro pulled it back. "You go with Will. Work this out. Our sofa pillows can't take any more beatings."

"Great," Nico said. He wrestled Che into his rig and then shoved the leash into my hand. "It's your show. Lead on."

Nico gave Che the command, *find,* and nose in the air, the dog dragged me into the shadows on the trail. Nico hung back.

No questions asked? I could feel his unasked questions stacking up like bricks in the wall growing between us. I glanced back and caught his dagger eyes for a second before he cast his gaze down to the trail. Maybe Marcus was right, and I couldn't predict how Nico would react if I told him everything, but I was one hundred percent sure that as long as I kept my mouth shut, our friendship would die right here.

The deep, pine mulch petered out and my foot crunched loose rock. Che dragged me around the bend, straight into the spot where all hell broke loose Saturday morning. Memories, not Keeper-vivid, but bad enough, came to me on a gust of wind that swirled dry leaves around my knees. In their clattering, I heard Seth's snarling voice, felt the sting of rocks digging into my flesh as he hooked his arm around my throat.

Nico grabbed Che's leash. "Hey, man. Breathe."

I bent over, my hands propped against my knees.

"Must have been pretty bad," Nico muttered.

I scowled up at him willing my heart to stop hammering. "You think I won the lottery here?"

He found something to study in the naked branches over the trail. "Last night after Dad told me what he thought you guys do now, I figured you hadn't told me yourself because . . ." He stuffed the end of the leash into his armpit and crossed his arms. "Maybe you don't want a mere mortal like me around anymore. Maybe I should let you and Seth get on with your hero thing."

"Hero thing?" I gaped at him. "I've had my ass kicked twice in the last three days. This aura crap at school? You can have it! I got up at the butt-crack of dawn this morning *to hunt for a rotting corpse.* This is no hero gig, Nico. My life is a freak show." My throat went so tight it was a struggle to keep talking. "If you can't handle that . . . If you want to chuck our friendship, just say so."

He kicked a rock off the path. "I figured you were the one chucking our friendship."

"What the hell made you think that?"

"Oh, I don't know. Maybe the dance committee election, all the lies!"

"I didn't lie to you," I said in a small voice, "I just left some stuff out." Nico snorted at that thin distinction. "You think anything like this has ever happened to me before?"

"No, but we're friends, why couldn't you trust me with it."

"I do trust you. This just feels . . ." Telling Reen yesterday hadn't felt this dangerous. I looked at my shoes. "This will change everything, Nico," I whispered. "If I bring you into this freak show, you can't unknow what I tell you, you know? It'll change things between us." That thought sent a flutter of panic through me.

"You've always been a freak, primo," Nico said with a faint smile. "Have a little faith. That never stopped us from being friends." The smile quickly faded. "The way I see it, either we risk it *together* or, you leave me behind."

I swallowed hard. He was right. It was all or nothing with us. Always had been. I nodded. "What do you want to know?"

He licked his lips, looking around. "Well, you got possessed right here?"

"Seth gets possessed. I listen and take messages."

Nico got a more detailed version of what I told Reen because *he* stopped me with questions every ten seconds. When he finally ran out of them, he looked a little stunned.

"Soooo, Seth's the Bridge, but you're the one the ghosts come to talk to. He's architecture, you're the destination?"

I blinked a couple of times. That turned Marcus' expendable Keeper theory on its head a bit, but I couldn't say Nico was wrong. "That's about it." I knelt next to Che, checking his halter. "There's one more thing. It's heavy." I glanced up to see Nico's eyes widen for a second before he braced himself and nodded for me to go on. "My dad didn't die in the line of duty, not as a cop. He died as a Bridge. Part of what I have to do as Seth's Keeper is keep him from dying that way too."

"Dios," Nico breathed. There was a long silence. "Don't tell me anymore. This is too much." I gave him a worried look, and he reached over Che to grip my shoulder. "I mean too much to get hit with all at once, you know?"

"Oh, I know, believe me."

"Okay, okay," he said nodding to himself. "My best friend talks to dead people. I'll repeat that about seven hundred times a day. Eventually, it'll soak in, and then you can hit me with the rest. We'll work this out but there's got to be ground rules."

"Yeah? Like what?"

"No more lying. Don't give me some lame excuse every time you go on a ghost hunt."

"Hey, who'd I call with the scoop last night?"

"You call what you said last night the *straight* scoop?" His voice was angry again.

I grimaced and ducked my head. "Okay, I'll level with you from now on. Except for the spirits' personal stuff." Nico's dark eyebrows bumped together over his nose, and I held up a hand. "Like your dad said, respect for the dead."

He shrugged grudgingly. "Respect for the dead. Yeah, okay. But just so you know." He looked up from Che's floppy ears. "If we find a rotting corpse today, I'm gonna run away flapping my arms like a freaked-out toddler." He gave me half a grin.

It wasn't his usual hundred-watt, not even close, but I'd take what I could get. "I'll be right there with ya, man."

CHAPTER THIRTY

C he shook his head hard enough that I expected
his jowls to fly off. After a couple of zig-zagged
snuffles, he settled in and took off down the
narrow, rocky trail unconcerned by the rolls of loose
skin slumped over his eyes.

"Can he see?" I asked and fell in beside Nico, feeling
more like myself than I had in days.

"Doesn't matter. When he's workin', he's nothing
but a nose with a dog attached anyway."

Following switchbacks down the steep ravine, we
walked into a hushed, refrigerated twilight in the rocky
creek bed. Wisps of mist curled over the ground.

"Eerie," Nico whispered, stumbling as Che jerked
the leash.

Stones tipped and clopped as we picked our way
across a dark ribbon of water. Che pulled us onto a flat
shoreline spotted with black, shiny pools. He snuffled
along until the leash unspooled completely and then

nose in the air, he gave a single huff that left a cloud over his head.

"He's definitely caught a whiff of something," Nico said.

"Like what?"

"Human blood, tissue."

"Look at these." I squatted down, careful to keep the seat of my jeans out of the mud. "Boot tracks." Dark depressions lined up along Che's path.

Nico studied them as we started moving again. "Two people. One big guy, one smaller. See how much deeper one set is than the other? The edges are still clean too."

"So?"

"So, that means it hasn't rained since they were here. That gives you a time frame."

"Go, Jim Bridger," I said, rapping his shoulder with the back of my hand.

"Dad's the master tracker. He could track a deer across a—" Nico put his arm out to stop me. "Did your guy die of lung cancer?"

Five pale cigarette stubs lay among the rocks beside the rippling water. I would have taken a hundred dollar bet that they were Vic's brand. "No, it wasn't cancer," I whispered. Che let out one, sharp woof.

"He's found something." Nico said, looking none too anxious to find out what.

Che was doing a high-stepping dance around a deep, muddy hole when we walked up. Nico stayed back and hauled on the leash. "Come 'ere, big guy." Fishing a biscuit out of his pocket, he knelt, rubbing Che's ears. "Who's a good boy!"

I approached the hole, scanning the mud around it.

"Somebody had a knock-down-drag-out fight here," Nico said. "See how the mud's all churned up, all the slide marks."

"Yeah." I bent down. The hole was deeper than some we'd passed. Oily, black water glistened in the bottom. It looked like an animal had clawed out pits on either side. "Did Che make these claw marks?"

"Nah, he knows better than that."

I was about to stand to see if a little height would make sense of what I was seeing when the sun tipped into the ravine. Through the sheen on the top of the water, a tiny, white object reflected the light. I reached down and pried it out of the mud. It was about the size of a corn kernel, shiny and hard. I held it between my fingers, shook it in the icy puddle to rinse it off and then laid it in my open palm.

"What is it?" Nico asked.

"Oh no," I whispered, staring from the thing in my hand to the glistening pool. The gouges beside the hole shifted, slowly making horrible sense. This was where our guy died. This was where somebody pushed his face into stagnant water. He'd clawed those gouges in the mud, fighting to breathe. Fighting for his life. Right here.

His shiny, white tooth lay in the palm of my hand.

I jumped back. The tooth flew out of my hand, arced up and then disappeared into the hole again with a soft plop.

"What? What'd you find?"

I crab-walked backwards. Mud oozed between my fingers. Ruby red leaves spotted the bank like blood. I couldn't tear my eyes away from that damned hole.

"Get up! Che's still on the scent. Come on!"

Nausea made my skin go hot, but I swallowed hard, slapped my hands clean against my thighs, and then caught up as Nico trotted behind Che.

"What was that?" Nico asked.

"A tooth."

"Human?" I could only nod. "Your ghost didn't die in a hiking accident, did he?" I shook my head. "Dios mío," Nico whispered.

"I left it there," I croaked, still trying to keep my breakfast down. "Is a tooth enough evidence for the police?"

"CSI could probably tell two guys fought back there, somebody got a tooth knocked out, but you'd need a body to prove anything else."

A gravel road up ahead curved out of sight through an opening cut into the steep embankment. A thick chain hung between two pylons with a *No Trespassing* sign dangling from it. "Where are we?"

Nico gave a sharp whistle and hauled on the leash. "Che, hold! That's the cemetery service road, I think. Somebody drove a couple of cars from there down to the creek." He pointed up the road, then back behind us, where several sets of tire marks squashed waffled lines into the creek bank. Che sat impatiently outside the chain with his nose pointed up the road. "He really wants to trespass."

"There's a lot of dead bodies up there," I said. "Won't that confuse him?"

"No way. He's tracking the scents he picked up from

235

that hole, whoever used to be attached to that tooth or the guy who fought him, nobody else."

"Give me the leash. You stay here. Your dad'll kill you if you do anything illegal." I nodded toward the *No Trespassing* sign.

"It's not illegal to go into a cemetery. Besides, Seth'll kill you too."

Kill me and follow me. I knew there was a good chance that his spidey sense had gone off. Finding that tooth sure felt a lot like getting slammed onto the hood of a truck. He'd be on his way as soon as Lola picked up our trail. My brother wasn't ready for acres of dead people no matter how much control he thought he had.

"Fine. We need to hurry." I lifted the chain for Che and soon, all three of us were on cemetery grounds. Nico looked uncomfortable as the tops of tombstones came into view. "How could Che have gotten a scent off of that tooth?" I asked to distract him.

"This dog could get a scent from a single skin cell stuck on blade of grass." He slanted his eyes my way. "He'd have no trouble if, for instance, somebody threw a body into the back of a truck and carried it up this road."

Cold wind hit us at the top of the hill. The road turned from gravel to pavement and the weedy brush became a well-manicured lawn. With a whoof, Che trotted right into the grass. Nico hopped behind him like he was in a minefield, trying to avoid stepping on any graves.

I hoped I was wrong about where Che was headed, but he barked and started his high-stepping dance exactly where I knew he would, around the temporary marker on Martha Janine Pearson's brand-new grave.

"No. This can't be the right place," I said.

"Don't listen to him boy. He doesn't understand the power of the nose." Nico pulled a biscuit out of his pocket and Che swallowed it in one bite. "Che says this is it. Did somebody kill an old lady? Either that tooth belonged to Martha, or somebody got this grave marker wrong. Your ghost's body is in the ground right here." He jabbed a finger at the high, curved mound.

I focused inside, waiting for the cat to take a few laps across my grave, but felt nothing. I hadn't gotten a spike of heat from my new talisman, so our spirit must not be bothering Seth either. If this was where his body lay, and I knew in my gut that it was, then our spirit must be wandering. *Where?*

"Will!" Seth's shout echoed across the ravine. I could see him on the switchback trail through the bare branches on the other side of the creek. He and Dr. Muro were almost at the bottom with Lola straining at her leash.

I grabbed Nico's arm. "Would it mess Che up if there was somebody else in that grave too?"

"No. It wouldn't matter if they were stacked in there like Pez. He could still pick out the one he's tracking."

"Come on!" I hauled Nico back toward the service road.

"Dude, you think somebody dumped your guy on top of that poor, little, old lady? That's just sick."

"Yeah, sickness fits with everything else we know about this case." Since his work was done, Che ran beside us instead of dragging us along. "You're brilliant, pup," I told him. "Sorry I doubted you." He cocked an eyebrow at me and lolled his tongue smugly.

We made it down the hill and jumped the chain just as Lola dragged Seth into sight.

"What happened?" Seth asked taking in my muddy jeans. "What did you find?"

I gave him a cold grin. "Hard evidence."

CHAPTER THIRTY-ONE

Reen looked achingly beautiful in a sweater the colors of blueberries and cream. It was hard not to reach across the table in the library and wrap one of her curls around my finger. My heart felt sore from how hard I had to work to keep it caged when I was with her. It was a flimsy-assed cage, and being this close was like dangling Faye Ray in front of King Kong.

Nico and I had made it to school in time for second period. Vic hadn't been anywhere near the front desk when we checked in late. Good thing. I wasn't sure I could have resisted smashing his face into the visitors' log. We'd discussed Snow Ball decorations with Maia during lunch, and then Reen had asked to meet me here. I assumed she wanted an update on Vic.

"It's over," I said in a low voice. "At least our part of it. Seth's talking to the police right now." Our spirit would have to find his own path from here. I had no idea what to expect when he passed on. Choirs of angels? A

239

tunnel of light? Would I even notice?

A few fat raindrops plunked against the floor-to-ceiling windows. The gray cloudbank I'd seen on the horizon at dawn had swollen into general gloom.

Reen shifted in her chair and tapped her gel pen on the table as if she had an invisible notebook there. "So, you said the talismans worked," she said, not meeting my eyes.

"Like a charm. You're amazing." It was a simple statement of fact.

Her lips curved up a little, but her gaze stayed on the pen. *Tap, tap, tap.* She shifted in her chair again. "I owe you an apology, Will." When she finally glanced up, her eyes held none of their usual self-assurance. Gripping the gel pen as if the tapping had been its idea, she rushed on. "I betrayed your trust."

My stomach did a painful, little twist. *God, what now?*

"I was confused. I needed help, so I talked to my grandma about you and Seth. She remembers what happened the night my house burned down a lot better than I do. And she knew your grandmother. They kind of ran in the same circles."

Marcus was right. We couldn't trust anyone to keep our secret. Or he was delusional to think BridgeKeepers had ever been a secret around here in the first place.

"Do you want to know what she told me?"

I swallowed and nodded, still waiting for the gut punch I expected her to deliver.

"A Keeper's aura, your aura, is intense. It has to be to attract attention across the veil. All that energy can't help but spill over to troubled souls on the living side too. That's why it affects people like Anthony and the others." She tucked a curl behind her ear. Faint, rosy spots bloomed on her cheeks. "I remembered how it was with us when we were little. All these feelings bubbled up, but I didn't trust them. What if it was just your aura? What if I was one of the troubled ones?"

Feelings? The crescent of dark eyelashes against her pale brown skin mesmerized me as she stared down at the table. Quietly, she reached out and slipped her hand over the back of mine, her fingers cupped the base of my thumb. I didn't dare move.

"Last night," Reen said very softly, "Grandma helped me realize that what I'm feeling right now is natural, not *supernatural* attraction . . . to you. I'm not troubled like the others. I lost my parents, but that was a long time ago." She squeezed my hand tighter, but still didn't look up. "What I need to know is, have I blown it? I've been so cold to you lately. I don't even know if you have feelings for me. We were just babies when . . ."

Rising from my seat, I leaned across the table, lifted her chin, and kissed her. Muffled voices in the library, and the slow plunk of rain against the window, disappeared. The universe began and ended with her lips, warm, soft, tasting of vanilla. Perfect. I pulled away far enough to give her a chance to stop us, to say something.

She sighed against my mouth and then pulled me close again. At the small of her back, my hand found her soft, blueberry sweater. My other hand slid into the hair at the nape of her neck. Every cell in my body felt polished into a mirror-bright shine.

Someone cleared their throat. Loudly, as if this

might have been the third of fourth time. "You're in the library, remember?"

Library? It wouldn't have surprised me if we'd floated to the ceiling. It took a long time for us to separate and sink back into our chairs.

"Sorry, Mr. Antone," Reen said, a little breathlessly. "We'll get to work."

"Good plan." The librarian gave us a look that let us know he'd be back to check.

"I'm not glowing, am I?" I whispered, half serious. A pleasant hum was running through me as if I'd been badly out of tune for months and somebody finally set my strings right. She gave a little laugh, and I smiled or kept smiling.

"I have something to give you before Mr. Antone comes back." She reached under the table to rummage in her backpack and came up with her hand clasped. Tipping her palm, she let a crystal the color of raspberry jam drop from it, dangling by a black, leather string.

"It's my garnet," Reen said.

"The one from your charm bracelet?" She nodded. The crystal was cool and surprisingly heavy when I lifted it in my fingers. "It's beautiful."

"Yes, and useful too. Garnets enhance the natural gifts of whoever's wearing them. For me, it was my Sight." She touched a finger to the center of her forehead. "But now it'll tune itself to you like your talisman did." She smoothed my fingers open, dropped the necklace, and then folded both of her hands over mine. "I give this gift with an open heart. Do you accept it freely?"

The phrase sounded formal, Her brown eyes were

242

solemn. I probably had no idea how complicated accepting her gift might be, but complicated was fine by me. "I don't know what natural gifts I have to enhance, but, yes, I accept. Thank you."

"You're welcome. I'll put it on you, okay?"

"Sure."

"I don't think I can pry your fingers apart."

I glanced down. "Oh sorry." I unclenched my fist, and when Reen lifted the crystal by its string, it left a cylindrical, pink impression in my palm. Her touch sent goose bumps across my scalp and down my shoulders as she brushed my hair aside, and I tipped my head forward, eyes closed. *Breathe.*

That lemon cookie scent wafted from her hair while Reen arranged the crystal over my heart and tied the leather string. With her warm hands resting on my shoulders, she began to whisper.

"What are you saying?" I asked, whispering too.

Her hands tightened until she finished, and then she hopped onto the table facing me, her feet dangling. "Oh, I guess you could call it a little spell."

"I've been under your spell since I was five, but I think I have the right to know if I'm going to sprout a tail or something. I mean was it from the voodoo side of your family?"

She looked down and said quietly, "I didn't have much time to learn from Mom. That spell was from Dad's side, my grandmother."

"What did you say?"

"You have to promise not to laugh."

Grin like an idiot? Probably. Laugh? Never. "Promise."

"A lot of Wiccan practitioners use rhyme. It melds the words to the intention of the spell, but I'm no poet." She cleared her throat. "Here goes . . . Mother Earth enfold your son. Strengthen. Guide. Protect this one. Gifts of the Keeper ever be, Strengthened by the gifts in me." She looked down at her swinging feet. "I just thought since you're new at this, you probably need all the help you can get. Not that I think you'll be a bad Keeper." She leaned down, kissed me lightly on the lips. "I think you're incredible."

I rose halfway from my chair intending to ignore Mr. Antone's warning when my phone went off.

"No," I breathed. "It's my brother. Just a second." I walked a little way from the table. "Tell me your talisman didn't just go off," I whispered into the phone. If Seth got a signal every time I kissed Reen, I'd cut his bracelet off myself.

"No, it didn't. What's wrong?" He sounded almost panicky. "Did something happen?"

"Nothing you need to know about. Is Vic in a deep, dark cell somewhere?" Silence. "Seth? Did they arrest Vic?"

"No. Is he still in the building?"

A worm of fear wriggled in my gut. "No idea. I didn't see him this morning."

"Don't leave school until I get there. I'll pick you up."

"I've got my bike. When the rain lets up—"

"Will, he thinks he got away with murder. If he finds out that we went to the police . . . He knows who you are and where you live." That shut me up like a slap. "Wait for me."

Reen hopped off the table when I started back to her. "Is everything okay?"

"Are you riding the bus home?" Vic didn't know Reen's name and address, but he knew her face. She nodded. "Good. Don't wander around by yourself tonight."

A spark of fear came into her eyes. Stepping close, she picked up the crystal at my neck, rested her forehead against mine, and whispered her spell again.

I imagined the words flowing into the garnet, the same way I'd pushed the bees into my rock. I didn't know if it would work. Wasn't sure her Wicca was real. But I closed my eyes and took it in.

Reen was right, I needed all the help I could get.

CHAPTER THIRTY-TWO

Saggy, gray clouds still hung overhead as I strapped my bike into the rack and then slipped into Seth's car after school.

"I told you to wait inside," he said, pulling away from the curb behind a minibus carrying most of the girls on the volleyball team.

"You think Vic would do something with all these people around?"

"He's dangerous, Will."

The fact that as BridgeKeepers, our new sphere of acquaintances included a murderer bore repeating. The reality of it festered like a splinter in my brain. Eventually, my mind squeezed the whole concept out, and denial scabbed over the wound. "Why isn't Vic sweating in some interrogation room?"

"You remember Tom Shikles?" At my blank expression, he prompted. "Think precinct Christmas parties when we were kids."

I frowned for a second and then groaned. "Sergeant Shikles? The cop who played Santa? Are you telling me he wouldn't help us because . . . You've got to be kidding. I was six! His beard was totally fake. The other kids weren't buying it either. He could have at least heard you out!"

Seth waved me quiet. "He did. He remembered you though, and a lot of other things that I got the feeling he'd spent the last few years trying to forget."

I frowned. "Marcus said nobody on the force knew about them."

"Doesn't mean they didn't have uncomfortable suspicions."

I looked at Seth's grim face and wondered how hard it must have been to walk into the station again after all these years.

"The sergeant says there's no evidence that a crime's been committed."

"But the body, the tooth!"

He shook his head. "A body *allegedly* buried in somebody else's grave. A victim we don't even have a name for. The sergeant said the guy Che tracked could have gotten into a fight down at the creek, lost a tooth and walked up that road to pay his respects to Martha Janine Pearson. We don't know if Che was following a dead guy or live one."

"We sure as hell do! Didn't Dr. Muro explain how the dogs work?"

Seth sighed. "It's a Catch-22. There may be solid evidence *in* the grave, but without solid evidence *outside* it, there's no way the police will ask the Pearson family for permission to disturb it. And remember, nobody's even been reported missing."

"What do we have to do? Get Vic to sign a confession?" I slumped in the seat fuming. We had a runaway Megan, and a violence-prone creep terrifying her mother. We knew where the victim's body was buried, but if we couldn't get to it, and the cops wouldn't accept testimony from the dead guy himself, Sgt. Shikles was right, our evidence was pretty flimsy. I rubbed my thumb across the hard edges of Reen's crystal, trying to figure out our next move. Apparently, my brain wasn't one of the gifts her crystal could enhance.

Seth slowed as the light ahead turned yellow. "The sergeant said he and Vic aren't exactly friendly, but he wasn't willing to bring him in for questioning." With his eyes still on the road, Seth pulled a folded paper out of the glove compartment. "I got this from the license plate ID service. Vic's last name is Nash."

I sat up and took the paper. "So, we have our ghost's last name too. It'd be the same as his brother's." Reading Seth's note, I frowned. "This says that Vic's address is 5502 Ridge. Not Megan Smalley's house?"

Seth shook his head. "No. I looked up that address. The house on Ridge belongs to Robert and Carolyn Sterling." He made the turn into our neighborhood. "If the Sterlings are connected to Vic somehow, they might know his brother too."

"Ridge is only a few blocks away. Let's head over there."

He gave me a flat-eyed glance. "How'd the direct approach work out for you yesterday? When we get home, I'll google the Sterlings. You order pizza."

I didn't like it. I was itching to *act*, but my stomach was making noises like an underwater mariachi band, and that was the only itch I could scratch right now. I ordered pizza.

Waiting in the basement, I picked up my guitar, hoping that wandering through a song or two would focus my thoughts. It had worked when we debriefed with Marcus. *Marcus.* Was he having better luck getting answers than we were? Maybe he'd already talked to Grams. Maybe even Dad. Was he on his way back right now? Could he help if he walked in the door tonight? Twenty minutes later when the doorbell rang, I ran upstairs and threw the front door open.

"Whoa! Hey there." A stick figure in a bright red 'Zah King cap squinted at the ticket on the pizza box. "You must be hungry, Misterrrr uh, sorry can't make this out. McCurty is it?"

"That's me," I said, feeling like an idiot for being so disappointed.

"Have to make sure we've got the right name, ya know." He wrestled the pizza out of the warming cover. "Big trouble if I hand your pie over to somebody else."

I stared at him, a crazy idea growing. He wasn't wearing any special uniform. Just the 'Zah King cap.

"That'll be $15.23 with your coupon," the pizza guy said, squirming a little under my scrutiny.

"Oh sure, sorry." I started to hand him a twenty, but then pulled it back. "Hey, how much would you take for that cap?"

Smiling, I closed the door. My guitar had loosened up a few synapses after all. The pizza box burned my palm and the steam rising off it sent my belly into a gurgled concert, but sacrifices had to be made.

"Seth! Pizza's off the menu."

"Why?" Seth asked from the kitchen doorway. "The only Showy Chef dinners left in the freezer are meatloaf." He shuddered.

I waved the 'Zah King cap at him. "I've got an idea."

"I can't believe I let you talk me into this," Seth muttered as we walked past a blue Volkswagen Beetle parked in Robert and Carolyn Sterlings' driveway.

Big, ranch-style houses lined Ridge Street. Somebody had a fire going and the smell of wood smoke mixing with the sweet scent of damp leaves made the neighborhood feel friendly.

Balancing an ice-cold pizza in one hand, Seth adjusted his brand-new cap. He'd left Dad's bomber jacket at home, opting for a lighter deliveryman-style black windbreaker. My hoodie was the best I could do for a costume, but I was just backup.

"This'll work. We're in the right place." I rubbed the middle of my chest where an intense wave of sadness was oozing into the hollow spot. There was no doubt in my mind that this house was the place our ghost had wandered to. "Just ask the questions like we planned."

"Why do I have to do all the talking?" Seth asked.

"Because you wouldn't stay home." *Safe behind the threshold.* "And the cap fit you best. Ring the doorbell."

After a few seconds, the porch light flicked on making two huge pots of mums flash rusty orange. A girl with dark hair as glossy as hot fudge, looked out. Her gaze flicked to the pizza box in Seth's hands.

"We didn't order any pizza," she said with a beautifully apologetic smile.

Seth didn't say his lines. The wave of sadness filling my chest grew into a tsunami, and I forced a good customer-service smile onto my face. "Hi. This is for . . ." I squinted over Seth's shoulder at the top of the box. "Mr. Nass? I'm sorry I can't make out this handwriting."

"Is it, Nash?" the girl asked frowning. "That's my brother, but there must be a mistake. Vic doesn't live here anymore."

Her brother? Their mom must have adopted Vic out of pity when the carnival left town. No way he shared DNA with this girl. I squinted at the box some more. "Oh, there's a note here. I guess Mr. Nash ordered this for someone else." This was the big one. I tried to keep it cool. "Does his brother live here?"

The girl frowned some more. "No, Matt's got his own place."

Matt! Our ghost had a first name! I shot a triumphant glance at Seth, but he was staring at the girl like he might cry. His head tilted in a way that made me worry about what or who he was listening to.

"But that doesn't make sense either." The girl went on, leaning toward Seth to get a better look at the top of the box. "What does the note say?"

I blocked her view pretending to study the imaginary note myself, determined to confirm Matt's last name and then get the hell out of there. "Matt Nash? That's your brother's name?"

She raised her chin. "No, his name's Matt Sterling.

Vic's our half-brother." She said it very distinctly like she wanted to make sure we understood and then turned and called over her shoulder. "Mom, would you come here for a minute?"

Matt Sterling, Vic's half-brother, we had what we came for, a full name and the connection. "We probably just got the wrong address," I said to her quickly. "We'll take the pie back to the shop and get this straightened out. Seth, we should go."

Seth's hand shot out to catch the edge of the door. "Abby," he said, his voice strained. The pizza box dropped out of his other hand and hit the porch with a soft thud.

My talisman burned. I shook my wrist and then grabbed Seth's shoulder. "Seth, come on," I said, twisting him around. His body swung toward me, but his eyes stayed locked on the girl's. He was rooted to the spot, solid as a fence post. And his skin glowed translucent white.

"Matt's here," he said in a raspy whisper. "I'm going to let him cross."

"No! Are you crazy?" I hissed. Abby's puzzled look changed to an I'm-about-to-call-9-1-1 glare.

"What's going on?" An older woman, about a head shorter than Abby, peeked around her. Matt's mom. Just great.

Abby put an arm out to keep her mother behind her. "Is this some kind of joke? Are you two friends of Vic's?" Suspicion and hostility put a little vinegar into her voice.

"Will," Seth gasped. "He's begging. He's got to talk to her." He tore his eyes away from the women in the doorway and looked at me. His face went calm. "Get ready."

"Don't. Don't!" I said, even as I stepped back out of his reach.

Light gushed from Seth's chest.

CHAPTER THIRTY-THREE

O nly the Keeper sees the light. Good thing. I could tell by the women's faces that what they *did* see was bad enough. Seth, head back, eyes wide, a weird mix of terror and bliss on his face. The flood of light narrowed to a tractor beam over his heart, tight and focused.

My talisman seared my wrist until Seth's light flickered twice and sank into him. His shoulders bowed like he'd taken on weight . . . Matt Sterling's weight. Matt's face molded Seth's into the mask I'd seen Saturday morning; both, and neither of them. Tears pooled in his eyes, glistening in the porch light. There was no more bliss in them, just desperation.

"Seth," I bit my tongue, started over. "Matt, why are you here?"

One of the women gasped. I didn't look up in time to see which one, but Mrs. Sterling had a two-fisted death grip on her daughter's outstretched arm. Her eyes were wide and locked on Seth's face. Knowing that at least one of the Sterling women saw *something* gave me hope that they wouldn't slam the door in Matt's face.

Seth's lips quivered. After a couple false starts, Matt/Seth said, "Abby."

"What is this?" Abby asked, her eyes narrowed. "I don't know what you're up to, but this isn't funny. Get off our porch!"

"Abbster!" Matt/Seth said in a don't-mess-with-your-big-brother tone I recognized. "Vic knows. He's looking for you. Both of you." Abby slapped a hand over her mouth and started to press her mom back out of the doorway. "Abbster, please!"

"Stop calling me that!"

Seth flinched. We were so screwed if Abby kept pushing him away.

"Honey, look at him," Mrs. Sterling breathed, leaning past her daughter. "Matthew?"

Matt/Seth frowned and pulled his eyes away from Abby. "Mom?" His face crumpled. The next word came out with a flood of tears. "Mom."

My feet ignored all of Marcus's warnings and I stepped across the porch to take hold of Seth's shoulders again. "I'm so sorry, man." Cold radiated through his windbreaker. "Matt, I'm so sorry, but please, keep it together. Talk to us." I willed my sweaty palms to calm him somehow. And somehow, it seemed to work.

He took a shaky breath, steadied. "Abby's not safe here, Mom. She should be hiding with Megan."

"Not safe from whom?"

"From Vic," he snarled. "He'll hurt her, Mom. She

has to hide!"

"Oh my God," Mrs. Sterling whimpered.

"Stop this!" Abby looked back and forth between her mother and Seth. "I'll go. I'll do whatever you say."

She didn't believe she was talking to her brother. She was playing along to get rid of us. I hoped it worked. "Matt, you heard her. You have to go, now." The look Matt/Seth turned on me was a hundred percent, *who's gonna make me?* This was why you didn't channel the same ghost twice. They got way too comfortable under your Bridge's skin. But Mrs. Sterling let out a muffled sob, and Matt/Seth's face softened. He reached out to wipe a tear that trailed down her cheek, but she flinched away from him. Seth's hand dropped slowly to his side, and Matt turned to me with a hard, level look.

I got the message. I damned well better take care of his family.

I caught Seth as his knees gave way. Matt's continued presence nagged at me, but it was faint as if this visit had weakened him as much as it had Seth. With the Sterling women staring at us, I realized I had no exit strategy. All I wanted to do right now was get Seth back across our threshold. The Mustang, parked a couple houses down, seemed a million miles away.

"You made him a promise," I said to Abby, pulling Seth's arm over my shoulder and turning to leave. "Find somewhere safe to stay for a while."

Mrs. Sterling pushed past her daughter. "Come into the house. Please."

"Mom!" Abby said. "We should be calling the police."

"No, Abby," Mrs. Sterling said, her eyes never leaving

Seth. "I have to know more. Please, come in."

Seth started to tremble. This little freak show had gotten us Matt's full name, but we needed more dirt on Vic if we wanted to jump-start a police investigation. And maybe, just maybe this threshold offered as much protection as ours. "I'm Will McCurty," I said. "My brother, Seth, channels spirits. Are you sure you want to invite us in?"

For a heartbeat, Mrs. Sterling looked like she might take back her invitation, but then she gave me a tiny nod. "Come in."

Making a wide circle around Abby who hadn't stopped glaring at us, I guided Seth through the front door. Relief warmed me when the whisper of Matt's presence faded away.

There was a comfortable after-dinner smell on the air, roasted meat and warm bread that made my empty stomach rumble. A fire crackled in the fireplace adding its glow to the twitchy light coming from a TV that was on, but muted. I chose a spot closest to the fireplace and lowered Seth into the corner of their couch.

Mrs. Sterling switched on a floor lamp. The fireplace mantel was a wide expanse of polished wood and framed pictures. Three people smiled out of one that caught my eye. Abby, in cap and gown stood next to a couple that must have been her mom and dad. On her other side was a tall, rangy, guy, same dark brown hair as Abby, not much older than Seth. Had to be Matt. He had his arm around her waist and smiled down like his little sister was the cherry in his lemonade every damned day.

"What's wrong with *him*?" Abby asked, jerking her

chin at Seth.

My brain was too scattered to come up with anything other than the truth. "It's ghost sickness. Could we borrow a blanket, please?" Mrs. Sterling lifted a knitted blanket from the back of a chair. She stepped back next to Abby the moment I took it, watching us like we might explode.

The blanket was soft and stretchy as pizza dough. I wrapped it around Seth's shoulders and sat down close enough that our knees and shoulders touched, hoping to share some body heat. It seemed to help. He dragged the 'Zah King cap off his head, let it drop onto the couch and hunched into the blanket.

"Your brother channels spirits?" Mrs. Sterling asked, sounding like she was sure she'd regret bringing this up again but couldn't help herself.

I nodded slowly.

"Don't give us that bull," Abby said through her teeth.

"Abby, you spoke to him," her mother said. "You *saw* him."

"I don't know what I saw." Abby snatched the graduation picture off the mantel and clutched it to her heart. "My brother. Is in Lawrence. Buying a wrecked '67 Impala." She punched every word like she'd make them true by sheer force of will. "He's going to haul it back here in a couple days and restore it."

"Vic told you that, right?" I asked.

"No, Matt did. Last week," she said with her chin high.

That stopped me. Had we gotten it wrong? Wrong house? Wrong brothers? But then the last ten minutes screamed through my head, every word, every detail. I

258

winced. Forced the images into a dark little corner to wait till I could vomit them out in a Sharing. We had the right house.

Mrs. Sterling sank to the edge of a chair and wrapped her arms tightly around herself. "I've seen things in my life that I can't explain. Both miracles and curses." She turned to Seth and me. "I'm not sure which you boys are offering, but I know in my heart who I saw." Lines of sadness deepened on her face. She was beginning to realize what having BridgeKeepers in the house meant about her son.

"Abbster," Seth said, his voice almost a whisper.

Abby jabbed a finger at him. "No! You don't call me that."

No, you don't. Matt's gone. You're not supposed to remember a thing. Crap!

Abby kept her hostile game face on for about two more seconds then dropped her forehead into her hand. "This is unbelievable." She collapsed into another chair, twin to the one her mom perched on, staring at the framed picture in her lap. "I haven't been able to get hold of him. It's not like Matt to ignore my texts. He's Mr. Reliable, ya know?"

I nodded and glanced at the Mr. Reliable currently in the room. Seth's eyes were closed, but his head was up, listening.

"He said he was going to talk to Vic before he left town," Abby said.

"Would they have met at Nickerson's Nature Reserve?" I asked.

Abby looked at me, surprised. "Matt loves that park.

He even knows a back way in so he can roam around there at night. He would have picked someplace peaceful like that. It wasn't going to be an easy conversation."

I knew just how badly his plan had gone. It must have shown on my face.

Abby gave us a stubborn look. "Vic's a creep, but I can't believe he'd . . . They might have fought, but Matt can't be . . ." She clamped her lips closed and shook her head in quick, hard movements.

"Maybe Matt's hurt." Mrs. Sterling sat up, looking like she'd found a life vest bobbing on a stormy sea. "In a coma somewhere. I've heard of people near death leaving their bodies, contacting loved ones for help."

"We have to find him!" Abby jumped to her feet.

I didn't want to crush the wave of hope they were riding, but it seemed kinder than letting the wave build. "Wait. We searched the park this morning, with dogs. We found . . ."

Seth squeezed my arm. "Nothing," he said. "We found nothing. He's not in the park, Abby. If we're going to find him, we need to figure out what happened when he met Vic." The women looked momentarily lost, their hopeful momentum smashed against Seth's certainty.

"Abby," I said into the silence. "What did Matt want to talk to Vic about?"

CHAPTER THIRTY-FOUR

Abby looked like she might bolt, head out to Nickerson's and search the whole park in the dark by herself. But finally, she sank back into the chair. Her gaze shifted to the muted TV where a freaky-looking kid, supposed to be a ghost I realized, picked two guys up by their necks and flung them down a staircase.

"I had an outdoor birthday party when I was ten," Abby said. Mrs. Sterling hunched forward, putting her face in her hands. Abby kept her gaze pointed at the pint-sized ghost laying into the guys on the TV. "Everybody was out in our backyard. We'd eaten dinner, had cake, and opened presents. The kids were chasing lightning bugs." She flashed a little smile that quickly faded. "I came into the kitchen for something. I don't remember what. Vic was there. He told me he had one last present for me up in his room."

"His room?" Seth asked quietly.

"He's our half-brother. Mine and Matt's. He was living here at the time." Seth nodded and Abby let her gaze wander back to the TV. "Anyway, when Vic took me upstairs, he shut the door and brought a brand-new Malibu Barbie out of his closet. She was naked."

An image rose in my mind of a book falling to the floor in the school library, Reen, Missy, and me following it down – *Invisible Girls: Speaking the Truth about Sexual Abuse.* Seth's hand tightened on my arm, and I realized I'd started up out of the chair. This story was giving me a powerful urge to pace, but I made myself settle back.

Abby's voice was steady. "He laid her bikini and sun hat out on his bed, all the little beach accessories. He knew how much I wanted that doll. He said I could only have her if I was naked too." Mrs. Sterling pressed her fingertips against her lips and stared at the floor. My skin crawled. I swallowed hard and turned to watch the TV screen with Abby. The ghost had one of the guys down on the ground, its hand stuck deep in his chest.

"I wasn't afraid," she said. "I mean, Vic's a bully, but he'd never touched me. I thought he was betting that I wouldn't do it so he could return the doll and get his money back. But I wanted that Barbie, so I pulled off my shorts." Abby gave a bleak chuckle. "I had my swimsuit on underneath. I thought I'd really pulled a fast one on him. I was so stupid."

"You were ten," Seth said quietly.

Giving Seth a grateful look, she went on. "I remember Vic licked his lips, and it was like somebody'd flipped a switch. My worldview turned upside down. Monsters were real." The framed picture of Matt in her lap creaked under her grip. "I couldn't move. My heart took off but the rest of me froze and watched him unbutton his shirt."

Mrs. Sterling let out a soft moan, and hearing it, Abby turned quickly with a smile spreading across her face, a genuine smile. "That's when Matt burst into the room. He was so mad and so scared, but he started laughing. He called me a goofball, said Barbie's tiny bikini wasn't going to fit me." Abby hugged the picture as a tear slipped down her cheek and into the crease of her smile. "He said that just because I was the birthday girl didn't mean I could show everybody my birthday suit. He talked and talked and had me and my clothes out of there so fast Vic just stood there gaping." Eyes fierce, she squeezed her mother's hand. "My big brother saved me. He was only fourteen."

"I thought he'd saved Victor too," Mrs. Sterling said so quietly that I almost couldn't hear her. "My ex-husband was a vicious man. Victor went to live with my uncle. We sent him through months of counselling. I'd hoped . . ."

"He was gone," Abby said, reaching over to squeeze her mother's hand. "Our lives were easier. We didn't think about it again, even when he moved back into town, until Megan Smalley came to us. She doesn't have a big brother."

"Oh Abby, why didn't you tell me she'd come?" Mrs. Sterling asked.

"We didn't know how bad it was, Mom, not at first. I couldn't get her to talk about it. She hasn't even told her mother."

"Why didn't you call the police?" I asked, getting to my feet despite Seth's grip on my arm. "We don't have enough proof to get an investigation started, but if Megan told them her story—"

"She won't talk to the police. Vic's got her completely twisted up." Abby stood too. We faced off across the living room rug. "She half believes that what he did to her is her fault. Vic threatened to post her pictures on some porn site if she told anyone. She's terrified, close to suicide. She needs time."

I caught the blanket that dropped from Seth's shoulders as he pushed himself up beside me. "Megan will have the time she needs, if you're sure she's somewhere safe."

"She is now," Abby said. "I called a hotline last night after she told me the whole story. A shelter came and picked her up. They wouldn't even tell *me* where they took her."

"Is there somewhere *you* can go?" he asked.

"Yes!" Mrs. Sterling popped out of her chair.

"No, Mom! I'm staying to find Matt."

"Honey please, you can spend a few days with Aunt Katie, or Uncle Geoff."

Seth put his hands lightly on Abby's shoulders. "Go. Let Matt have some peace, at least about you. We'll find him."

Abby looked away. I could see she didn't want to give up on mounting a search herself, but I also knew that even with ghost sickness, Seth in full-on, big brother mode was tough to resist. She pressed her lips together and nodded.

"Thank you." Seth turned to her mother. "Mrs. Sterling, would you call the police and report Matt missing?"

"Yes, yes of course," Mrs. Sterling said, a shadow passing over her face again. "I'll get a few of Abby's things first, then I'll make the call." She hurried from the room.

"Do you have your phone?" Seth asked Abby. "I'll give you my number."

"I think I left it in my car!" Abby said, frantic, as if her missing phone was the final straw that could break her.

"It's okay," Seth said. "Will, would you find something to write on."

"Look in the kitchen." Abby pointed a trembling finger. "There should be a note pad on the counter."

I was glad to get out of that room and paced around the kitchen island looking for the notepad. "I should have broken the bastard's arm when I had the chance." I knew ten pressure points that would have made him sorry he'd ever touched Megan.

You're not in the revenge business, boys. Head down that dark path and all three of you are lost. Marcus' voice rumbled in my head. My pacing slowed. Evidence. Vic would get away with murder and worse if we couldn't find enough to get the police involved. Mrs. Sterling's call would open the door, but whatever we did next, it had to happen fast. I had a feeling that finally identifying Matt had started an avalanche that would either carry us to the end or bury us.

The notepad lay on the counter with a mug full of pencils beside it. As I picked up a pencil, the garage door rumbled up. Abby's dad must be home from work. *Super, another heart to break.* Hurrying, I jotted down Seth's number and ripped the paper off the pad. I made it all the way across the kitchen when the door to the garage swung open. Plastering on a polite smile, I turned to meet Mr. Sterling.

The man who walked through the door wasn't Abby's dad.

CHAPTER THIRTY-FIVE

He wasn't in uniform, but even with his back to me, shoving the door open with a beefy shoulder, I knew who it was. Vic took a fast, deep drag on his cigarette, blew a gust of smoke into the garage, and then tossed the butt. I heard a yelp and a curse from someone following him.

"Mom," Vic yelled as he turned around holding a smashed box. "Somebody left a pizza out on the front porch." He looked up, saw me, and gave a startled jump. I knew the moment when he realized who I was, because his eyes went wide with fear. My face had probably made exactly the same trip.

Vic took a couple stiff steps in my direction. "What are you doing here?" he hissed in a shaky whisper. If he hadn't suspected that I knew he killed his brother before, he did now.

"Hi, Vic," I said loudly, praying that Seth and Abby were paying attention.

The guy coming in behind Vic stopped short. "Hey, I know you." He half-smiled, half-sneered around a purple wad of gum. "You're the kid I annihilated at the hapkido tournament."

I took my eyes off Vic long enough to take a good look at the guy. In sparring gear, with a Day-Glo orange mouth guard he'd look just like . . . *Oh shit.* It was Chomper.

He elbowed Vic. "You should've seen this kid fight, he was decent. Couldn't handle me though."

I gave him a thin smile. "Makes perfect sense that you're a friend of Vic's."

"Shut up," Vic said. "How'd you know this was my house?"

He stepped closer, and I glanced over my shoulder. Seth was moving to the front door, struggling to take Abby with him. She looked like she couldn't decide if she was scared enough to run or mad enough to come in here and tear Vic a new one. I had to keep stalling.

"Your house?" I asked. "I thought Mrs. Smalley's house was your house." Vic curled his lip. I held up my hands. "Hey, I had no idea you lived here. I'm just the pizza guy." I pointed to the greasy box in his hands. "Had a little accident."

"Pizza guy, my ass," Vic said, he didn't sound as scared anymore.

Dropping the box on the counter, he came around the island. When I stepped up to block his view into the living room, Vic reached for the front of my hoodie, but hesitated, probably remembering what had happened the last time he tried that move. As his hand dropped to his side, I felt a twinge of disappointment. No utility belt or holster this time. This would be a fair fight.

"Vic, who the heck is this kid?" Chomper asked, looking like a confused cow chewing its cud.

"This is the punk who came sniffing around my place looking for Megan."

Chomper's chewing slowed. The same fear I'd seen in Vic's eyes slowly filled his. Was he involved in this too? I felt my lip curl and had to remind myself that it would not be a good idea to start a fight in Mrs. Sterling's kitchen.

"Where's my mother?" Vic raised a fist. "What did you say to her?"

I started to back up but was stopped short by somebody behind me.

"Victor! You didn't tell me you were coming over!"

Mrs. Sterling walked around me like I wasn't there. She put both arms around Vic's waist, tucked herself under his chin, and pressed her cheek against his barrel chest.

Vic's whole body relaxed. "Mom," he said, his voice full of relief. He wrapped his arms around her and closed his eyes. They stood like that for several seconds oblivious to me and Chomper.

I was grossed out and a little pissed-off, but that hug showed me that even fratricidal pedophiles could love their moms. And she loved him, even after all she'd heard tonight. The contrast to my mom was so stark, I felt a pang of envy.

Vic kissed the top of her head. "You okay?" He looked over at me, worry back in his eyes. "Is this kid bothering you?"

She broke the hug but kept a hand on his arm. "He's

just delivering pizza, dear. He dropped it on the porch." She turned to me. "If you expect a tip young man, you'll make this right."

"Um, well . . ." I said, trying to get my brain to work as fast as Mrs. Sterling's. "I'll head back to the shop and get you a fresh one."

"I should hope so." Mrs. Sterling flapped her hands, shooing me out.

Vic's thin lips contorted, probably holding back words he couldn't say in front of his mother. We kept our eyes on each other as I backed out of the kitchen. Chomper followed, still looking confused and worried.

"Don't forget your cap, young man," Mrs. Sterling told me sternly.

"No ma'am." I took one long sidestep to the couch and swept the 'Zah King cap up to my head. Giving Vic a tight smile, I pointed to the logo. His eyes narrowed to slits. I walked backward till my elbow hit the front door.

"Don't worry about the boy, Victor," Mrs. Sterling said as I pulled the door open. "I'm sure he'll get things straightened out." She cupped Vic's cheek in her hand and made him look away from me. "Now, introduce me to your friend."

Weird, the woman was all of five-foot-three, but she made Vic look even smaller. Out on the porch at last, I collapsed against the door gulping cold, clean night air.

By the driveway, Seth had a finger stuck under his leather bracelet, holding the stone away from his skin. Abby gripped his elbow like she'd hauled on it to keep him from charging back into the house. "Are you okay?" he asked.

"Man, I'm tired of answering that question."

"I'm tired of asking it," Seth said.

"I'm fine, thanks to Abby's mom. She's somethin' else."

"You have no idea," Abby said. "She's the only person Vic has any respect for. She'll keep him busy for a while, but you two better leave."

"And you," Seth told her. "You can't go back in there. Is the blue Volkswagen yours?"

Taking her by the arm, he led her quickly around a very familiar, black truck now parked in the driveway. It still had my face-print rubbed into the grungy hood. Cupping my hands against the glass, I looked in the window. All I could see were junk food wrappers and crushed energy drink cans. I checked the flatbed in back—sparkling clean. "Huh."

"Anything?" Seth asked me as Abby opened the door of her toy car.

I shook my head. "Not anymore."

The dome light flicked on in the Beetle and Abby leaned in. "I'll put your number in my phone before I go—Oh!" Backing out slowly, she turned with a pair of black leather gloves in her hand. "Matt left these in my car. We went to a movie last week," she whispered, stroking them with shaking fingers.

I blinked, my eyes suddenly burning. *What the hell?* After an hour of backstory and a couple of pictures on the mantel, I could see Matt's hands in those gloves, ten and two on his steering wheel, warm and alive. I looked out into the shadowy yard, a little desperate for something to focus on besides Abby's raw grief.

"I hope you guys are a couple of delusional

sociopaths," she whispered, "And this is all a really sick joke."

"We'll help him," Seth promised, gently guiding Abby into the driver's seat.

I could only swallow and nod my agreement.

We watched till her car disappeared around the corner, then started for ours at a crooked jog. "Hey, Mrs. Sterling can handle her son," I said, touching Seth's shoulder to slow him down. "She'll buy us time. Don't push it."

"I'm not pushing it," he grumbled, but he slowed to a walk. He did a controlled collapse into the Mustang's leather passenger seat, leaving his feet on the curb. I got a whiff of clean sweat as he scrubbed a hand over his face.

Bracing myself on the roof, I leaned down to him. "Is Matt still trying to get your attention?" My hand rose to my chest and I frowned. "I'm getting nothing."

Seth listened for a second or two. "Me too."

"Seems like with Abby and Vic in the same place, Matt would be all over us."

"Maybe spirits get crossover sickness, same as my ghost sickness. Even though he really wanted to be here, I had to pull him across this time, like the old grave at Muddy Bend." Leaning back, Seth dug his car keys out of his pocket and held them up to me.

I stared at him stupidly. "You want me to drive? That's illegal! I don't even have a permit." I'd been old enough for months, but I just hadn't worked up any interest. "How bad are you feeling?"

Before Seth could give me an answer, a sickeningly

familiar voice came out of the dark behind us.

"Hello, boys." Vic growled.

CHAPTER THIRTY-SIX

"I'm talkin' to you," Vic said, like he was surprised I'd be so rude as to ignore his polite greeting.

I heard a squeaky chuckle punctuated by the sound of cracking gum. Vic hadn't come alone.

Seth jammed his keys back in his pocket and grabbed my wrist. His palm folded around my bracelet. Both talismans were warm. "Don't provoke him," he breathed, pulling me half into the car. I nodded and started to back out, but Seth pulled me in again. "But don't hold back like you did yesterday if he starts something."

"Thanks for the advice. Just stay out of my way." Seth lifted weights and ran miles, but he'd never hit anybody in his life. I straightened, meaning to block the two men's view of him, but my brother shouldered me aside and stood up next to me. Ten seconds ago, I wouldn't have said he could stand at all. I gave him a what-the-hell-are-you-doing look. He ignored it.

"We don't want any trouble," Seth said.

"I'm not the one bringing trouble," Vic said. "Your boy here was sniffing around my girlfriend's daughter. Now I find him at my mother's place." His eyes darted back and forth between Seth and me. "I want to know what the hell you said to her. She's talking about Matt going missing. And where's my sister?"

"Stay away from her," Seth said. Vic forced a nasty laugh.

Chomper took it up a beat late and stepped up, toe-to-toe with Seth. "Who's gonna make him, pizza boy? You?" In one brutal movement, he sucker-punched my brother in the gut. Seth let out a hard cough and went down.

My head exploded—or maybe imploded. Liquid lightning flashed from my talisman, up my arm, and then sizzled in the middle of my chest.

Reality shifted.

I stopped feeling the cold in the night air and felt only its pressure flowing against my skin, measuring the space between me, Keeper, and my Bridge. Breathing in the scent of Seth's sweat, I could taste the fear in it. His heartbeat and choked coughs were the only sounds reaching my ears.

In the next second, my awareness expanded, not far, still tight, focused, taking in the threat—Chomper. I reached for his shoulder. Vic dove for me. I blocked, shoving his hands off-target. Driving my palm up, I felt his nose collapse like a plastic cup. Vic staggered back, clawing his face.

Chomper lifted Seth off the ground by the front of his jacket. I punched the soft spot between his hip and ribs. Chomper howled, arching back. I grabbed a fistful of his hair, bashed his face against the edge of the car door, took him by the belt and collar, spun him around, and heaved him at Vic. They ended up in a tangled pile on the lawn ten feet away.

"Get in the car," I ordered Seth.

He struggled to stand, clutching his stomach. "No, I won't leave you out here."

Vic and Chomper were already getting to their feet behind me. Their groans, the smell of blood, the movement of the air, told me exactly where they were. "Seth, get in the car. You're making it harder. I can handle them." My Bridge looked at me like he wasn't sure who I was, but he clambered into the passenger seat. I slammed the door, mimed locking it. Seth glared, but the locks clicked. He was dialing his cell when I turned back to Vic.

Standing, Vic swiped his knuckles across his mouth. "You cocky, little prick." Blood poured from both their noses, giving them matching, glossy black goatees in the dark.

"We're gonna bus' up tha' pretty face o' yours," Chomper added. "You're gonna scream like a lil' baby!"

Their fear and anger tasted like vinegar in the back of my throat. "Let us leave now," I said evenly, "and I won't hurt you anymore."

"Hell with you!" Vic's fist shot past my jaw. I grabbed his wrist. Jerked it high, pivoted behind him, and landed a palm strike to the back of his head. His forehead bounced off the Mustang with a metallic bong. Smelling Juicy Fruit, I drove my elbow backward.

"Bwuuh!"

A giant wad of gum sailed over my shoulder to splat against the back of Vic's neck. He twisted around, swung again. I ducked, came in low, and drove my fist into his doughy gut. His butt rocked the car on its way down to the curb.

Seth pressed his face against the window as Vic's body slid past. Our eyes met. His were wide, terrified, searching mine. I saw him yell something into his phone.

Chomper's hiccupping breaths drew me back to the last target standing. I raised a knee and side-kicked him across the grass. Both threats were down, but every twitch they made drew my eye, every groan vibrated in my ears. I stepped between them, ready to make sure they stayed down.

"Help us. He's crazy!" Chomper whined.

Seth's heartbeat, the theme song running in my head, jumped. I snapped my attention back to the car. He still had the phone to his ear. He was staring out the rear window. "No!" he said, his shout muffled by the glass.

"Shoot!" Vic yelled. "He's high on something! He has a knife!"

Seth threw himself against the passenger door. The dome light flashed on, but Vic's body kept him trapped inside. His scream sailed through the open crack. "There's no knife!"

My tight focus blew outward. Flashing lights. Shouts. Heavy footsteps. A storm of new information flowed over me.

"Down on your knees! Get your hands where we can

see them. Do it now!"

I dropped into fighting stance.

CHAPTER THIRTY-SEVEN

"Shoot the son of a bitch!"

"No! Wait!" Seth yelled.

My Keeper instincts held my focus in a zone that spread out around my Bridge like dark, still water. Down deep in this zone, everything was simple. Every sound, every scent, every movement caught my attention. Find the dangerous stuff, ignore the rest. If it threatened my Bridge, take it out.

But something kept pulling me up out of that still quiet. When my head broke the surface of the zone . . . confusion . . . chaos. "Get your hands in the air! Do it now!" People in uniform rushed in from the street, circling the Mustang.

"He doesn't have a weapon!" Seth's frantic voice.

"Stay in the car, sir!"

My connection to my Bridge hummed. He was scared. Find the threat. Take it out.

No. Something's wrong. Think. I shook my head. *What's going on?* The first drop of sweat I'd felt all night trickled down my side. Seth scrambled over the gearshift to the driver's side. He threw the door open and jumped out into the street.

The man in uniform swung the gun around. "Stop right there!"

I dipped back into calm, still focus. Gauging the distance to the man with the gun, I dropped into a half-crouch.

"Will! Don't you dare move!" Seth's voice pinned me.

"Shoot him!" Vic yelled. "You think that little shit'd be the only one standing if he didn't have a knife?"

"Shut up!" Seth's voice was shrill. "Will. Do what the police say. Put your hands up."

Police?

"Is he high on something?" The man in uniform asked, weapon pointing back where I wanted it, back at me.

"No! Listen to me, Will." Seth brought his volume down to his calm-in-an-emergency voice. "It's over. Everything's all right. Do you hear me? Just do what they say."

My brain clicked back online. It correctly interpreted the man in front of me. *Cop. With a gun.*

Chomper's prediction about me screaming like a baby? I came close, really close.

"Show me your hands, son."

There were more cops behind me. I forced myself not to guess how many. The officer in front of me and I established a relationship. I spread my arms out like

280

he asked. They shook so badly it looked like I was trying to fly off.

"Down on your knees now."

I nodded. When a guy's right he's right. I was about to fall down anyway. The officer holstered his weapon, approached slowly. I appreciated that. I was still teetering along the edge of the zone. Sudden movements—not good.

"Put your hands behind your head. I'm going to check for weapons."

"Don't have any." My voice cracked.

"He's not carrying anything," Seth said at the same time.

"Just let me check for myself."

I concentrated on not breathing in gulps while he patted me down. I couldn't say he was gentle, but he was quick. I hardly had time to panic as handcuffs snapped around my wrists.

"He's clean." The officer pulled me up by one elbow and pushed me out into the street.

"Seth?"

"I'm here." Seth had his own officer too. Everybody had one. "It's all right. Go."

My officer took a firm grip on my shoulders and pushed me toward a patrol car lit up in the dark like a pinball machine. He waved off another cop, "It's okay. I know this kid."

I twisted around, checked the name tag above the badge. *Santa?* Tom Shikles carried a little bulk around his middle, his cheeks were round, and his hair white and curly, but right now there was no merry twinkle in his eyes. "Sergeant Shikles?" I croaked.

The man's lips curved up like a bow—a ticked off, worried bow. "Have you taken any illegal or prescription drugs tonight, Will?" he asked, official, brusque.

"What? No."

"Have you been drinking alcohol?"

"No." The man's face stayed hard, professional. His eyes flicked back and forth, probably gauging the size of my pupils, waiting for me to twitch or foam at the mouth. I forced myself not to fidget.

Finally, Sergeant Shikles let out a breath and then scowled long and hard before he said, "You're going to be it, aren't you?"

"Sir?"

"You and your brother. You'll be the thing that makes me give in to my wife and retire."

"I, um, sorry?"

He sighed irritably. "When I talked to Seth this morning, I didn't think you two were planning an ambush. In fact, I'm sure I made it perfectly clear to your brother that you should stay away from Mr. Nash."

I tried to point, but only managed to wrench my wrists against the cuffs. "He jumped us. Seth called you, didn't he? Why would he do that if we'd been ambushing somebody?"

Sergeant Shikles frowned. "We didn't respond to Seth's call. Mrs. Sterling called in a few minutes ago."

I looked past him. Mrs. Sterling stood on her front porch, arms tightly crossed, watching.

"There are two men on the ground over there." The Sergeant crossed his arms too. "Grown men with bloody

282

noses." He cocked one snowy white eyebrow. "You son, don't seem to have a scratch on you."

I couldn't help it, I fidgeted. The cuffs tightened. "We didn't come here to fight." I'd tried to avoid it or end it even after the zone swallowed me. Hadn't I? I felt sick, weak-kneed. An ambulance rolled up, lights, no sirens. Cops waved the paramedics over to Vic and Chomper. The sergeant watched them and then looked back at me with a sour expression on his face.

"We came here to get information," I said. "And we got it. Vic's a murderer. He killed his brother. He—"

Sergeant Shikles held up hand. "Seth told me your theory. Did Mr. Nash confess tonight? Did any witnesses come forward? Do you have any physical evidence that a crime has been committed?"

He seriously wanted to know. And I seriously wished I had something, anything, to tell him. *There's a girl in hiding who won't talk to you,* didn't seem like a helpful answer. I stared at Sergeant Shikles' black shoes.

An argument rose over the low rumble of idling engines. "That's a lie!" Seth's voice punched above the others. Vic had an ear-lock on an officer taking notes. Seth said something I couldn't make out over the roof of his car. I moved in that direction.

Sergeant Shikles grabbed my arm. "Hold it," he said.

Seth's cop had hold of his elbow too, and turned him around. Seth wasn't cuffed. That was a relief, but despite the anger in his voice, he leaned against the Mustang like it was the only thing holding him up. The officer that'd taken Vic's statement flipped the page in her notepad and started to walk in our direction.

"Stay right here," Sergeant Shikles told me.

"Yeah. Okay." I stayed by the patrol car while the two cops decided our fate in the middle of the street. I wanted that hyper focus back. Instead, I just shivered and tried not to let my eyes wander over to where the paramedics were working on Vic and Chomper. The light was good over there. The blood was red. But they didn't bring out gurneys, and Vic was waving the paramedics off.

When he came back, the sergeant's face was grim. "Do you know Megan Smalley?"

"Yes. I mean, she's a friend of a friend at school."

"Mr. Nash says you know her better than that. He says you're stalking her. That she ran away from home because she's afraid of you."

"That's a lie," I said quietly.

"He said you came to her house. Frightened her mother."

"I'm not the one Mrs. Smalley's afraid of."

"But you were at the girl's house? This girl you don't really know?"

He waited, but I couldn't think of any way to contradict what he'd said. Vic had twisted things up. He was good at that. No matter what I said now, it'd be my word against his, and I looked a lot more criminal tonight than he did.

"Why did you come to the Sterlings' house tonight?" Sergeant Shikles asked.

My heart jumped, and a 3D, IMAX movie of Matt's family reunion ran through my head. I needed the Sharing but swallowed hard, forcing the images down. "Mrs. Sterling wants to report her son missing,"

I managed.

The sergeant's snowy eyebrows rose at that. He put a hand on my shoulder and squeezed just hard enough to make me wince. "Let me tell you how I see things right now." He tipped his head toward Seth and Vic. "Your brother and Mr. Nash gave conflicting statements. Who threatened who, who started the fight. I've got to say it's pretty clear who ended it." I winced again. "If Mrs. Sterling does report her son missing, and her story conflicts with what Mr. Nash has said, I'd guess he could be convinced not to press assault charges against you. Given the situation, my options are to bring all of you in for fighting in public. Or none of you." He looked me in the eye. "Do you want to sleep in your own bed tonight, son?"

I ground my heel into the grit on the side of the road. "Yes, sir."

"Good. Go home. Stay away from Megan Smalley and her mom."

"I'm not the one—" Squeeze. I shut up.

"If a missing person report comes in, *we* will handle it." The sergeant turned me around. "Deming," he barked, as he unlocked my cuffs, "Bring the other Mr. McCurty over here. I'd like to have a talk with Mr. Nash."

I rubbed the circulation back into my hands. Officer Deming brought Seth over. He looked exhausted, but managed to put one foot in front of the other. Deming unlocked the back door of the squad car and tucked us inside. I stared over at the ambulance where the sergeant and Vic stood talking. Drizzle speckled the window. Cold leached from the squad car's hard plastic backseat straight through my jeans. I could hear the heater going full blast up front, but the bulletproof barrier only allowed a trickle of it to ooze up from the floor.

Seth had closed his eyes and let his head drop back. He was quiet for a long time. "Will, what happened back there? I've never seen you fight like that."

I pulled my hoodie tight around my ribs and tried to hold in a shiver that had little to do with the cold. "I'm not sure. When Chomper sucker-punched you, I just—"

"Lost it?"

I didn't answer for a minute, remembering the feel of the zone. Focus, calm, total certainty about the mayhem I was dishing out. "No," I said quietly. "The opposite. It felt like I completely, totally found it. Everything was exactly right. I was exactly right. I did what I'm supposed to do."

"Which is?"

I looked at him. "Protect you." He rolled his head my way and opened his eyes. We stared at each other. "Do you think I'm crazy?" I asked, really wanting to know.

"No," he said on an exhaled breath. "I feel the same way when I let the light go. It's what I'm supposed to do." He frowned. "But Will, you were about to launch yourself at Sergeant Shikles. He had a gun."

"Yeah, it was pointed at you. He swung around when you jumped out of the car."

"But if he hadn't recognized you, if I hadn't stopped you . . ."

Seth didn't have to finish the sentence. I shifted uncomfortably on the hard plastic. I'd been wondering since Marcus told me how Dad died whether I could put a bullet in my own chest for Seth. Now, I had part of my answer. In the zone, I'd take one. I swallowed. "Yeah, that's kind of disturbing."

Seth snorted softly and closed his eyes again. "Whatever this thing is, you've got to control it."

I sighed. "I'll work on it." But if Marcus never mentioned this little Keeper quirk, maybe it never happened to him. Maybe he didn't fall into the zone and that's why he couldn't handle the situation the night Dad got killed. Maybe this wasn't something I wanted to control.

"Vic knows we're after him," Seth said, eyes still closed. "He can't figure out exactly what we know, but he's scared." A crease appeared between his closed eyes. "He'll make a move tonight."

I nodded slowly. "He'll bolt. Or come after us. What should we do?"

After a long pause he said, "We've got to talk to our only witness."

CHAPTER THIRTY-EIGHT

"Are we nuts?" I asked, already pretty sure of the answer.

Seth had asked for a Sharing before we got sprung from the squad car. Marcus was right about there being less drama with practice. I managed to keep my crying jag fairly short. Seth got a few minutes rest afterward while we waited for the cops to write up our warnings, but he still felt bad enough to let me take over driving the Mustang as soon as they were out of sight.

"You do realize there'll be a lot of dead people there," I said. "It could be a mob scene."

"I don't think so. Most souls pass on all by themselves, remember? I can handle it."

The leather steering wheel scrunched under my hands. "Matt's getting way too comfortable under your skin, man. I think he has ideas about staying and working this out with Vic himself. What if he takes your body and runs?" The thought made my throat go dry.

I hit the brakes at a red light. Half a second before the engine died, I remembered to jam the clutch to the floor. Seth winced as the car coughed and shimmied.

"Matt won't run," Seth said once the car had settled. "I step aside when he takes over but I'm not totally helpless." He laid a palm against his chest. "I'm still in here."

Of course. Where else would he go? But was Seth's confidence fact or wishful thinking? "What does it feel like?"

Seth stared out the windshield. "Like he and I are in separate rooms of the same house. I can't hear or see what's going on between you two, but I sense the tone of it like muffled voices through a wall. And I wait."

"Wait for what?"

He shrugged. "A sense of satisfaction or resignation. There's a change in the tone. I think it comes once you convince him that we'll take care of things. If he doesn't leave on his own, I push him out."

That first time on the trail at the nature reserve, had Seth pushed Matt out? Or had Matt left on his own because it wasn't *satisfying* to talk to an unconscious Keeper. A green glow came through the windshield when the light changed. I eased my foot off the clutch but kept our speed five miles under the limit, stalling.

"We're in totally uncharted territory here," I said. "Letting a spirit cross multiple times isn't just something Marcus never heard of, it's something he specifically told us *not* to do. What if I can't convince Matt this time? What if you don't sense any change in the tone?"

"People's lives are at stake," Seth said quietly. "We

have to try."

It was nerves making me argue. Seth was right, we had no choice. We needed proof *tonight*. The only source of information we had left was Matt.

Rain spattered the windshield. I fumbled in the dark, trying to find the wiper switch, until Seth reached over and turned them on.

"The crossings have weakened Matt," he said. "I think the longer he's stuck In Between, the harder it is to leave, whether he's heading forward or back across the veil. Matt will be strongest right on top of his body."

"You're sure about that?"

"Even after a hundred years, I pulled echoes from the graves at Muddy Bend. I'll pull Matt across one more time, but you'll have to get him to talk fast."

"Yeah, I've had so much luck controlling our conversations so far."

"You kept me from losing it tonight on the Sterling's front porch."

"Matt, you mean," I said, eyeing him. "I kept Matt from losing it."

"Right." Seth shook his head. "I meant Matt."

"Seth, you're remembering too much."

"It's only Matt's feelings that stick." I opened my mouth, but he held up a hand. "And a word or two here and there. Look, Abby and Megan are Matt's priority. Putting Vic in jail will make them safe. You'll just have to convince him of that."

I took in a deep breath, trying to steady my nerves.

"You can do this. I trust you," Seth said. "Trust yourself."

"I'll get right on that."

It was close to eleven o'clock when we pulled into the cemetery. Seth kept his eyes closed as we wound along the road that Marcus and I had walked Sunday morning. I was ready to slam on the brakes and get the hell out of there if my talisman so much as tingled, but the stone and my brother stayed quiet.

Pulling off the pavement, I took us a little way down the gravel service road before I stopped. I rolled my shoulders to loosen the iron bars that had rusted across them, and we sat for a minute listening to the thwok-slap of the windshield wipers. Seth didn't say a word, just pulled his phone out of his pocket and dropped it in the glove compartment. Neither of us had on rain gear and we were about to get very, very wet.

"Here we go," I muttered as Seth climbed out. Reen's crystal tapped my chest when I dropped my phone in with Seth's. Catching the garnet between my fingers, I whispered, "Give me some mojo, Reen. Enhance whatever the hell I'm going to need tonight." I tucked the necklace back under my shirt and dug around in the glove compartment. It yielded one penlight the size of a Sharpie and a road hazard glow stick.

"It's different at night." Seth said, leaning against the Mustang, staring into the murk at the top of the hill.

Cold rain plastered my hair against my skull before I could flip my hoodie up. "Nah, graveyard, dark stormy night. I'm up for a game of hide-and-seek, just like the old days." Clamping my teeth together, I stopped babbling, cracked the glow stick, and handed it to Seth. As he shook it, and a yellow cloud of light spread around us, I flicked on the penlight. An anemic beam pushed its way to the gravel at my feet. I could almost make out my shoelaces.

"Mrs. Pearson's grave is over there." I swung the penlight and a fuzzy slideshow of tombstones glowed and disappeared. Seth squared his shoulders then stepped off the road. The soggy ground gave under our shoes like the cemetery lawn was one giant slice of moldy bread. Every few feet, my brother lifted a hand from his side, hesitated as his palm brushed against a tombstone, and then let it drift back. If I squatted down to watch him from the height I'd been as a little kid, Seth could have been Dad.

My talisman sparked at the same instant that Seth flinched and stumbled sideways. I grabbed his elbow. "What?"

"That grave," he panted, jerking his chin back behind us. "Who's in it?"

I pointed the tiny light at the stone. Its surface was shiny white, brand-new. "Robert Cavanaugh."

Seth nodded. "Remember that name. He wants to talk to you."

We closed the distance to Matt and Mrs. Pearson's crowded grave, shoulder to shoulder. Seth tossed the glow stick, and it rolled up against a monument, splashing the sobbing angel with a yellow haze. The mound looked sunken. Rain had polished the raw chunks of dirt glossy smooth.

I dropped the penlight into my pocket, and as my eyes adjusted to the dark, I made out the white pylons holding the chain that marked the rim of the ravine a few yards away. If there'd been a moon, even a few stars, we could have seen the hillside and the park trail across the creek. As it was, it looked like the world ended beyond that chain. Seth hadn't taken his eyes off the grave.

"Is Mrs. Pearson more than an echo?" I asked. "Will she get in the way?"

Seth stretched his hand out over the mound, cocking his ear toward it. "There's only Matt. I can barely feel him though."

"Keep your signal focused, man. We only want to call Matt."

With his mouth set in a determined line, Seth nodded. "Let's do this."

He closed his eyes, and I took the first long, slow breath with him. As the familiar warmth started in my stone, Seth's face and hands went translucent, raindrops caught in his hair sparkled like a fiber-optic Christmas tree. His hand snapped open, and the beam shot from his palm, spearing the grave. His chin jerked up. Wide-eyed he stared into the falling rain.

Nothing happened.

Seth's breathing changed to short gasps spaced too far apart, but his beam still pulsed laser bright.

Still nothing.

"Come on, Matt. I'm here," I said through my teeth. "Come on." Shaking all over, Seth began to sway, and without thinking, I grabbed his shoulder to keep him upright.

A shock of rampaging bees stampeded from the spot between my eyes, down my arm, and out my fingertips clenched on Seth's shoulder. He gasped.

Jerking my stinging hand away, I jumped back. "Ow, ow, ow! What the hell was that?" I remembered all the times in the past few days that I'd instinctively touched him to try to share some warmth or lend him some calm. *The Keeper is a source of strength, sometimes great strength for the Bridge.* Grams' words from Halloween night echoed in my mind. Seth, rigid and trembling, looked as if that beam hitting the grave was a hundred-pound barbell that he couldn't put down.

Swiping rain off my face, I stepped close again. "Okay, big brother, I'm going to ignore Marcus and trust my instincts here. You pushed a little light into me, I'll push a few hundred bees into you." I swung my arms in a couple of ready-or-not test runs then latched on to his shoulders. And pushed.

Sucking in air through my teeth, I managed not to groan as energy surged into my hands. Seth's weight sagged against me. I forced my breaths to slow until his fell into rhythm with mine.

"Red Rover, Red Rover, send Matthew right over," I chanted tightly. "Let's get this over with, man. Come talk to me."

CHAPTER THIRTY-NINE

The smell of stagnant water pressed across the space between Seth and me just as Matt's features oozed out of his pores. I tightened my grip and kept my voice low. "Easy, Matt. Come on. Just one more time, we need your help to get this done."

"Abby? Megan?" Matt/Seth rasped. The strangely familiar eyes rolled and then settled on mine.

"Yeah, it's me again," I said. "The girls are safe for now, but Vic's hunting them."

Their faces creased into double exposure scowls and a moan started deep in Seth's throat. I shook him. "Don't go ballistic! Listen to me. The police need proof that Vic killed you."

He lifted a lip showing teeth. Seth's hand, still blasting light, pointed a rigid finger at the grave. "Murderer," he snarled.

"Mrs. Pearson was there first, man. The cops won't touch it." Matt moaned again and jerked a shoulder out of my grip. "Listen!" I grabbed his jaw and brought our dripping faces nose to nose. "If we put Vic in jail, the girls will be safe. Do you understand? There's got to be something we can tie directly to Vic, a fingerprint, hair, drop of blood. Think CSI."

He went still. Totally. Not even blinking the rain out of his eyes. Turning slowly, he stared down the service road. "Where's my car?"

I frowned. "Your car?" He jerked a nod. "Vic told everybody you'd left town. He must have stashed it. There's something in it?" Matt/Seth looked past me, eyes going dark with something I hated seeing on my brother's face. His lips moved and I leaned in. Cold breath sent goose bumps rippling down the side of my neck.

"My blood," he whispered, "on his clothes, stinking mud."

I pulled back. "The stuff he wore when he killed you. It's in your car?" Another nod. I felt a jolt, like I'd missed a step on the stairs. Images fast-forwarded. My face smashed onto the hood of Vic's truck, the garage door rumbling up, Mrs. Smalley backing out past a second car hidden under a canvas tarp. "The idiot stashed your car in his own garage. That's it. That's enough to put Vic away!"

A smile like the glint off cracked ice flashed across Seth's face. Cruel. Cold.

"Yeah, revenge isn't a high priority for you at all," I muttered and let go of Seth's shoulders, shaking my fingers out as the burning faded. "No more juice for you. Your mom reported you missing, and we'll call the police with a tip about the car. That's enough to get a warrant to search the garage." *I hope.* "Vic'll be in a cell before morning. Megan's safe, Abby too." I took a step back. Watching. Waiting. *Come on, Seth, end this.* Matt's anger kept burning in Seth's eyes, but the light spearing the grave sputtered. I felt stupid with relief when he let out a rasping moan and the glow sank back under his skin. "Whoa, I gotcha. I gotcha." Seth clung to me till a tide of shivers passed.

"Was it enough?" he asked, teeth chattering. "What did he—"

"Don't ask me! Not here." I couldn't fall into a Sharing and keep him on his feet at the same time. "We got enough. Shikles is going to love it." I didn't mention that it was only enough if Mrs. Sterling had really reported Matt missing. And if a tip about the bumper I'd seen in Mrs. Smalley's garage was enough for the sergeant to get a warrant. And if Vic hadn't panicked and moved the car already. No, I didn't mention any of that.

"Let's go home," I said. "We'll defrost then call the cops."

"No. Our phones are in the Mustang. Call first. Get warm at the station."

"Fine." I rubbed rain off my face, then pulled Seth's arm over my shoulders and hooked my fingers in the waistband of his jeans. "I'm getting too good at hauling you around, man."

"S-sorry."

"You still hearing echoes?"

"No. Bridge is out." He made a relieved sound, not quite a laugh.

"Good." We turned around carefully as I let Seth get

297

his feet untangled. For half a second, I considered going back for the glow stick at the base of the angel, but I didn't have three hands. "Hey, we have another surprise for Marcus."

"Hm," Seth said, concentrating on putting one foot in front of the other.

"Yeah. You pushed a little light into me. Turns out I can push . . ." The low grind of tires rumbled under the patter of rain. I froze. Two cars were on the road ahead of us.

"You can push what?"

"Shhh." The engines stopped. Hinges screeched. There was one muffled slam and then another. I jerked Seth down into a crouch and knelt beside him.

"Who is it?" he whispered.

"Can't see. Stay quiet." Movement. Men's voices. Clanging sounds. What the hell were they doing, unloading farm equipment?

"The old lady's over there," someone said loudly. "Pass me one of the Maglites."

Vic.

"She's a cougar, takin' a dirt nap with a younger man." Chomper let out a fit of nervous giggles and then moaned. "Damn, my nose hurts."

"Stop whining."

Two long, white cones of light appeared by the road. *Shit.* I looked frantically for cover, but the gravestones in this section only reached our knees.

"They're here for his body." The snarl in Seth's voice sounded very Matt-like.

I pressed a finger to my lips.

"Sonofabitch!" Chomper shrieked. Seth and I cringed as one of the lights swept by an inch from my shoes. "That angel! It's . . . it's glowing, man!" Another beam swooped past.

"Move," I breathed, shoving Seth in the direction of the service road. The watery slaps of his unsteady feet made me wince. What looked like two plastic pup tents with legs knelt in the angel's glow. Vic and Chomper wore dark, oily rain ponchos and both carried spades.

"It's just a glow stick." Vic blew out a loud, breathy laugh. "Did you pee your pants, short bus?"

"No," Chomper whined. "What's it doing here?"

"Hmph." Vic's flashlight swept the chain along the ravine in a wide arc headed straight toward us.

I grabbed the back of Seth's jacket and shoved. "Run!"

He stumbled. Stopped. "Not without you."

Damn. I spun around.

Two Maglite beams hit me square in the face.

CHAPTER FORTY

Fuzzy blue and yellow balls bobbed behind my eyelids.

"What the hell is this?" Vic snarled. "You two again?"

Seth weaved and steadied himself with a hand on my shoulder. What did it take to drop me into the zone? The only thing buzzing through my system was adrenalin. Did I have enough mojo left to pump some of *that* into Seth?

I'd hardly thought the thought when Seth's hand clamped down on my shoulder. He let out a quiet gasp. Something was happening. The contact between us was the only warm spot on my body. Squinting into the flashlight beams, I edged us backwards. "Really weird running into you again, Vic. Sorry we can't hang out."

"How do you keep ending up in the middle of my business?" Vic's voice sounded strangled with panic.

"What business do you have in a cemetery in the middle of the night?" Seth asked. The breathless quiver

300

in his voice was gone.

"I didn't tell 'em we'd be here, Vic," Chomper said. His flashlight jerked down to the ground, then back into our faces, then down again as he stumbled around and over tombstones, circling right to cut us off.

"Is your brother the only one with you, McCurty?"

Tombstones and raindrops flashed and disappeared as Vic swept the beam around. Maybe he expected a SWAT team to pop out and yell, *Boo!* If only.

"We called the police," Seth lied, his voice stronger still.

Vic spun and lit up Matt's soggy grave. It obviously hadn't been disturbed. He put the light back in our faces with an edgy chuckle. "Sure, you did. I bet they're just dying to come out in the rain for you two again."

"Vic, we can't get what we came for with them hangin' around." Chomper cracked his gum, snap-snap-snap, in quick succession. "Just run them off!"

"Shut up. Let me think!"

"What's to think about?"

"Get back to the car," I whispered while they argued. "Call 9-1-1. I'll make sure they don't take off with Matt's body."

"Forget it. Not doing that again," Seth said. "Are you zoning out, or in, whatever?"

"No." *Damn it.*

"Well, something's happening to me. Feelin' kind of a rush."

I heard a grin in his voice and frowned. "Are you high?"

"Look at that kid!" Chomper's voice cut above Vic's.

301

His flashlight shined into Seth's face. "What're you smiling at, you crazy little shit?"

"We can take 'em," Seth said into my ear.

"No, that's a bad idea. Don't . . ." He moved to stand beside me.

In the heartbeat between one step and the next, his fingers left my shoulder and my senses flashed into the dark. I registered the scent of the rain-swollen creek in the ravine, the wind chime clatter of branches on the hillside in the park, the position of every tombstone within fifty feet, and dismissed all of it. I drew my focus in.

Beside me, my Bridge's heart thudded strong and steady. His boots made soft squelches in the wet grass as he bounced on his toes, anxious to move. I unzipped my rain-soaked hoodie and shrugged it off. Still blind from the flashlights, I closed my eyes to let my other senses lead me.

The rain made a sharp tap against Vic's plastic poncho. He was a crystal-clear target. I could almost hear him sweating.

A flashlight hit the ground with a soggy thud. "You don't scare me, boy," Vic snarled.

I opened my eyes just in time to watch the tip of his spade swing through the beam of light on the ground. The handle slapped into his palm, giving him a two-handed grip. I let my knees go loose, brought my fists up, ready for his charge. But Vic stepped backward and shoved Chomper toward me.

"Go get him, you moron!"

Full of the tang of Chomper's fear, my nostrils twitched. His panicky scream turned into a battle yell as he charged, lifting the heavy Maglite like a club. I blocked it just short of my skull and twisted his arm back. He dropped the light. With a solid kick in the ass, I sent him lurching and stumbling over tombstones. Seth let out a harsh laugh.

Roaring curses, Vic charged. I met him with a side kick that stopped him short and changed his roar to a grunt but didn't send him far. With furious slaps, he smeared my shoe print off his poncho, then cocked the spade over his shoulder like a baseball bat. I dropped under the swing and swept out a kick that scythed his legs out from under him. Vic lay gasping like a landed fish.

"I've got the other one," Seth growled low in his throat. My Bridge was yards away from me, circling in the shadows, but I heard his voice as if he'd whispered in my ear.

"Seth, stay out of it!"

He popped up behind Chomper, jerked the back of the man's poncho over his head, and then dragged his struggling captive backwards. Seth's calves hit a low tombstone and he and Chomper toppled over with Seth's arms still locked in a bear hug. I leapt after them.

Something slammed into my shoulder blades, dropping me flat. Pain flickered my hold on the zone. I rolled onto my back in time to dodge the sharp edge of the spade slicing down like an ax. A soggy thwack splattered mud into my ear. Scrambling to my feet, I arched backward, away from another wild swing but felt the kiss of icy air as a slice opened in my t-shirt. *Enough!*

I lunged under his next swing, wrenched the damned spade out of his grip, and flung it into the dark. While

Vic cursed, I drew the cold, calm of the zone around me, took a wide stance, and then exploded off my back foot. A solid roundhouse kick sent the bastard skidding across the grass in a plume of muddy water.

Vic staggered up gasping, one arm clutching his chest. "You're dead kid, dead!" He turned and ran sloppily up the hill toward the road.

A scream out of the dark made me zero in on Seth again. I vaulted a headstone, splashed into a puddle on the other side, and reared back, arms wheeling when a Maglite beam hit my chest. Mud-streaked, soaking wet, and grinning, Seth was on the other end of it.

"I gave him some of his own medicine," he panted, waving the heavy flashlight. He aimed the beam to show me Chomper on the ground, moaning and holding his bandaged nose. "Consider that payback for the Hapkido tournament," Seth said, and swung the light back to me. "You okay?"

I inspected him head to toe. Except for the manic grin on his face, my Bridge seemed to have come through this fight without a scratch. I took a deep breath and his gravitational pull on me loosened.

"I'm good," I said.

"Where's Vic?"

"Done. He ran off. Let's get out of here before he—"

A sharp crack split the night air. I barely registered a red flash by the road when something slammed me off my feet. I hit the ground, fire exploding in my side. My connection to Seth and the zone snapped.

Too much information flooded in, cold rain, cold ground, pain enough to drown in. Something hot and slick, spread across my waist, rolled down one side of my belly. I flopped over to all fours.

"Will!"

Seth's voice was ragged with terror, but I couldn't find the zone. I tried to stand up, but the world tilted, and my left hand and knee hit the wet ground again.

"Shoot him again! He's getting up!" Chomper's voice.

Shoot me? I looked down to where my hand clutched my side above my hip bone. Crimson ribbons flowed out between my fingers. Blood dripped from my knuckles and mixed with the rain sparkling in a flashlight beam. *Oh, God.*

Vic stomped down the hill. I wanted to run, but the pain was too distracting. I couldn't get anything to work right. He stopped so close that all I could see was the dripping edges of his poncho and his muddy boots.

"Little shit," he muttered.

"Sick bastard," I gritted out.

He swung the butt of his pistol down. And everything went black.

CHAPTER FORTY-ONE

Cold air hit my burning skin. Rough hands yanked my shirt up. Somebody moaned. It sounded familiar. *Me?*

"Bastard! Leave him alone you son of a bitch!"

Seth's cursing! This is bad, very bad.

"I just winged him." Vic sounded disappointed. "Bleedin' like a stuck pig though."

"He needs a hospital!" Seth said from very far away.

"Wake up, McCurty!" Vic added a kick to his request.

Groaning, I opened my eyes to a blinding wash of light. Sharp-edged, black shadows stretched from men, trees, tombstones, everything vertical. They'd moved one of the cars so that its headlights pointed down from the road. The skin over my ribs was waxy pale in the bright light, sandpapered with goose bumps. A jagged gash above my jeans oozed hot blood across my belly, down my back. *I'm shot. Shot!* I started to shake.

"Will! Look at me."

Seth's don't-mess-with-me voice snared my attention. I tore my eyes away from my body and got them to sync up with my ears. Seth was on his knees in front of Matt's grave. Chomper held him down pressing the handle of a spade against his shoulder. Seth's shirt was ripped. Blood dribbled from his lip. He looked pissed, and so damned scared.

"I'm back." I'd only managed a whisper, but my brother heaved in a breath like it was the first one he'd taken in a while.

"About damned time," Vic snarled.

When he reached for me, I tried to sink into the mud, but he hooked his fingers into my t-shirt and hauled me to my knees. A whimper slid out as bile burned my throat.

"Who told you I'd be here?" Vic snarled.

"No one. We *didn't* know!" Seth said.

"Bullshit!" Vic smacked the back of my skull.

I curled forward, jaws clenched, trying not to heave up my empty stomach.

Vic took sloppy steps back and forth in the mud. "That little whore ran straight to my sister. Abby figured it out, didn't she?"

Little whore? "Megan's fourteen, you pervert. She has a name."

He jerked me up by my hair and jammed the hot gun barrel under my jaw. Sulfur burned in my fast, shallow gasp.

"It was Matt!" Seth yelled. "We came here for him."

"What do mean you came for Matt?" Vic nervously pulled the barrel away from my throat then jammed it back.

"Matt's dead, stupid." Chomper shifted from foot to foot behind Seth, looking at Vic. "You told me he's dead, right?"

"He is dead," Seth said, twisting around so he could face Chomper. "We came to talk to him."

Vic let go of me. He charged Seth and backhanded him across the face. "You want to try to sell me some bullshit ghost story? Fine." He raised his arm, and I cringed away from the huge gun-shaped shadow that stretched across the ground.

"Don't!" Seth yelled.

"Vic! Stop." Chomper grabbed Vic's arm and pushed it down. "I don't want any part of murder."

"You're already part of it," Vic snarled. "You came when I called that night. You drove Matt's car away from the creek."

"I didn't know you'd killed him," Chomper whined.

"Who do you think's going to believe that?" Vic shoved the pistol into his belt and then gave Chomper a hard, measuring look. "We'll stick to the plan. All we have to do is get the body out of that grave and into Matt's car. Then you'll take another little drive."

"What are you gonna do with these two?"

"Don't you worry about them." Vic threw an arm around Chomper's shoulders. "You won't even be here. Drive the car half-way to Tulsa and torch it out in the middle of nowhere. Shove it off a cliff if you want to."

Chomper swallowed, shifting guilty looks from me to Seth. "Yeah. Yeah, okay." Spade in hand, he walked over to the grave eying it warily.

So, one of the cars up on the road was Matt's.

Vic's bloody clothes were probably still in it waiting to disappear with the body. We'd be back to having no proof. Not that any of that mattered, I realized with a shiver. Our BridgeKeeping days looked to be numbered.

"I'm going to help my brother." Seth started to get off his knees.

Vic pushed him back down, but Chomper was watching like Vic might blow our brains out any second. Vic changed his mind and gave Seth a shove. "Sure. Take care of baby brother."

Poking the muddy mound gingerly with the tip of the spade, Chomper asked, "How deep did you plant him?"

"A couple feet at the most." Vic joined his partner.

Seth scrambled over and knelt in front of me. The rain had nearly stopped. The blood trickling from his split lip was an undiluted red line. "Ahh, Will," he moaned. His hands hovered, moving to my shoulders, then to my elbows, like he didn't know where it was safe to touch. I started to pull my hand away from my side to let him see. "No, keep pressure on it."

"Try to get to the car," I whispered. "The phones."

Seth shook his head. "Shut up."

"Damn it, Seth. We've got to do something before he moves Matt's body." *And shoots us both and throws us in with poor Mrs. Pearson.* Vic had been smart with Matt. If Seth and I hadn't caught on, nobody would have found that body. He was smart about Chomper too. I was willing to bet Vic would make sure that Chomper got caught. Probably make an anonymous call to the police himself. He'd time it so Matt's car and the evidence were burned but poor, dumb Chomper got caught with the gas can and matches in his hands.

"Matt's back. Do you feel him?" Seth asked. "He really, *really* wants to talk to his big brother."

A new shiver of terror went through me. Where was my cat? All I could feel was desperation in the hollow of my chest, and that was all mine.

"I can pull Matt across again if you help me," Seth whispered. He glanced over his shoulder. Chomper had made some progress slogging mud off the grave. Vic squatted behind him, eyes on us, probably trying to figure out a smart way to get rid of us. "I think when Matt's body is above ground it'll make it easier. The closer I am to the remains . . ." He gave me a quick, hard smile. "If you have a better idea, I'm dying to hear it."

I squeezed my eyes shut. The only energy I had left was the quivery effort it took to keep myself up on my knees. Even if by some miracle I could give Seth enough juice to pull Matt across, I didn't trust our ghost to ever leave again. The fourth time was not the charm. But Seth wouldn't make a run for it without me. If we stayed here and did nothing, we'd both end up dead.

The Keeper is expendable. Marcus lived with a nightmare of regret because he couldn't save my dad. Did I really have nothing left? I was still upright, wasn't I? If I gave Seth everything, could he pull Matt over?

"Oh, oh hell," Chomper gasped. "Here he is."

"Get hold of the tarp," Vic said. "Pull!"

Muddy sucking sounds came from the grave. No time left for doubts. I trusted my brother, now I had to trust my Bridge. "Okay," I breathed. "Do it."

Seth's answering smile was desperate. He clamped

his hands on my shoulders, let his eyes fall closed, pulled in, one, two breaths, and started to glow.

CHAPTER FORTY-TWO

Light flickered over Seth's skin. Weird to see him lit and feel nothing. Cold, hollow. No zone. No bees. Nothing. Tears stung my eyes. Not the sting I hoped for.

"Pull, damn you!" Vic's yell rose into the wall of dark above the headlights and echoed across the ravine.

Chomper let out a loud groan. "He's movin'. I've almost . . . got him."

The slick, squelching sound made my stomach roll. "Help," I rasped. "We need help."

A fingertip of pressure nudged my chest. Warmth like a soft, exhaled breath bloomed under my muddy t-shirt. It was the crystal, my little spark of Reen. I let out a shaky sigh as the garnet's warm touch sank through my skin and lit a spark in the empty hollow of my chest. There was hunger in that spark, but all I had left to give was my rapt attention, so I fed that to the crystal. The spark turned to flame. Grimacing, I stoked the little fire

312

with pain. I had plenty of that, and fear, a giant supply, memories, Seth aglow at Muddy Bend, Marcus at the door, Reen's kiss. Bits of me flowed into it like puffs of wind whipping up a brushfire. Pressure built under my skin, but it wouldn't leave me. I couldn't push it out to Seth.

"Pull!" Grabbing Chomper by his armpits, Vic heaved him backward. A long, heavy fold of canvas slithered out of the muddy hole. Chomper dropped it and rolled away gagging. "Drag him to his car," Vic ordered without looking down.

"You drag him," Chomper panted. "I'm soakin' wet. I'm covered with—"

"Drag him to his car!" Vic roared, jerking the gun out of his belt.

Chomper shrank back. "Okay, okay." Wiping filthy hands on filthy jeans, he grabbed the corners of that horrible load, threw his weight backwards and started toward us.

I jerked my left shoulder out of Seth's grip. As his arm dropped, I caught his wrist with my bloody right hand. His talisman felt cold, dead. I pressed his palm flat against my chest. "Take what you need." His fingers closed around a wad of my t-shirt, scooping up Reen's crystal with it. He squeezed.

My heart jumped, squirming like a hamster held too tight. The flame inside me sputtered. *Breathe. Don't fight it, give him everything.* Energy gathered around my heart. I nudged it toward the crystal in Seth's fist. He rocked back, and I let out a groan. A firestorm gushed from my chest as if a physical hole had opened. Light flashed out of Seth, white and diamond-hard, then sank into him in the next heartbeat.

Chomper's muddy backside appeared over Seth's shoulder, dragging Matt's body closer.

"Matt," I croaked. "Now. Or never." It was hard to get my lips to move. Hard to steal even that speck of energy back from Seth. As Chomper struggled by, the sweet, sickening smell of rotting flesh closed my throat. The canvas shroud, slick, black, shining in the headlights, slithered up beside us, and Seth's free hand shot out. Mud oozed between his fingers.

"Hey!" Chomper said, flopping onto his butt. "Let go!"

Six feet back, Vic pointed the gun at Seth's head. "Let go, you freak! What are you doing?"

Good question. After that burst of light, Seth was tombstone still. There was no tractor beam that I could see, no aurora-borealis-glow under his skin. I squinted at my brother's face tilted slightly up and back like he had his ear cocked toward Vic. Just my brother's face. No change. No second soul remolding his features. I hadn't given him enough.

Seth's breaths came achingly slowly. A single word rolled past his lips, "Pervert." He looked like he was talking in his sleep. His fist twitched on the canvas, and then, he let go and raised that hand, fingers spread wide, arm straight out. Light shot from his palm, so bright, so focused, it would have looked solid but for the raindrops falling through it.

Vic and Chomper couldn't see Seth's light, but they stared at his open hand, then looked back at me.

Frowning, Vic followed my gaze to where the column of light . . . ended. His mouth dropped open. A hiccupping click left his throat like a deep-down scream knocking to get out.

"What's wrong? Vic?" Reluctantly, Chomper looked back over his shoulder. His face stretched into a manga mask of horror.

Matt looked just like the picture on Abby's mantel, jeans, green t-shirt, denim jacket, his sister's dark hair, pale skin. Seth's light skewered his chest. He looked almost as solid as Grams had, but he was the only thing in the graveyard not casting a long, black shadow.

"You'll pay, murderer." Matt's lips moved, his face was full of pain, but there was no sound. Not from him. The only voice was Seth's, dripping with the hurt on Matt's face. Their mouths formed words in unison.

Vic swung the gun back and forth, trying to decide whether to point it at the poisonous voice coming from my brother, or at the ghost of his. "This can't be happening," he whispered. "This can't be real. You're dead!"

"You held me down," Matt said, eyes only for Vic. He took a step. Seth's hand followed, streaming light like a movie projector. "Choking. Fighting for air." Seth's voice shook. Tears ran down Matt's cheeks. "Did you feel me die, brother?"

I saw the oily, dark water in the hole down by the creek, the claw marks dug on either side of it. I groaned and the sound flowed to my brother.

Silently, Matt threw his head back. "Look at me!" Seth screamed.

Nightmare. Matt's dark hair thickened. Slimy clumps

315

stuck to his neck, his cheeks. Mud oozed and slithered over his shirt, mixed with the blood that dribbled from his nose and mouth, plopped off the ends of his fingers. The smell of stagnant water mingled with the fear and sweat and death in the air.

Chomper let out a hoarse scream and scrabbled backwards toward the road.

"Stop this! Stop it!" Vic chose a target.

BAM! BAM! Double-fast slaps on my eardrums. Echoes bounced across the ravine. Over and over. Finally, the click . . . click . . . click of empty chambers. A truck door slammed, and an engine roared to life.

"No! Don't leave me!" Vic lurched sideways, trying to do an end-run around the completely uninjured specter of Matt. "Don't leave me here!" Moving headlights made the long, black shadows arc wildly around us. My body swayed with them. Only Seth's grip on my shirt kept me from keeling over.

Seth closed his fist. Matt and the light winked out. Then he shifted his arm, opened his hand, and Matt reappeared directly in Vic's path. Vic cursed, rearing back.

"You freaks!" Vic panted as he gaped at Matt. "You're doing this!" Jamming a hand into his pocket, Vic scooped out the contents. Bullets dropped into the mud. "Make him go away!" Vic managed to thumb one bullet into the chamber. He raised the gun. This time the target was me.

Matt flickered into Vic's line of fire, then lunged at him, his mouth open in a roar that Seth screamed into my face. Both fists hit Vic's chest, solid as flesh, but not flesh. Lightning sucked straight from my guts made the fizzy scent of ozone fill the air. Falling, Vic dropped the pistol and clawed his chest.

I sagged into Seth's hand. Images of Grams' fingers moving across the table at the Heartland Café came to me, vivid as a Sharing. I'd known instinctively that her touch could wound me, as loving as she would have tried to make it. Matt wanted blood. His touch would do more than wound. He loomed over his victim.

"I . . . I didn't mean to do it," Vic sobbed, crab-walking backward, digging his heels into the muck. "Please. I'm your brother."

"Your brother's dead." Matt silently mouthed the words that Seth spoke out loud. Vic took a few clumsy swings, but they passed through air. Matt kept punching. Every strike stopped my breath and shoved Vic closer to the edge of the ravine. "Megan's just a kid. How many others have you hurt?"

Vic stumbled over the low chain fence between the pylons. Arms wheeling, he cried out as loose rocks cracked and popped like hot grease on the way down the cliff. Matt shoved his fist *into* his brother's body, and Vic's cries turned into strangled gurgles.

Matt's fury burned with the fire inside me. His terror, betrayal, the horrible grief, I felt them all, *shared* it as it fueled me, an echo chamber that made Seth more and more powerful.

"Don't let him do it," I whispered desperately. If Seth waited for a sense of satisfaction from Matt before he ended this, I had no doubt that Vic would be dead. I tried to pull out of Seth's grip but barely managed a shrug. Trying to reverse the flow of power felt like trying to suck a roaring flood back through a sippy straw. Vic's gurgles shrank to wheezes.

I had to do something. Reen's garnet, my tiny arrowhead, and Seth's talisman, all of them were burning now, but they were rocks, all three, just rocks. Cold, dense, stone. That essence was what I needed. I concentrated on their stillness. Willed the stones to gather the chill in the night air, the freezing damp seeping up through the mud, ice from my rain-soaked hair. I pulled the cold inside me like the mud filling Matt's grave. The flow of fire slowed. "Stop. You've got to stop," I said as my teeth started to chatter.

Matt turned.

"I won't—let you do it."

He frowned at me, for a hundred years. The power died a little more and a little more until finally, Matt slowly pulled his hand out of Vic's chest.

Vic swayed, head lolling. I couldn't do a damned thing but watch as his body tipped backwards and disappeared over the edge of the ravine.

One sharp cry.

Silence.

Seth closed his fist. Matt winked out then reappeared standing over the muddy corpse next to us. "They're safe now," his lips said in Seth's whispered voice.

Cold, heavy as flowing cement, seeped in now, smothering the fire, smothering me. "You've got to go," I mumbled.

Matt frowned, confused. "Where?"

"Bad stuff's In Between. Follow the Light." Matt

looked down at Seth's beam of light, weaker and flickering, but still hitting his chest. "No, not his. The other one." How could he not see it? Hell, I could see it. When I focused, it got brighter, closer. I felt it's warm current, much stronger than the cold flowing into me, drawing me toward it. An invitation. A promise.

"It's right there." I barely formed the words around my last breath. "Follow me."

CHAPTER FORTY-THREE

The closer I came to the Light, the stronger the gentle grip of the current became. Matt slipped past me, a whiff of something sweet and sad. Gone.

The beacon hit me full force, like I'd been standing in Matt's shadow. It was liquid sunshine like Seth's, but a river of it, calling, pulling me along. It felt like the most natural thing in the world to dissolve into it.

Grams rolled over and through me till I couldn't tell where she ended, and I began. Without any conscious thought of my own, I stopped moving. The current passed me by. I was trapped, baked inside a giant cinnamon roll.

"Grams? Am I dead?"

"No, child. You have to go back."

"Why?" I asked. Then, "How?" There was no forward, no back. Just the pull of the Light.

"Follow Seth," she said. "Can you feel him?" She loosened her hold on me, and I was bobbing in the

Light's current like a toy boat on a long, long string in Seth's fist. All at once, I figured out where I was.

"We're In Between. Is Dad here?"

"He's holding the entity at bay."

"We have to kill it. I can help him from this side!" I pulled against Seth's tether.

Grams folded around me again. "Not yet, Will. Your work is with Seth. Help your father and me by keeping the entity from collecting more troubled souls. Focus on your brother now."

Seth's grip made ignoring him impossible. Feeling its relentless pull, I began to remember fingers and toes, skin, separateness.

An oily taint touched the Light's current. Rot, breaking glass in the dark, a razor blade in a candy apple. Wrongness. And hunger. When I noticed the dark entity, it noticed me.

"Go! Hurry," Grams said. I shrank back, wanting to disappear into her again, but she was gone. There was only Seth, too far away.

Like a blast of summer wind, my *father* swept me up! Gun oil and soap, love, longing, sadness, all too intense to bear, too intense not to. For the space of a heartbeat, our atoms blended, and I felt how proud Dad was of me, how much he loved both of us, how hell-bent he was on protecting us. Dad tore me away from the Entity, pushing hard against the current. I shifted my attention back to the stubborn tug of Seth's string.

There was up and down again. Here and there. Then I was falling, and Dad was gone.

Gone. I felt like I'd lost an arm, half my heart.

Crushing grief smothered me. I dragged in my first breath and sobbed out the next.

"It's all right. It's okay," Seth panted beside me. His hand was clamped around my talisman, pressing the stone into my wrist. I blinked up into his face.

"Seth, Dad was . . ." Bright blistering pain didn't want me opening my eyes. No way.

"I know. I felt him too."

Nico said urgently. "Keep breathin', primo!"

Nico?

Reen's breathless voice. "Yes ma'am, he's conscious."

Reen? I concentrated on taking deep breaths, trying to clear my head. I had to be hallucinating. Who else was here?

"We don't have a blanket, everything's wet," she said, panic edging her words. "Are they almost here?"

"A blanket!" Nico said. "In the pup truck! Be right back!"

"You're going to be okay, Will," Reen said. "The ambulance will be here in just a minute."

Her voice was a cool splash sharpening my muzzy thoughts, washing away the lingering grief. I dragged my eyes open, carefully this time. A loose mess of soggy curls dangled above me. A line of snotty nose tears ran down her upper lip. She looked beautiful.

"What are you doing here?"

She put a warm hand on my cheek. "You called me." Her chin trembled as she tried to smile. I shifted, intending to wipe her tears away, but the cold ground did a carnival ride routine that made my stomach roll. I panicked until black spots popped across my vision. *Oh good. Much better to pass out.* I'd hate to puke right now, even if Reen turned out to be a hallucination.

I don't know how long it was before I woke with a few brain cells on active duty. Hours? Days? I wiggled my fingers and toes, relieved to find them attached and working. I wasn't so sure about my head. Memories bobbed around in there like bubbles in molasses. I cringed away from them, not wanting to poke anything that might pop into a sense-o-rama Keeper replay.

"Where am I?" I croaked. Seth pulled his nose out of the book on his lap, his physics text. Homework. A smile slowly spread on my face.

"The hospital," Seth said, "Are you really awake this time?"

A sharp, disinfectant smell and the soft whirs and beeps of monitors confirmed Seth's answer. He fumbled around at the edge of my white cotton blanket till he found a clunky controller and pushed a button. The hospital bed hummed me up to sitting. Tubes snaked down from an IV pole into the back of my hand. My mouth tasted like the soles of my Converses.

"You look like crap," I told Seth. A bruise under his left eye drooped onto his cheekbone, and purple spread from the cut on his lower lip across half his chin. Crusty, red scabs topped his knuckles, but his shirt was clean, he'd showered at least.

Seth raised an eyebrow. "Should I hand you a mirror, little brother?"

"No way." I could tell how I looked by how I felt. Under the room's only window, a long, narrow sofa had another hospital blanket and pillow squashed into one

323

corner. "You slept here last night?"

"Well, sleep's not exactly the right word." Seth's mouth twitched in a tired grimace.

"The hospital's got to be as bad as the graveyard. People die here, man. Have you been home at all?" The dark circles and stubborn look on his face told me the answer to my question. "We've got to get out of here." I flung the blanket off and tried to swing my legs over the side of the bed. "Owww."

Seth grabbed the blanket and threw it back over me. "Lie down! You've got twenty stitches in your side." He eased me back onto the pillow.

"Fine." I nodded toward the duffel tucked under Seth's sofa bed. "I guess Mom's been here."

He took a while adjusting the pillow before he answered. "No, Nico brought some stuff over. Mom's still at the recovery ranch where Grandfather took her. The hospital faxed her the insurance papers though. She got you this private room."

"Oh." My chest ached, a familiar pain that had nothing to do with the fight at Walnut Glen. "Hopefully this retreat or whatever will do her some good. She'll be home soon," I said, convincing neither of us. "Hey! Where's Vic?" When the question popped out, I was shocked those hadn't been the first words out of my mouth. "Is he . . .?"

"Alive. Probably wishing he wasn't. He broke his leg and most of his front teeth in the fall. Were you awake when the sergeant was here?"

"Thought I dreamed that." I rubbed my forehead. "I'm surprised he didn't haul you down to the station."

Seth pulled the blinds on the window open, and sunshine flooded the room. "He didn't insist on it."

Translation—Sergeant Shikles realized it was easier to question Seth here rather than drag him away from my bed and chain him to the back of a squad car.

Seth sat back down and looked at me soberly. "Vic has a weird burn." He touched his chest. "Right here. It's deep enough they'll have to do skin grafts. The sergeant said it looks like he was struck by lightning."

Wincing, I closed my eyes. Vivid graveyard images boiled up out of the slow-moving goo. "Not lightning."

"Figured that. I'll ask for a Sharing as soon as you're up to it."

I just nodded, forced the memories down, and waited for my breathing to slow. But then, "Matt's car!" I jerked up off the bed. Such a very bad idea. "Ooooow!"

"Stop doing that!"

"But the car. Did I tell the sergeant to look in Matt's car?"

"Yes, you told him, me, and everybody walking by when they wheeled you in here. They found the bag of bloody clothes. Relax." Seth pulled the blanket up as I sank back. "The forensics guys have plenty of evidence. They got the big guy with the gum too. Can't get him to shut up about the pictures Vic was peddling." Seth gave me that tired smile again.

"Did they find Megan? How's her mom?"

"The police didn't tell me much. Megan's still at the shelter. I can't imagine what her mom's going through."

After we'd sat silently churning that thought around, I said, "Looks like we solved our first case. Scooby-Doo and Shaggy couldn't have done it better."

Seth snorted. "Not so sure about that. We were very, very lucky."

One down, the rest of our lives to go. Bruised, battered, exhausted, my brother, my partner. For the rest of my life. Funny, that thought didn't weigh me down the way it had a few days ago. I reached for Reen's crystal. All I felt around my neck was a tender spot. "Seth, where's my—"

"Right there, in that plastic bowl." He pointed to the table cluttered with his notebooks and pens.

Beside a pink jug with a bendy straw in it was a kidney-shaped bowl. Smiling with relief, I picked up the crystal from where it lay beside my bracelet and let it dangle from its leather string. Red sparks danced on the white blanket covering my knees. "Reen really showed up, didn't she? And Nico? Not a hallucination?"

"No, not a hallucination."

"How the hell did they know we were at the cemetery?"

Seth opened his mouth, closed it, then shook his head. "I'll let Reen explain that. She and Nico will come by after school. Pretty sure you've got yourself an honest-to-goodness girlfriend."

The tops of my ears felt warm, but I couldn't keep what was probably a goofy grin off my face. Seth smirked, patronizing as hell. "What about you?" I asked. "Abby Sterling sent some pretty clear signals the other night."

Seth stopped smirking and crossed his arms. "She was traumatized. And I'm not sure it'd be right."

"Well, don't call her before Matt's funeral, man, but

eventually. Life goes on."

"I don't mean that," he said. "My life's not normal. BridgeKeeping didn't do Mom and Dad's marriage any good."

"Who said anything about marriage?"

Seth scowled stubbornly down at the floor.

"Ooookay, so, what you're telling me is you're going to take a vow of chastity? Swear off girls?" He glanced at me sideways. "Seriously?! You're walkin' the road to forty-year-old virginhood?"

Seth sat up. "That's not what I . . . I'm not a . . ."

I burst out laughing. "Ow! Ow! Man, your face. Stop it. Turn around or something."

"You think this is funny?"

"Oh crap, I wish it wasn't." I pressed the bandage, afraid I'd pop one of my brand-new stitches.

Seth went narrow-eyed. "Reen's due here soon. I could help you get cleaned up, and by the way, you stink, little brother. Or I could press the button there and call the nurse to come give you a sponge bath. She's a real nice lady. Probably spiff you right up."

My laughing jag died instantly. "You wouldn't do that. Would you?"

Seth only smiled.

CHAPTER FORTY-FOUR

"The gunshot knocked me right out of bed!" Reen was perched on the edge of the chair Seth had vacated. She pushed up the sleeves of her fuzzy purple sweater and leaned her elbows on the side of my mattress. "I could tell it wasn't just a random nightmare. When you didn't answer your phone, I called Nico."

"A hysterical girl on the other end of the line at one o'clock in the morning really punches through the sleep fog," Nico said, standing next to Seth on my other side.

"I wasn't hysterical," Reen protested.

Nico fluttered his hands around his head, pitched his voice to a squeaky shriek. "Wake up! Wake up! Something's wrong! Will's dying!" Reen tried to scowl at him, but the look they shared held a lot more affection than annoyance. "When she told me you were in a cemetery in her nightmare, I knew exactly where we'd find you."

It was great to have them here, but their story got more and more disturbing the longer I thought about it. I picked up the garnet and let it dangle by the string. *Light of the Keeper ever be, Strengthened by the light in me.* "Did your spell make this happen?"

"Spell?" Nico's grin broadened.

Reen smiled and shook her charm bracelet out of her sleeve. "I wore that garnet on my bracelet for years. When I passed it on, it tuned itself to you like I said it would, but I guess my spell kept it connected to me too. When you got into trouble, I just knew. Isn't that cool?"

I frowned down at the innocent looking bling. "Take it back."

"What? Why?" Reen asked.

The hurt on her face made my fingers clumsy, but I untied the knot and tried to press the necklace into her hand. Reen jerked back. The garnet fell, staining the white hospital blanket like a drop of blood. "What if you'd pulled up before Vic ran out of bullets?"

"She had *me* with her," Nico said, indignantly.

I glared at him. "Was there a bulletproof vest under your lucha libre robe that I missed?"

Seth cleared his throat. "You, Will, are a hypocrite. I'm going for coffee. Nico, you're coming too."

"No thanks." That earned him a raised eyebrow from Seth. "Oh. Oh yeah. Fine." He threw a good-luck-pal look over his shoulder as they walked out.

"You could've gotten hurt," I said, a little less sure of my position after Seth's parting shot, but still not willing to drop it.

"Or, if I'd had any clue that the garnet would work

329

like that, I might have been ready," Reen shot back, hands on her hips. "We might have gotten there early, called the police, and *nobody* would have gotten hurt." She stuffed a stray curl behind her ear, her eyes daring me to challenge her logic.

Who was I kidding? If the crystal hadn't given me that extra kick in the pants at the end, and if Reen and Nico hadn't shown up when they did . . .

"Come on, Will," Reen said, softening. She knew she had me. "This isn't a murder-a-minute kind of town. Next time you're in a supernatural situation, you'll probably just need a potion or something."

"You make potions too?" I asked, and then sighed. "Of course, you do."

She smiled. "None that actually work . . . yet." Leaning the curve of her hip on the bed, Reen plucked the crystal from the blanket. "Please keep wearing it."

When she leaned toward me with one end of the leather string in each hand, I didn't stop her. Silently vowing that I wouldn't let wearing her crystal put her in danger, I rested my forehead in the soft spot between her neck and shoulder and breathed her in.

"You didn't cast the spell this time," I whispered after she finished the knot.

"I'm about to." Her breath was warm against my mouth, her kiss soft and slow.

"Knock, knock! Sorry to interrupt," Nico said with zero sincerity.

"Barge in much?" I asked. Reen linked her fingers in mine.

"Seth said to make sure you aren't totally wiped

before I let everybody come in." Nico walked over to Seth's makeshift bed and started folding the blankets, turning it back into a couch.

"Who's out there?"

Nico and Reen exchanged a look. "Well," Reen said. "We've had a little trouble with the Snow Ball committee."

"Everybody and their gerbil want to join, man! You caught a murderer! Well, actually, they're giving Seth all the credit for that, but you're his little brother." He stuffed the blankets underneath. "You're the most famous kid in town and they don't know the half of it."

"How many people volunteered?" I eyed the door, wondering if a horde might invade any second.

"Oh, thirty or so," Reen said. She squeezed my hand quickly. "Don't worry. They're not all out there, but we do need to figure out what to do with them."

I waited for a surge of panic, sweaty palms. We had four, maybe five weeks before the Snow Ball. Plenty of time to build six-foot snowflakes, book a DJ, and ask Reen to be my date. Heading the committee and attending the dance just didn't measure up to my new definition of terrifying.

"Bring 'em in," I said. "Let's get the *ball* rolling." I got the groans I deserved.

EPILOGUE

There was no casket up front at Matt's funeral. They'd cremated his remains. Not much else his family could do after he'd spent days in the ground wrapped in nothing but a canvas tarp. Mother Nature had had plenty of time to start the whole ashes to ashes, dust to dust process. The large sanctuary was packed, and the pastor's voice sounded tinny piped to us over ancient speakers in the very back of the church. I wasn't listening to her anyway. This far back, the people who had come to pay their respects felt free to whisper.

"Best mechanic in the county," a man next to Nico said. He looked like he'd just come off a road crew despite wearing a Sunday suit. "DaVinci with an engine. Wouldn't let anybody else touch my car. I don't know where I'll take it now."

I knew a whole lot about Matt's death. It was strange that at his funeral I'd finally learn about his life.

"He was such a nice young man," a lady in a knobby

wool coat told Reen. "Never met a stranger. That boy could strike up a conversation with the man in the moon." She shook her head. "I feel bad for his mother, this has to be so hard on her. His own brother," she tsked. "Thank goodness, they got that monster behind bars."

Reen's soft fingers tightened around mine. When the service ended, we shuffled along in the reception line that snaked down the aisle and out into the hallway. Abby stood up front beside her mom and a kindly looking man who must have been her dad. Their eyes were red-rimmed and puffy.

"What are you going say to her?" I whispered to Seth. He hadn't taken his eyes off Abby since we got in line.

He looked startled. "No idea. Shut up."

"Will." Reen tugged on my hand and pointed.

I followed her finger to the line of people behind us and spotted a slice of profile eyeing us from behind the road crew man in the Sunday suit.

"That's Megan," Reen whispered.

Nico turned too. "*The* Megan? The girl Vic . . ." He couldn't finish the sentence.

"The girl Matt died for," I finished for him. I shot a glance at Seth, but he was still locked on Abby. "Save my place," I said, and stepped out of line.

Megan Smalley had pale blond hair like her mother's, but hers looked like somebody had hacked it off at her shoulders with kindergarten safety scissors. Missy stood beside her. They both wore jeans and plain sweatshirts, Missy's gray, Megan's black. Missy flashed me her silvery smile, but the look Megan gave me did not encourage me to get close.

"Hi." I'd never met this girl but knew too much about her. "I wanted to introduce myself. I'm—"

"I know who you are." Her voice was deep, at odds with the paleness of everything else about her. She crossed skinny arms over her chest.

"*I* asked him to go to your house, Meg," Missy said, giving me an apologetic look. "I was worried. That's how he got involved." She reached over and worked her hand into Megan's tightly crossed arms until she'd loosened them enough to twine their fingers together.

The silence turned even more awkward. Megan didn't know me. I wasn't the guy who saved her from Vic. That was Matt.

"Well, I wanted to make sure you were okay."

Megan said nothing, but Missy replied, "Thanks, Will. I'll see you when everybody gets together to paint decorations." She turned to Megan and said hopefully, "Maybe we'll both come."

Megan didn't look like there was a chance in hell that would happen, but I said, "Sure. That'd be great."

When we reached the Sterlings, Abby caught Seth off guard and turned his polite handshake into a hug. She pulled back, but not far. "Would you come to the graveside service? Both of you. It's just for family, but . . ."

"Of course," Seth said.

She squeezed his hand in both of hers, her forehead creased with worry. I had a feeling I knew why she wanted us there.

Nico maneuvered the pup truck into the traffic jam leaving the church. I watched Reen watching me out of the passenger window until they turned the corner and then I walked back to Seth. At the edge of the parking lot, he stood, hands in his pockets, looking out at the tombstones studding the lawn.

"Getting much attention?" I asked.

He shrugged. "Not yet. You?"

"Not a thing." I gave him a half-smile, but I think he knew I was worried. My cat hadn't made an appearance since the fight. I told myself that most souls passed on without a stopover In Between. It might be weeks before somebody else's troubles filled the hollow in my chest.

Seth put a hand on my shoulder. "Be patient."

We followed Matt's family down a winding paved path to his new grave. They'd chosen a site far from Mrs. Pearson. I was grateful for that. No offense to the elderly lady, but I never wanted to see that corner of Walnut Glen Cemetery again.

Sheltered by pine trees at the bottom of a small hill, Matt's new spot felt secluded, peaceful. The pastor gathered us around a neat square hole in the ground. Finally, a place of his own.

"Some believe that a tragedy like this is part of God's plan," the pastor said, her black robes billowing. "But I believe that on the night Matt died, it was God who shed the first tear." She took Mrs. Sterling's hand and gave her a gentle smile. "But God's not grieving now, Carolyn. Matt's home."

Fresh tears streaked Mrs. Sterling's face. Her husband put his arm around her, and I couldn't stop a twinge of guilt at my part in the pain she must be going through.

"Can you hear him?" Abby whispered as her parents knelt to lower Matt's urn into the ground. "Is he really at peace?" Mrs. Sterling heard Abby's question and looked up at us, waiting for an answer too.

Seth turned to me and shook his head. He wasn't hearing anything. I thought about what Grams had said, how even she didn't know exactly what lay beyond In Between. But I'd sensed something powerful in the Light that Matt followed. Peace was as good a word as any to describe it. It didn't matter if my cat was on duty today or not, I'd seen Matt go. Here at least, I could ease their pain. I shook my head.

"You don't need to worry about him anymore," Seth said quietly. Abby let out a shaky breath, squeezed her mother's hand, and knelt beside her parents.

Thick, stubbled grass crunched under our shoes as we walked back to the top of a rise. The cemetery spread around us like a small, orderly city.

"Let's head over to the grave that got my attention the other night," Seth said. "Robert Cavanaugh, right?" I stopped, and Seth looked back at me. "But not if you don't feel up to it."

He was trying not to push, but I could tell by the gleam in his eyes that he *needed* to set the light free. If I was honest with myself, I'd have to admit that I was ready too. I'd learned a thing or two. Getting a chance to answer a spirit's call on purpose instead of bumbling into an ambush would feel pretty damned good.

I stiffened my spine and gave Seth a shove to get him started down the hill. "Maybe this'll wake my cat up. Mr. Cavanaugh probably just wants to say, 'Tell mom not to give my figurine collection to cousin, Walter.'"

"Absolutely," Seth agreed. "He could have a million

dollars stuffed in a mattress that he wants to unload."

"A definite possibility." Out of the corner of my eye, I caught a flash of sunlight off chrome. A dark shape sped along the cemetery road toward us. "Seth, look. Is that—"

"Marcus. It's about time." Seth waved and fast-walked down the hill to where Marcus pulled the big Harley to a stop.

I hesitated, not wanting to overwhelm the guy with my enthusiasm at having him back. He was still an unattached Keeper and the hackles rose on my inner guard dog's scrawny neck. "Down boy," I muttered when Seth waved for me to hurry up. At least the dog was on duty. That gave me hope for the cat.

Marcus took off his helmet and his dark eyes immediately found mine.

I'm cool, I made my smile say as I sauntered closer. "Hey, Marcus."

He gave me a nod. "So, it's all over? I got a newspaper in town. That was quite a story."

"Piece of cake." I got a sideways glance from my brother and dropped the good-humor act. "We handled it." There wasn't much about the *way* we handled it that Marcus would approve of. "What about you? Did you find a team that would help?"

"I found one, yes." Marcus looked at Seth, then away.

"Don't worry," Seth said. "Will told me everything."

There hadn't been any point in keeping the truth about Dad's death from Seth after the last Sharing. He'd felt the dark entity's touch while I was In Between. "Seth handled it better than I did."

Marcus nodded as if that's what he would have

337

expected, but he didn't start talking.

"Marcus, just spill it," I said. "Grams told me we can help. We just need to know how."

"Grams told you?" He looked up sharply. "What do you mean, Grams told you? What the hell have you two been doing while I was gone?"

Oh, so very, very much. But that story was for later. "Marcus, can we kill the damned thing or not?" I asked.

Marcus studied us, worry plain on his face. "They've figured out a way, but . . ."

The silence that followed that *but* was ear-splitting. A twist of fear knotted my stomach, but then Seth caught my eye. Fear shimmered in his gaze too, but it couldn't overshadow his sheer, stubborn determination.

Shaking my head, I snorted softly. "Sibling BridgeKeepers, Marcus, we're a whole new breed."

Seth smiled.

Marcus narrowed his eyes and looked back and forth between us. "It's going to be a long, hard road, boys."

I shrugged. "We'll figure it out as we go."

The End

ACKNOWLEDGEMENTS

It's no exaggeration to say that BridgeKeeper wouldn't have grown from a little ghost story bouncing around in my head to the book you hold in your hands without an army of wonderful people.

To Sherry Bushue, the creator, captain, and heart of her publishing company, The Big Fig—thank you for embracing BridgeKeeper so wholeheartedly, and for helping me learn to dream as big as you do. To my editor, Jenn Bailey, your insights and advice made putting my story out into the world less terrifying. Thanks to cover artist, Cristina Bencina, I'm humbled to think that my story inspired your beautiful work. Judy Hyde, copy editor extraordinaire, I'm grateful to you for so many things, but especially your detail-oriented mind. And Tessa Elwood, I never imagined how elegant seventy-eight thousand words could look!

Writing a novel takes persistence, patience,

optimism, and a circle of kindred spirits to keep you going. The wise and wonderful writers of the Wednesday group are my circle. My heartfelt thanks to my friends and critique partners—Judy Hyde our unflinching leader, Elizabeth Bunce whose generosity and ever positive perspective made me braver, Roz Bethke, Sherry Bushue, Victoria Dixon, Michele Helsel, Erin Mos, Ann Parr, Roderick Townley, Wyatt Townley, Judy Schuler, and Lisha Cauthen. Erin said that BridgeKeeper was like a kid she drove in a carpool for years who's now headed off to college. Well, thanks to all of you for your patience through a lot of carpooling. And to all the rest who offered the encouragement and honest criticism that kept me on the path, thank you!

I'd also like to thank Angela Gillette, who made leading fiction-writing programs and working with teens at the library part of my job for fifteen years. Thanks to Hanna Taylor at Square One whose expertise made dipping my toes into social media less daunting. And to all the teens—you guys are the bravest writers I've ever known. Keep putting your hearts on the page.

And finally thank you to SCBWI, the Society of Children's Book Writers and Illustrators, whose great workshops, retreats, and conferences introduced me to new friends and the world of professional writers and publishers.

L. S. Moore

L.S. Moore has lived many places, including Rome, but calls the Kansas City area where she was born and raised, home. After studying theater at the University of Missouri, she moved to Chicago to try her hand at acting and became a professional bartender and cookie baker. Finally, her passion for storytelling found its outlet in writing. When she isn't crafting ghost stories for young adults, she's walking about cemeteries indulging her obsession with gravestone designs or cultivating her garden, growing bushels of veggies for her husband and two sons.

Cristina Bencina was born on Long Island, New York. She studied illustration and received her BFA at the School of Visual Arts in New York City. She creates artwork with digital and mixed media techniques.

Over the years, Cristina has worked in book illustration and other various jobs. She has experience on a wide range of projects including wrap-around dust jackets, book covers, interior narrative book illustrations, portraiture, album covers, advertising illustrations, conceptual artwork, and more. Her artwork has been selected and featured in various annuals and exhibitions such as *Spectrum: The Best in Contemporary Fantastic Art, American Illustration, The Society of Illustrators in NYC.*

Cristina currently lives in beautiful, sunny Colorado with her husband and two dogs. In her spare time, Cristina enjoys reading, gaming, swimming, and photography.

Tombstone tourism takes me all over the country looking for haunting sculptures like these. LSM

THE BIG FIG
Visit us at TheBigFigBooks.com

An imprint division of The Little Fig
P.O. Box 26073
Overland Park, Kansas USA
View us at www.thelittlefig.com

First Paperback Edition: August 2023

ISBN 978-1-63333-069-6 (pb)

Library of Congress Cataloging-in-Publication Data available

Printed in the United States of America